Also from J. Conrad Guest:
One Hot January

Watch for other titles by
J. Conrad Guest
from Beckoning Books at
www.secondwindpublishing.com

Backstop:
A Baseball Love Story in Nine Innings

By

J. Conrad Guest

Beckoning Books
Published by Second Wind Publishing, LLC.
Kernersville

Beckoning Books
Second Wind Publishing, LLC
931-B South Main Street, Box 145
Kernersville, NC 27284

This book is a work of fiction. Names, characters, locations and events are either a product of the author's imagination, fictitious or used fictitiously. Any resemblance to any event, locale or person, living or dead, is purely coincidental.

First Beckoning Books edition published
November 2009.
Beckoning Books, Running Angel, and all production design are trademarks of Second Wind Publishing, used under license.

For information regarding bulk purchases of this book, digital purchase and special discounts, please contact the publisher at www.secondwindpublishing.com

Cover design by Stacy Castanedo. Front photo courtesy of Colette Marine Lindemann and back cover photo courtesy of Jonathan Hunt. Author photo courtesy of Stephen Sommerville, Sommerville Photographie

Manufactured in the United States of America
ISBN 978-1-935171-31-7

For Dad, a lover of the game who showed his love as best he could.

My thanks to Zinta Aistars for her fine editorial eye on content, without which Backstop's story would be sadly lacking.

"Baseball is a game where a curve is an optical illusion, a screwball can be a pitch or a person, stealing is legal and you can spit anywhere you like except in the umpire's eye or on the ball."

— Jim Murray (1919-1998), sportswriter and
1990 Pulitzer Prize winner

"Life is a ballgame, but you've got to play it fair."

— Sister Wynona Carr (The Ballgame)

"Got a beat-up glove, a homemade bat
and a brand-new pair of shoes.
You know I think it's time to give this game a ride.
Just to hit the ball and touch 'em all—a moment in the sun.
It's gone and you can tell that one goodbye."

— John Fogarty (Centerfield)

Pregame

October 27, 1996, Detroit, Michigan

I'VE PLAYED FOURTEEN YEARS IN THE BIG LEAGUES, twelve behind the plate and, when my knees started to wear, the last two alternating at first base. You know me. I play for any team in any city in America with a major league ball club. You cheer me when I deliver—and I boast my share of late inning theatrics—and boo me when I don't. The sportswriters in this town have called for me to be traded nearly as often as they come to me for a colorful quote in the aftermath of a tough loss or in the afterglow of a hard-fought win. I don't think of myself as outspoken, but I say what's on my mind; sometimes, when something I say makes it into the morning edition, they somehow manage to make me sound erudite. Most of the time I find it amusing. I learned long ago not to pay attention to what the press writes or says about me, for good or bad. This game is filled with ups and downs—no other career or avocation, save for maybe your local television weatherman, forgives failure three out of four times in exchange for that one in four accomplishment in starting or extending a rally, or driving in the winning run—and I'm hard enough on myself without trying to please a prejudiced press or fickle fans.

War is hell. I don't speak from personal experience, but I imagine when the bullets start to fly and the bombs drop, no kid in a trench fights for his country. Thoughts of honor, glory and duty are replaced by the survival instinct. Baseball is like that, not in the sense that we lay our lives on the line, but we're a close-knit fraternity, a pretty exclusive membership. We're driven to excel the result of competition—not only against the opposition, but also with our teammates. I can strike out with a runner in scoring position, but when the next hitter goes out and brings the runner home I'm all grins. That's part of the beauty of baseball—that a teammate lifts you up when you fall short. Next time it'll be my turn.

Yogi Berra said that baseball is ninety percent mental and the other half is physical. As a catcher, I love getting inside the heads of unsuspecting batters, especially the young ones. I think nothing of telling a batter a fastball is on the way and then calling for it. Always amazes me the number of batters who can't catch up to it even when I tell them it's coming. One rookie was so frustrated he turned around to question my ancestry and then asked me why I'd told him I was calling for a fastball. I only laughed and said, "Did it do you any good?" His next trip to the plate I told him to look for the change and he was so far out in front looking for the heat I nearly fell over laughing. I got so far inside that kid's head he went oh-fer the weekend. And the Splendid Splinter called pitchers the dumbest sons of bitches he ever saw.

That baseball is a humbling game is an understatement. The mental part of the game comes in letting go of my last at-bat, whether I struck out or hit a homerun. Step into the box thinking mechanics—keep my head down and my hands back—or about my previous at-bat and chances are I'll head back to the dugout in short order. I work on mechanics during batting practice, and I do my thinking in the dugout, watching what the pitcher throws under certain circumstances; I think about the situation, how many outs, runners on, while I'm on-deck. But once I step in to face the pitcher and I note the defensive alignment, which can tip me off on how they plan to pitch to me, I look for the pitch I want to hit and trust that my mechanics are sound. Of course that can change should I fall behind in the count and I have to shorten my swing to protect the plate as the pitcher expands the strike zone, but the onus is on the pitcher to make me swing at the pitch he wants to throw. Focus on anything other than the pitch I want to hit and more than likely I'll record an out.

I spent a year in the minors; I hit well enough, for average and with above average power, and caught well and threw out enough runners to earn a good look the following year at spring training. I was fortunate that I had a good preseason, so the team took me north. I worked my ass off to stay in the majors. I might not have Hall of Fame numbers, but I've rarely been cheated at the plate. Sure I've had my share of oh-fers, but I've also accumulated some three-for-fours and four-for-fours along the way, too, and five Gold Gloves to boot. I was voted to the All Star team six times during my prime. I haven't won a World Series, but this could be the year as I get ready to take the field at home in game seven of the Fall Classic. I'm proud of my career. I've played the game the way it was meant to be played, with adolescent joy, and have been paid well for playing this kid's game I love so much. I've put up numbers good enough to have played my entire career for the same team, a rarity in this modern era, and I'm thankful each and every day I take the field, which isn't as often as it once was, even with the Designated Hitter rule.

But hey, it's time. I've got on my catcher's gear and I can hear the crowd outside the clubhouse, through the tunnel that leads to the dugout ...

First Inning

I RECALL HOW, as a boy, the last day of school seemed to spill out onto an endless summer of baseball. The first day of school, after Labor Day, seemed nearly as remote as old age. I'd wake up early so I could get my chores done and then, after lunch, head down to the schoolyard with my buddies to play ball; if they didn't feel like playing or were unavailable, I'd head down anyway, hoping to play a pick-up game. Didn't matter to me that I didn't know some of these guys—all I wanted to do was play baseball.

After dinner, it was listening to Ernie Harwell call Tigers games—Baltimore, Boston, Cleveland, Washington, and New York in the East; Chicago, and Minnesota on Central Time; and those West Coast games against Oakland and California, back when the Angels played for the entire state of California and not just the city of Anaheim, that started at 10:05. I lied in bed with my earplug nestled into my ear so my parents didn't know I was still awake listening to Hall of Fame announcer Ernie Harwell call the games— "Strike three called ... he stood there like the house by the side of the road." No one calls a game the way Ernie does; he's simply the best. I've done a few pre-games with Ernie, who once interviewed Cobb, and it's always a rush.

Playing baseball any time of year is special. Opening day is grand, when all the teams are tied for first place, every player's stats are identical, and every team's hopes for a good season—to be in the pennant chase come September—are high. They talk about the dog days of summer being difficult, and sometimes, like when you've all but been mathematically eliminated from the postseason by the All Star break, it's not so much fun coming to the park. But that's when you start manufacturing fun and reasons to play well—to stay out of the cellar, for example, or end the season with more wins than some other team near you in the standings, even if they're in the National League, or playing spoiler for some other team that still has postseason ambition. But when you're in the hunt with the season winding down—a game or two in front of the Yankees who are coming on strong, or trying to catch the Blue Jays who seem to win on those nights you do and lose when you lose so you can't make up any ground, and you can't help but scoreboard watch from the dugout—August and September seem the shortest months of the year.

For me, coming to the ballpark has never been a chore. The sights, the sounds, the smells: the scent of fresh-mown grass, the feel of lumber in my hands, dirt in my spikes, grass stains on my uniform, the crack of the ball off the bat—a foul ball, a Texas league popup, the long ball into the empty seats in left field during batting practice—each one has a unique sound all its own. I look forward to coming to the park; there's always something I want to work on, some facet of my game I want to improve. At this stage of my career, I can't rely just on experience; I'm fighting old age. My reflexes are slowing, and my knees feel the constant ache of more than sixteen hundred games behind the plate, despite a rigorous workout routine to stay in shape. Yet to me it's all splendid, even the aches and pains. I feel blessed to be able to play this grand old game, maybe because I know there's more sand in the bottom bell than in the top bell of the hourglass. But playing in October, the dog days of summer past, the Divisional Playoffs and Championship Series over, under the lights with autumn's chill in the air and with all the marbles on the line, that's what it's all about. And for me it's extra special, because this is my first Fall Classic, and I feel like a rookie all over again. My heart is thumping, there's a spring in my step ...

AS I WAIT FOR THE FIRST BATTER TO STEP IN, I turn to home plate umpire Tim Welke and ask him if he'll give us the outside corner tonight.

"That depends on how much trouble your young rookie phee-nom has with his control," he tells me.

I nod. "Stewart will have his best stuff. Belt high or letter high?"

"Don't you be telling me my strike zone, Backstop. I've been calling balls and strikes since you were but a glint in your daddy's eye."

"That's what worries me, Tim. When was the last time you had your prescription checked?"

Welke chuckles as I crouch and the batter digs in. I refer to most ballplayers as batters; indeed, in my humble opinion there are few pure hitters in the game. In my mind, Gallegos is a batter. I mention, matter of fact and trying to downplay the moment, that he must be thrilled to be here. He snorts and tells me they're going to beat us. I grunt and, disavowing his words for the mere bluster that they are, tell him that's why we have to play the games.

I call for the fastball, down and away; a moment later I hear the siren's song of the seams and feel the sting of the baseball in my mitt … "Stri-eeke one!" Welke calls out. Gallegos glares at him as the fans roar their approval. "Good call," I affirm, although I, too, think it was off the corner. "I like your strike zone," I add. I figure if we get that call all night, we'll be tough to hit.

September 1968

THE YANKEES ARE IN TOWN FOR A WEEKEND SERIES. It's late in the game with the Tigers comfortably ahead, and Denny McLain is on the mound. The Tigers are destined to win the World Series next month, coming back from a three-game deficit against the Cardinals to do it. McLain will win thirty-one games, still a major league record for the modern era, but Mickey Lolich will win the series MVP, pitching and winning three games, including the decisive seventh game, and hitting a homerun in game two—the only four-bagger he ever hit in his sixteen-year career.

I'm ten years old and sitting alongside my dad behind first base at old Tiger Stadium—at the corner of Michigan and Trumbull in Detroit—when Mickey Mantle steps up to the plate. Beyond the twilight of his career, he's in that crepuscular place reserved for athletes who have overstayed their welcome in a game in which, at some point, experience no longer counts. He's lost his timing, along with much of his grace, and he routinely swings wildly and misses pitches that, a few years earlier, he would have sent into orbit. McLain looks in to Freehan for the sign; he shakes off the first as well as the second. Then he leans back, steps off the rubber, and holds up the ball for Mantle to see, seeming to ask Mickey where he'd like the pitch. The crowd, which has grown complacent with the home team's lead, senses something is up. Mantle gamely swings his bat—arcing it gracefully through his wheelhouse—to indicate where McLain should leave the ball for him. McLain nods, goes into his windup … and bloops the ball right where Mickey wants it … and Mickey returns the favor by launching the ball into the right field bleachers. The crowd erupts. Mantle has certainly hit longer and more important homeruns, but the crowd perhaps has seen the writing on the wall, although they may not yet have read the text: this is Mantle's final appearance at Tiger Stadium, and the homerun will count as the next to last round-tripper in his illustrious career. Mantle would retire from baseball the following spring.

"He should be fined, maybe even suspended," Dad tells the ten-year-old boy I once was.

"Why?" I ask with all the innocence of my youth.

"He's paid to get Yankees out," he tells me angrily. In my youthful naiveté, I'm not certain his anger isn't directed at me for asking such a silly question. "He's paid to get opposing players out, not serve up pitches for them to drive out of the park."

Years later, after it was reported that Mantle had a bad liver, I realized Dad had known more about Mantle's off-the-field behavior and drinking habits than I did when I was ten, and that that perhaps played a part in his reaction that long ago afternoon.

The game has changed since Mantle's day, and so has the off-the-field behavior of its fraternity. Much of today's substance abuse comes in the form of performance-enhancing drugs ... but that's another story.

I can't remember not wanting to play baseball. I watched what few games they telecast back in the 1960s and listened to as many games as I could on the radio. I remember Dad taking my sister and me to our first ballgame at Tiger Stadium—Fred Gladding pitched for the home team against those same Angels and won 4 to 3. I remember walking up a ramp and catching my first glimpse of the playing field—we had a black and white TV, so I was unprepared for the brilliant, picture-perfect green of the turf under the lights. I elbowed my kid sister and said, "Look, there's the field." She sneered and told me, "No it's not, that's a picture." I spent the evening learning how to keep score in the program while my sister, bored, counted the lights above the porch in right field. I dreamed of roaming right field, as Al Kaline was doing, already assured of his place in the Hall of Fame, of making spectacular catches to the delight of the home crowd, of hitting the ball all over the field, of setting records and of winning the World Series.

My folks had other ideas. They let me play sandlot ball but put the kibosh on my playing organized ball in school, fearing I'd get hurt. I played anyway, making the varsity squad after forging Dad's signature on the injury waiver. The shit hit the fan when my folks found out, but Coach Heathcliff talked to my dad, told him I had real talent. Dad, who'd joined the Marine Corps to escape a stint on the assembly line at Ford Motor Company, bought into Heathcliff's pitch, for a time anyway.

After high school, University of Michigan offered me a scholarship to play baseball as a Wolverine, and again my parents got squirrelly. Actually, I thought Dad was kind of high on the idea, but Mom convinced him otherwise, and he was accountable to her, not me.

"Look, what do you want from me?" I asked.

"I want you to come to your senses," Dad said. "Major league baseball, that's a pipe dream."

Both Dad and Mom wanted what was best for me, and they both thought they knew what best was: they wanted me to play it safe—get my degree and spend the next forty years working nine to five for someone else. I saw that as a sentence, one that would end up with me, age sixty-five, regretting that I'd never even tried, disgusted with myself that I'd given up my dream, sans the pipe, for what my parents had wanted for me.

I was six or seven years old when I took a spill from a bike that didn't belong to me. It was too big for me, and I was riding too fast and lost control. I landed hard, the bike on top of me, and promptly burst into tears. Dad, who'd watched the entire proceeding from a lounge chair on our porch, crossed the street in no great hurry. Perhaps he already knew what hadn't yet occurred to me: that I was crying more from having given myself a good scare than from being hurt, although I'd banged my ankle pretty hard. He carried me back across the street and, once he'd determined I had suffered no real damage, scolded me for being so reckless. The lesson he wanted to impart was to avoid risk.

"I'm going to college, and I'll get a degree," I said, "but I want to play baseball."

"But major league baseball—"

"Is for a lucky few," I finished for him. We'd had this discussion before. "Well, who's to say I won't be among those few? You joined the service, risking your life overseas, to avoid the drudgery of the assembly line. At least in baseball I won't be risking my life." I could see he was beginning to waver.

Kaline had, a few years ago, turned down a six-figure contract, pissing off his teammates, and Pete Rose was still a couple years away from signing his four-year 3.2 million dollar deal with the Phillies; and while my ego wasn't so big that I put myself in their class, I was convinced I could play in the majors and earn a living, too. "Look, Dad. A few seeing-eye ground balls and bloop singles here and there over the course of a season spell the difference between mediocrity and superstardom. I've got some talent, and I'm hard-working. I can hit a curveball, and if I can learn to lay off the high inside fastball, I'll be able to work a count. I've a pretty good glove, too. After my playing days are over, maybe I'll end up managing, or in a booth doing color. If I don't make it, well, then I'll have my degree to fall back on."

Dad said nothing more, not then and not after I'd made it to the show; he died at age fifty-eight, the year before I was drafted. Maybe that's why I continue to play well into the twilight of my career: to ward off dying young.

Dad: Most of what I recall from my youth is that he was absent. Took me to a handful of ballgames, showed me how to throw a baseball and swing a bat but left the learning to me. He married late, at age thirty-five, after spending eight years in the Corps and serving on Okinawa, where some of the bloodiest fighting took place. Growing up I knew little of his wartime experiences. In youth we believe that little of what happened before we got here is of much importance. I learned, through several stern reprimands, that Dad was not an ex-marine or a former marine. He was a *retired* marine. I asked Dad twice, once as a boy and again shortly after he'd been diagnosed with colon cancer, when I was twenty-one, to tell me about his service years. Each time he refused. He was as proud of his service in the Corps as he was his Polish heritage. He attended many reunions, stayed in touch with a handful of his old buddies, kept his medals, his footlocker and uniform, the saber he took from the Japanese soldier he left no longer in need of it; but whatever he did on Okinawa, whatever he saw, whatever he endured, he took with him when he died.

I learned more about the marine who was my father after he passed away from reading books about the war. An older cousin told me she recalls her mother reading a letter her uncle had written on the back of a dead marine, and that for years he couldn't stand the sight of ketchup on the kitchen table. She related her favorite uncle's homecoming: "He was tall and looked so handsome in his uniform. He dropped his duffel bag on the landing and I squealed, 'Uncle Antoni, tell me some stories about the war!' He looked at me and his smile disappeared and he told me very sternly that I was never to ask him about the war."

Dad related to me, a few months before his death, a different, very abridged account of his homecoming: "I always felt cheated," he said, holding back his emotion, "because the family moved while I was overseas and I never felt the satisfaction of coming home." This simple statement seemed so contrary to the man I thought my father, who put little stock in materialism. After all, home is where one's family is, a house only so much brick and mortar.

Dad was a stranger to me, an enigma, who became less so only after his passing, upon my reflection of several snapshot recollections from my boyhood ...

"MY DAD WAS IN THE ARMY," I tell Larry, one of my boyhood chums. We're six years old and preparing to fight our own imaginary battle against the Japs in one of the jungles in our backyard.

Dad overhears my serious faux pas and, as I slip into what was once his backpack, corrects me in no uncertain terms: "I was in the Marines."

"Big difference," I say to save face in front of my buddy.

"There's a helluva difference," Dad tells me, and something in the tone of his voice warns against further dispute.

He then proceeds to explain to me and Larry that the Marines are a far more elite group of this country's armed forces than is the Army. "It's documented," he tells Larry and me proudly, "that in Europe army troops often panicked and fled the field of battle. Marines *never* abandoned their positions."

DAD KEPT IN TOUCH WITH A SELECT FEW OF HIS COMRADES, most of whom to me were merely names he mentioned from time to time, save one—Sgt. Major Stawicki. Stawicki I met several times, the last time when I was eighteen, shortly before Dad was diagnosed with cancer. I had already reached my adult height but still skinny. Stawicki looked at me approvingly before exclaiming to my dad, "God, he's a good-looking kid, Tony. We'll make a marine out of him, eh?" He promptly looked back at me and asked, "Do you like to kill?"

Yet Dad never talked to me about joining the service, even as he advised me against playing baseball. He never explained to me what I might be missing by forgoing a tour of duty during peacetime—the camaraderie, the male bonding. I realized much later, after I'd made it to the show, that I couldn't have made an informed decision without the information he had withheld from me. I was angry, but by then it was too late: Dad was gone.

I recall standing next to Dad at the foot of the Marine Corps Memorial in Washington, D.C. during one of the many Marine Corps reunions he attended. It was the summer of 1966. Earlier in the day, on a bus ride to the Marine Corps base in Quantico to attend an artillery demonstration, Dad introduced me to General Lewis B. "Chesty" Puller, the most decorated marine in history. Puller's son, Lewis Junior, proudly followed his father into the Corps, serving in Nam where he tripped a booby trap, losing both his legs, a hand and most of his stomach. He recovered well enough to become a lawyer, served on President Ford's Clemency Board, and ran unsuccessfully for Congress in Virginia. Battling severe depression as well as alcoholism, Lewis Junior won a Pulitzer in 1992 for his autobiography, *Fortunate Son*. Three years after the book's success, he committed suicide. That day on the bus, I heard the reverence in Dad's voice as he introduced me to this small and wiry man who, to me, seemed ancient. The best part of his life was obviously behind him, but he seemed an important personage to my dad, so I tried to hold him in some higher esteem.

That evening, at the foot of the memorial, as I looked at the names of battles during which marines lost their lives etched into the pedestal, many which I couldn't pronounce, I heard my dad hiccough. I looked up at him and saw tears coursing down his cheeks. It was the first time I'd ever seen my dad cry. It would be many years before I understood the why behind his tears.

"ALL RIGHT, give it some gas," my dad tells me, "and start easing the clutch out—not too much," he warns when the engine revs too high. I lift my foot off the gas; a blink of an eye later the clutch engages, the car lurches forward, and the engine stalls. *I killed it,* I think to myself morosely, waiting for my dad's reprimand. It comes in the form of a long sigh modulated in such a way that I can't help but notice his displeasure with me.

"Start it up," he tells me. I turn the key and the car lurches forward again. "Foot on the clutch," he barks, and I'm certain that this surely is how his recruits must've felt on Parris Island. My dad: the consummate marine DI. I expect that, once we get home, he'll have me run a mile in full gear.

I start the car and tease the clutch with my left foot while feathering the throttle with my right to get the car rolling. I'm accelerating now, still in first gear, toward the far end of the parking lot. The lot is empty on this Sunday morning, making it a good place for Dad to teach me how to drive the manual transmission in our 1965 VW Beetle.

"Shift it into second," he tells me as the engine revs escalate. I release the gas pedal and step on the clutch with my left foot, then shift the gearshift into second gear, engaging the clutch a moment after stepping on the gas. Dad admonishes me: "Slipping the clutch like that will burn it out prematurely." At the far end of the parking lot, Dad tells me to come to a stop and has me repeat the process of engaging the clutch and shifting into second gear. We do this several times, and the last two I manage to reach third gear. I'm noticing improvement in my technique.

"All right," Dad tells me. "Let's take her out onto Michigan Avenue." I think I hear a note of excitement in his voice and wonder whether he's getting into this as much as I am.

I pull out into traffic and accelerate from first to second to third gear, up to thirty-five miles per hour. Each time I take my right hand off the steering wheel to shift, the Beetle veers left. After a few iterations of this, Dad tells me: "If you didn't have such a death grip on the steering wheel, the car wouldn't swerve like that every time you take your hand off the wheel."

We hit a couple traffic lights. I'm getting more practice starting from a stop, once on an incline, and now, cognizant of keeping a loose grip on the steering wheel, the car no longer veers left when I take my hand off the wheel to shift.

We're approaching the city of Wayne. Once we get through downtown the speed limit jumps to fifty. I hope Dad won't make me turn around before I can achieve fourth gear. He doesn't, and by the time I pull into our driveway at home, I feel as if I'm ready to qualify for the Indianapolis 500. I want to ask Dad how I did but refrain; he, of course, volunteers no positive assessment. The moment recalls for me presenting Dad my third grade report card. I was mighty proud of my grades, but without looking away from CBS Evening News with Walter Cronkite, Dad set my report card on the end table, to be looked at later.

I RECALL DAD BEING MOSTLY ABSENT FROM MY YOUTH. When he was present, he was critical, never voicing approval until the final year of his life.

Just a few weeks before he checks into hospice, I take Dad to lunch at his favorite greasy spoon, where he seems to take great pride in introducing everyone to "my son." On this particular afternoon, I turn to lock the door while Dad takes a cautious first step down from the porch and toward the car. He suddenly loses his balance and takes a spill onto the concrete, hitting his knee hard. I bound down the steps, kneel beside him and, after making certain he isn't seriously hurt, help him to his feet. He attempts to hide the fear in his eyes by muttering something about his knee buckling. I draw a breath, ready to scold him for not waiting for me, for taking an unnecessary risk, but some distant memory—the memory of a father scolding his young son for riding a bike that was too big for him—stays my mild rebuke.

A few blocks from home, he breaks the silence by telling me what a pleasure it is to ride with me. "You're smooth and always in the right gear. You try to time the lights, anticipate traffic and avoid potholes."

I'm taken aback by this praise and manage to stammer something about having had a good teacher.

For two weeks, while in hospice, I watch Dad slip the rest of the way away from me. One afternoon, while I'm sitting at his bedside, his eyes suddenly flash open, he casts a furtive look at me and exclaims, his voice laden with paranoia, "Who are you?"

I wince inwardly, but place my hand on his to reassure him. "It's okay, Dad, it's me, your son."

The tension immediately leaves his face, and while I see no recognition in his eyes, the smile that breaks across his mouth assures me in return that he trusts my words. The smile lingers but a moment before he drifts off again, yet I'm convinced that in that moment I also glimpsed no small measure of pride.

Two weeks later, at Dad's memorial service, I spoke a few words; afterward family and friends told me that they were good words, spoken with eloquence. I thanked them because that was the polite thing to do, but I thought, then and even now, that they weren't nearly enough. That a man's life can be summed up in a few hundred words seems, somehow, wrong.

Maya Angelou had it right: Regardless of your relationship with your parents, you'll miss them when they're gone from your life.

NOW, so near the end of my career and sixteen years after Dad's passing, I wonder on those days I perform well whether Dad, wherever he is, is at all proud of my achievements. On those days when I do poorly, I'm convinced that those who've moved on to that other plane of existence couldn't care less what goes on in ours. I learned long ago to clear my mechanism of such negative thoughts; my failure to do so more than once turned a bad day at the plate into a prolonged slump.

WE GET GALLEGOS ON STRIKES, but Richards lines a comebacker off Stewart's right hip. I trot out to the mound, meeting the skipper and the trainer, and ask Stewart if he's okay. "I'm fine," he announces. He's rubbing the baseball between his hands, his glove held pinched between his left elbow and left hip, perhaps in an effort to keep from rubbing his other hip. "Well then, what did you make the skipper come all the way out here for?" I ask to cut the tension. Amused, he snorts. After a couple tosses to make sure he can continue, the skipper and trainer return to the dugout.

With one out, the count one and two and Richards on first, I suspect the hit and run is on and call for the fastball up and out of the strike zone; the batter, protecting the runner, swings and misses, and I fire a frozen rope strike of my own down to second base to complete the double play. After a half inning: no score.

Lakeland, Florida, 1982

I'D PLAYED THE PREVIOUS YEAR WITH THE TOLEDO MUD Hens, the AAA affiliate of the Detroit Tigers. I'd played first base for the Wolverines but did some time behind the plate, too, and so the Tigers signed me as a catcher. In my sophomore year, I caught a couple games for Steve Howe, the two-time All-Big Ten selection at U of M. Howe was a left-handed fire-baller who won rookie of the year with the Dodgers in 1980, a year before they beat the Yankees for the World Series. Howe was the poster child for substance abuse—alcohol and cocaine his drugs of choice. He checked himself into a clinic in 1983, but relapsed and was suspended from baseball for the 1984 campaign and six more times during the course of his seventeen-year career in the bigs, successfully appealing a lifetime ban in 1993. He signed with the Yankees in 1994 and recorded fifteen saves and a 1.80 ERA as the closer; however, he failed to match that performance the following year, was relegated to the role of setup and was released in 1996 after posting a 0 and 1 record with a 6.35 ERA. Steve Howe: just one story among many.

As a Mud Hen, I earned the nickname Backstop because of my ability to block pitches in the dirt. I had a strong arm but lacked the footwork to consistently throw runners out, nailing a paltry seventeen percent of attempted steals early in the season. But I worked hard on my footwork and improved to throw out twenty-eight percent the last month of the season. I was never going to be a Johnny Bench, but knowledge of opposing runners and game situations, combined with my strong arm, made up for my average footwork.

I was always a good hitter, able to work the count and drive the ball the opposite way, often into the gap in right-center for an extra base. Ted Williams may have hit .406 in 1941 as a dead pull hitter, but today's ballplayer has to be able to hit to all fields if he wants to hit for a high average and be considered a hitter and not merely a batter. I knew I'd never be a threat to hit thirty homeruns, but like Cobb, I thought the long ball overrated. I was committed to getting the bat on the ball to either get on base for the hitters behind me or advance the runners on base ahead of me. That, in addition to my ability to call a game along with my defensive prowess and commitment to improve my footwork, convinced the Tigers to take a look at me during spring training.

Cobb forever changed the way the game of baseball is played with his no-holds-barred-take-no-prisoners approach, but it wasn't until the modern era that players came to spring training in shape and ready to play, using the preseason to work on the basics. I came to Lakeland that year in the best shape of my life, ready to learn and convinced I could contribute. The Tigers gave me my chance—the catcher's position was mine to lose.

I played well my first preseason game, going two for three before being pulled late. But I knew the Cleveland pitchers, like ours, weren't showing their entire arsenals. Early on pitchers tend to work on their secondary and tertiary pitches, with little care given to working or fooling hitters. Our own staff ace, Seamus McGillicuddy, was intent on working on his split-finger fastball, which needed a lot of work—he was hit hard during his two innings of work—and the rest of the staff wasn't sharp either, so we lost 8 to 6.

After the game, most of the squad signed autographs. As a rookie, I didn't draw too many requests, but one came from a pretty blonde who had long, tanned, well-sculpted legs—I'm a sucker for beautiful legs. She told me her name was Liza, with a long "i", and I proceeded to autograph her program, *To Liza.* She smiled shyly when I handed it back to her and told me I looked good before asking me if the team intended to take me north when the Grapefruit League season ended.

"That's the plan," I said.

An awkward pause ensued during which I was slow on the uptake.

"Take me to lunch?" she asked, and I realized my faux pas in assigning the shy moniker to her smile.

I mumbled something about wanting to run some wind sprints, and then, after kicking myself for a missed opportunity, suggested dinner, to which she readily agreed.

"Seven okay, at the Overboard Tavern?" I suggested.

"I'll be there," she said and left.

Later, in the clubhouse, McGillicuddy, who'd overheard my exchange with Liza, gave me a ribbing over nearly blowing what he termed "a golden opportunity." McGillicuddy was married and had two kids, but I'd already learned he had a voracious appetite for sex and a penchant for making it with any young thing who showed interest. I recalled reading an item in the sports section the previous year, while I was playing for Toledo, which quoted McGillicuddy as never having sex the night before a game in which he pitched. I imagined that hadn't gone over well with his wife, who was left at home with the kids when the team went on the road. A star-struck rookie, I said nothing.

"Just don't let it interfere with your game," he warned, and I realized I'd just learned my first off-the-field lesson as a major leaguer.

NURSING A BEER, I was just beginning to wonder whether I might be stood up when I saw Liza approach wearing a white miniskirt and pale green halter.

"There you are," I said, standing; I wondered if she'd caught me looking at her golden-tanned legs, glistening with lotion.

"Fashionably late," she announced, sitting down. Gone was the shy façade I noted earlier. *She knows the effect she has on me,* I thought, believing her flirtatious appearance in dress was to please me.

After some small talk about her residence—she lived right here in Lakeland—the talk turned to baseball, and Liza surprised me with her knowledge of the game.

"The Tigers have been in need of a good catcher since Freehan," she said. "Not a Hall of Famer, Freehan, but solid."

"Agreed, but I wonder if he'd be a major leaguer in today's game."

"A bygone era," she said, "but I miss those players of yesteryear, before the era of big money players."

"Really. But can you fault us for wanting to be paid well if the owners are willing? It is, after all, to what I aspire—to be paid well for my contribution to the game and my team."

"No, I can't fault you. But with high salaries comes a certain arrogance. It *is* but a kid's game."

"True," I said.

"You won't let that happen to you, will you?" Her question sounded almost as if it were a tease.

"I hope not," I said, realizing I'd never considered how my accomplishment of becoming a major league ballplayer might result in arrogance.

"You're cute," she said. "All rookies are."

During dinner our talk turned small and I began to take notice of Liza's features. She was older than I first thought, late twenties, maybe thirty. I'd never really had a type other than a dazzling pair of legs, but Liza's deep Florida tan set off her bleached blond hair and blue eyes, and she had a set of cute dimples around the corners of her mouth, and so I began to wonder what might happen after dinner.

AFTER DINNER, Liza took me to her place where she undressed to reveal tan lines that really heated me up. As a lover, Liza didn't care much for foreplay, ignoring my compliment that I thought her legs spectacular, but she definitely liked to be in control. In her toad-like crouch on top of me, I watched her medium-sized breasts bounce and sway. I cupped the soft pliancy of her buttocks, but she took my hands and placed them on her breasts. I alternated between kneading her flesh and pinching her nipples, which prompted her to greater heights of pleasure, as evidenced by her intermittent squeals of delight. Still, for all the passion she displayed, it was a passion for her pleasure alone. She climaxed once, muttering a string of vicious obscenities, then twice more before rolling off me. I rolled between her legs and eventually poured myself into a now less than enthusiastic participant, after which I was left to my own afterglow. Liza quickly fell asleep without so much as saying good night.

Decidedly satisfied but disappointed and somewhat less than gratified, it occurred to me that I'd often heard women complain about being objectified for their body parts. While body parts had certainly played their role in leading me to this tryst, in that moment I understood what it must be like for a woman to be treated merely as an object on which a man spends his desire.

I AWOKE THE NEXT MORNING TO LIZA'S SOFT CARESSES, and we screwed again in much the same way we had the night before, with Liza lost in her own enjoyment.

Afterward, before I could catch my breath, Liza told me I'd want to get to Joker Marchant Stadium for the morning workout and that I was free to use her shower. When I got out of the shower, I found Liza asleep. I sat on the edge of the bed and gently caressed one of her legs. As I felt my desire return, I leaned over to kiss the inside of her right thigh; she in turn moaned her discontent and rolled over, leaving me to stare at her cold back. Confused, I suddenly resented her for using my celebrity to her gain even as I chastised myself for allowing her to use it in the manner she had. But I, too, had used that same status for my own, albeit imagined, advantage.

I sighed, resigned to the fact I'd pretty much gotten what I'd bargained for—not that much bargaining had transpired. This transaction was a done deal, so I dressed and left, making sure to lock the door behind me.

WE PLAYED THE YANKEES THAT AFTERNOON, a game which we won despite my going hitless and striking out twice. I'd been distracted by Liza's cold behavior.

After the game, I signed several autographs and spotted Liza, but she closed herself off from me, deliberately avoiding eye contact. I wondered whether my poor plate performance had something to do with her aloofness, but left for the clubhouse, leaving her to seek another pasture. Her reason for approaching me yesterday, to play me, hadn't yet occurred to me.

In the clubhouse, McGillicuddy again gave me the raspberries. When I didn't react, he finished, rather sternly, "I told you not to let it distract your play."

I said nothing to McGillicuddy then, even as his advice left its indelible mark.

I went three for four in our next game, driving in two runs with a dinger in a 6 to 1 win.

I SPENT THE REST OF THAT SPRING AND THE REGULAR season thinking baseball, trying to learn everything I could about the game, which included opposing hitters—their strengths and weaknesses, how I wanted my pitchers to pitch to them—and opposing pitchers, how they pitched me and how to adjust my approach so that I could hit them. I also worked on my footwork and my conditioning. I'd never before played a one-hundred-sixty-two-game season, and I worried about a late season slump. I finished the year on a fourth-place ball club batting .263 with sixteen homeruns and seventy-four runs batted in. Not bad for a catcher hitting in the bottom third of the lineup. I'd also thrown out twenty-three percent of attempted steals. I knew I could improve on all those stats next season, but I would need help from our pitching staff to catch more base stealers. They seemed almost nonchalant about holding runners, and none of them seemed in any real hurry to get the ball to me to give me a chance to nail some of the less speedy runners.

Yet for all my focus on the game, there were times when my thoughts drifted to my encounter with Liza. The way it ended—not that it had really started—no longer distracted me from my game, but I had wants. I occasionally took a lover, careful not to make them more than what they really were—encounters of the lonely. They all might have been Liza, differing slightly only in appearance, expecting nothing but a night with a major league ballplayer. Yet I always felt left untouched a more intimate need, which saddened me, so I began to question whether intimacy with a woman was another sacrifice I'd have to make for love of the game.

I'm nothing if not introspective, and I'm very hard on myself on the playing field; now I found I was hard on myself off the field, too. I loved the game, the road life, the fraternity to which I belonged, but I longed to share all of that with someone.

Yet this game is hard on families. I thought of McGillicuddy, with a wife and two kids, and still he couldn't keep his pants zipped. I hadn't yet played a full season and already I was tired of meaningless encounters. I feared if I kept up that lifestyle, I'd become just like McGillicuddy, sans a wife and family.

Fortunately, fate was on my side. *Un*fortunately, it waited until the following April before it decided to step up to the plate.

AFTER TREXLER LEADS US OFF WITH A DOUBLE, we're unable to advance him, finishing the threat with Reynolds going down on strikes, Lott flying out to center, and Miller hitting a groundball to first. No score after an inning.

Second Inning

IT'S TRUE: youth is wasted on the young. Stewart has a good fastball. In the mid-nineties, he has one of the best in the game, when he can locate it well and when he sets it up with his off-speed stuff. Unfortunately, when he gets into a jam, he figures the only way out is to overpower the batter with heat. He hasn't yet learned that a ninety-five-mile-per-hour fastball travels a long way when the batter is sitting on it—or as Kevin Costner says in *Bull Durham*: "Anything that travels that far oughta have a damn stewardess on it."

Here in the top of the second, Stewart wasn't even in a jam, merely frustrated that, after nine pitches, he hasn't been able to dust off the lead-off batter. I call for the curve, he shakes me off; I show three fingers for the slider, again he shakes me off. I know he doesn't like throwing his changeup to right-handed batters. *Might as well be throwing batting practice*, I think. I call time and trot out to the mound to discuss the situation as much as to let him catch his breath.

"You get the feeling Porter's sitting on the fastball?"

"It's my best pitch," Stewart says, hiding his mouth behind his glove.

"And he knows that, too. You've fed him six straight fastballs."

"He won't expect a seventh."

I ignore Stewart's lame argument. "Right now all you're doing is tossing him BP."

"I don't care, Backstop. I can get him out with my heater."

"I thought the point was to get him out period." That gets Stewart's attention. "Look, you've got eight other guys on your side who want to win, too, and we can help, but only if you'll let us."

"You're right."

"Okay. Trust me, we can get Porter with the curve—it was literally falling off the table in the first. If you miss with it and put him on, no harm. Higgins led the majors in double plays so it's likely we'll get two for one. If Porter fouls off the bender, we can come back with your heater." I hate having to treat kids with kid gloves, but part of being a catcher is being a psychoanalyst, playing to pitchers' egos, getting what you want by making them think you're giving in to what they want.

"Okay," he says.

I pat him on the rump and trot back to the dish, where Porter is smiling knowingly. "You tell the kid I'm sitting on the fastball?"

"Kids," I say as I crouch. "They think the answer to all of life's problems is speed and more speed." I think about what I've just said, and then, after checking to make sure Porter isn't peeking at my sign, call for the fastball. Stewart cocks his head; he looks like the proverbial dog, confused by my contradiction. I nod and flash one finger again, emphatically, and indicate inside. Stewart nods and goes into his windup; I set up inside and offer my mitt as a target. A moment later, I feel the sting of the ball as Porter, certain he was getting something off-speed, pulls the trigger too late.

"Shit!" Porter spits, knowing he's been duped. He heads back to the dugout shaking his head while I nod at Stewart, pointing at him with my gloved hand, thinking all the while he owes that strikeout to me.

Catchers get far too little credit in calling a good game. Hockey at least acknowledges the assist to the goal scorer, football the quarterback for completions and yards thrown; in baseball the pitcher racks up the strikeout and the catcher is left with no accolade. But that's my ego, which doesn't rear its ugly head nearly as often as it once did, in my own youth, and I remind myself of what I'd told Stewart out on the mound: the point is to get opposing batters out—how or who does it is immaterial. We got here playing as a team; whether we win or lose this World Series, we'd do it as a team. Focus on individual statistics or let our egos get in the way, and we were likely to lose it.

April 1983

IT WAS LATE APRIL, and we were in Chicago preparing for game two of a three-game set on a Saturday night. I love Chicago, for its many shops and restaurants. Typically, I head for the less touristy places, and since it was sunny and mild this Saturday morning, I left the hotel after breakfast on foot and headed up Michigan Avenue with no particular destination in mind, inclined to do a little window shopping. I hadn't gone far when I noticed a little shop that seemed to specialize in arts and crafts and souvenirs for visitors to the Windy City—one of many that I tend not to notice. However, I have a propensity for noticing attractive women, and in the window of this shop was a very striking woman who was setting up a display. I watched a moment, discretely, feigning attention on some of the items, mostly ceramics and wooden trinkets, but some jewelry, too—jade and amber, and turquoise that looked rooted in Native American origins, none of which interested me, all the while watching the woman. Twice she nearly made eye contact with me, but I was quick to look elsewhere. In between her glances, I noted her long dark wavy hair, tied back, and dark eyes under finely arched brows along with a Mediterranean complexion—she used cosmetics as they were intended, to highlight her features not hide behind—and a dimpled chin. Not a Kirk Douglas crevasse left by the hammer and chisel of a stonemason, but the graceful, sensuous recess as might be found on a sculpture of Helen of Troy on display at the Art Institute of Chicago. And while this woman's countenance might not inspire the launch of a thousand ships, I found the arrangement of her features and color alluring; yet mixed in with these physical qualities was elegance, a sophistication that hinted at substance. All of which didn't seem to fit with being a shop owner. This, too, I found intriguing. Unfortunately for me, she also had a beautiful pair of legs: not too long, and well-toned, gracefully shaped calves. Some might've found them too well-developed, even masculine, but they were the type I've always found irresistible—yes, the type that had, in the past, gotten me into trouble.

"Damn," I muttered. Then I shook my head and made off again up Michigan Avenue. I didn't get more than half a block before I turned around, came back and went into the shop, the bells above the door announcing my entrance.

"Can I help you find something?" the woman asked. She was behind the counter now where a small TV was tuned to the local morning news.

"Just looking," I said. She must've noticed me staring at her, or maybe she was aware of the time that had elapsed between my window shopping and entrance into her shop.

"I'm not for sale," she told me.

"No?"

"I'm not that kind of woman," she said, reigning in her indignity. I was certain that were I not a potential customer, she would've said something much more lethal.

"I'm sorry, miss," I said. "I didn't mean that the way it sounded." When she didn't say anything I added, "Are you the proprietor?"

"Yes." Her response seemed an effort to dismiss me; I wasn't to be put off.

"You like baseball?" I asked, noticing the sports segment of the morning news on the small TV. I was aware that I was about to commit my self-imposed cardinal sin of using my celebrity to my benefit. Yet what choice did I have? I'd managed to stick my spiked foot in my mouth and it didn't seem as if I could expect any help from the woman.

"No."

And I realized here was no baseball groupie, which was a good thing based on my past track record with that type; yet I was running out of options to make small talk. The woman looked at me again, more closely.

"Do I know you?" she asked.

"So you *do* watch baseball—I usually have on a cap with the old English D."

"No, I don't watch baseball, but I just saw a clip of you being interviewed after last night's game."

"Did the Sox win?" I asked, grinning.

"I don't know and I don't care."

"You're not making this easy are you, miss?"

"That's the idea."

"Look," I said. "We've gotten off to a shaky start. I only came in to ask if you'd like to have dinner tomorrow night, after the game and before I leave for Cleveland."

"I have dinner every night, whether or not you leave for Cleveland."

I laughed, although the woman's demeanor had not portended humor. "That's funny," I said. "I meant dinner with me."

The woman ignored me: "I'm a businesswoman. Do you intend to purchase something?"

I looked at some of the items for sale on the countertop, my eyes alighting on a dish of blue marbles, maybe three-quarters of an inch in diameter, painted to look like globes, the continents painted on the surface in remarkable detail. I picked one out of the dish and asked how much.

"Eighty-nine cents."

I handed a dollar bill to the woman, who in turn rang up the sale and handed me my change. I exchanged the tiny globe for my change and said: "There, I just gave you the world, so you can't turn me down."

The woman sighed, told me: "You come into my shop, insult me and expect me to be impressed by an eighty-nine cent bauble?"

"Not by the price, no," I said, "but by all it foretells. I was hoping to make up for some of my previous comments, which were not intended to be insulting." She seemed to soften a bit, but remained mute. "Come now," I added, "when was the last time someone offered you the world?"

The woman stiffened again, told me: "That's none of your concern."

"No, I suppose not," I said, "but from your response I can only surmise that whoever he was, he took it back."

The woman said nothing, but her complexion flushed, more from embarrassment than from anger.

"Look," I said, "I didn't mean to pry. I was only out for

a little window shopping—not for a woman, mind you—and I noticed you in your shop, and I thought to myself, now there's an attractive woman who doesn't have to work very hard at being attractive. On top of that, she looks intelligent, sophisticated. Beauty and brains is a tough combination to beat, at least for me." The woman softened again, and I added, "I tend to be clumsy in first encounters. It's not easy being a young man in the eighties. Women's equality has also won you the right to be selective in the courtship ritual, which is a good thing—but my heart was in the right place, and I'm sorry I made you angry, and really, it takes more muscles to manufacture a frown than to let yourself smile, and if you don't help me out here, I'll be forced to go on and on spouting off more and more inane axioms, trying in vain to make myself sound widely read, so please help me out."

Before she could help herself, she smiled to reveal straight white teeth from between full lips.

"Thanks," I said. "That's a great smile you have."

"So I've been told," she said, her tone much friendlier, although a wistful note accompanied her admission. "I have my parents to thank for braces, although sometimes I wish they hadn't straightened my teeth."

I realized here was a woman who, unlike Liza, didn't relish being looked at for her body parts. Perhaps she'd gotten burned by someone who saw her only for her beauty and not as a person, a businesswoman.

"Why would I want to go out with a baseball player?"

I shrugged. "I'm just a guy who happens to play ball."

"But you live in a fantasy world."

"I live in the same world in which you live," I said. "The stage may be bigger, but I'm just a regular guy trying to earn a living, same as you and everyone else."

"Playing a kid's game."

"Living out a dream," I acknowledged with a nod, "same as the research scientist who dreams of finding a cure for Parkinson's disease."

"But why would I want to get involved with a baseball player, even if you have just given me the world?"

I grinned. "I'm not asking you to get involved with me. I'm just asking you to have dinner, spend a couple of hours with me, get to know each other. After that ... who knows?"

"But you're a baseball player."

I laughed. "You make me sound like a leper."

"I'm sorry," she said, softening more. "It's just that—"

"You're not a sports junkie, you're intelligent, a businesswoman, and you think all athletes are jocks."

"Aren't they?"

"Some of us are—okay, most of us are. But some of us are intelligent and educated."

"And you?"

"I have a degree in communications, with a minor in journalism."

"So why aren't you writing for a newspaper?"

"Because writing for a paper is more respectable than playing ball?"

"I didn't say that."

"Not in so many words. But to answer your question, I *am* writing for a paper—the *Free Press* back in Detroit. I'm doing a weekly column, a sort of baseball journal by someone in the game. Think a non-fiction Ring Lardner."

"Never heard of him," she said, but she seemed to see me again for the first time, with some higher esteem.

"Look, miss," I said. "You're obviously a woman who resents being looked at, judged, for her beauty alone, but aren't you guilty of the same sin, judging me by my career?"

"I suppose I am at that," she said, looking down. "But what if I—" She cut herself off.

"What if you liked me?" I hazarded.

She said nothing but looked up again, trying, unsuccessfully, to withhold her smile, and I thought maybe she already did, or wanted to.

"If you did—like me—would that be so terrible?"

"No," she said. "But you're a baseball player, on the road most of the year. When would I ever see you?"

"Spoken like someone who doesn't understand the game," I said with a grin. "During the offseason I'd be around all the time. You'd probably be glad to see me go to Florida for spring training. Miss me and, hell, I'd fly you down for a vacation—stay as long as you like. During the season, well, I can be in Chicago a few days every month, on those days we don't play, and I could bring you to my place during home stands."

"But home—that's Detroit."

"It is," I said, "and you say that as if it's a worse place than Cleveland, the mistake by the lake. But aren't you getting ahead of the game? You don't even know yet whether you like me."

She looked at the tiny globe in her hand, and I determined that small gesture on my part had somehow endeared me to her. I continued with the pros of my argument:

"I've always thought of home as where I hang my cap at night. Home could just as easily be Chicago as Detroit. I love the Breezy City."

"The Windy City."

"I knew that," I said, my delivery indicating my faux pas intended. "Look, miss—what is your name?"

"Darlene."

"Darlene." I said, trying on her name for size. "I like that. It suits you." I gave her my name, told her also the name by which my teammates called me, explaining to her perplexity how I'd earned it, that it was not intended as ridicule, and finished by saying, "Look, I'm not asking you to marry me, I'm not suggesting you should sleep with me. I'm just asking you to have dinner with me. We can go Dutch if that makes you feel better, less obligated, and see how we get along, what we have in common. Let's leave the repercussions for later." She laughed, and I asked her if I'd said something funny.

"Repercussions," she repeated, her voice lowered in imitation of mine. And then, in response to my puzzlement, she added, "If I didn't know you had a penchant for writing, I'd think that was a big word for a baseball player."

"Penchant," I said, playing along. "That means proclivity, right?" She smiled warmly, which I found contagious and therefore I returned it, adding, "The pen is sometimes mightier than the bat."

Darlene laughed and said, "One thing you should know about me—I'm a traditional woman, so dinner is on you."

"Good," I said. "I like a traditional woman."

I SIT ON THE BENCH IN THE DUGOUT AND BEGIN TAKING OFF my chest protector; I'm due to bat third in our half of the second. After taking ten pitches to retire Porter, Stewart finished off the side on three more pitches, getting Higgins on a curveball that resulted in a high-hopper to short and Smith on a changeup he fouled straight up that I caught near the visitor's on-deck circle. What had started out as a high pitch count inning had ended with a more reasonable count.

Stewart sits down next to me and waits for me to finish taking off my shin guards; when I'm finished, he asks, "What was that all about?"

"What?" I ask as I watch Fernando finish his warm-up tosses.

"You came out to the mound and talked me out of throwing my fastball, but then you ended up calling for it."

I caught on Stewart's reference to "my fastball." Pitchers really are an arrogant lot, but like it or not they have to be. They have to take the mound thinking their stuff unhittable. If they don't, they start throwing the ball, aiming their pitches, and they lose their control, their command, and often end up getting hit. Stewart had shown flashes of brilliance all season long—throwing two two-hitters and two shutouts in four complete games—and during those moments he brimmed with a ton of confidence; yet when he gave up a few hits early in a game, that confidence turned into a cocky arrogance that often resulted in him getting shelled. A pitcher has to take the mound with a certain amount of swagger—what some might call arrogance. But there's a difference between arrogant/good and arrogant/cocky. The former is believing in oneself, the latter mere bravado. Although considered one of the bright young stars in the game, Stewart, due to his youthfulness, tended to fall into the latter category. When he got hit, instead of finding a way to get batters off-balance to set up his fastball, he often bemoaned that the opposition was hitting his best stuff. Impatient for my reply, Stewart intrudes on my thoughts.

"How come you changed your mind?"

I recalled my short exchange with Porter after my trip to the mound, how I'd gotten him thinking off-speed before calling for the fastball. A batter has maybe half a second to identify the pitch and decide to pull the trigger. Get him thinking off-speed and a ninety-three-mile-an-hour fastball seems even faster. You end up freezing him, or he'll swing at a ball that's already past him and in the catcher's mitt.

"Don't think about it," I tell Stewart. "This may be a thinking man's game, but when you start over-thinking, that's when you get yourself into trouble."

"Huh?"

"Never mind," I say. "You don't need to know the why. You've faced the minimum through two innings and have struck out three. Let me do the thinking."

Stewart says nothing as I watch what Fernando is throwing to Hernandez.

❧

DARLENE LIVED ON THE NORTH SIDE SO SHE SUGGESTED WE meet at 3rd Coast Café & Winebar for dinner, in an area of Chicago known as Near Northside. On the corner of North Dearborn and Goethe, it was far enough away from the more touristy main drag of Michigan Avenue, so I expected, on a Sunday night and based on Darlene's assessment of quiet ambiance and good food, to have a romantic dinner. While the rest of the team headed for the airport after the game, I hopped a cab into the city. I had already arranged another night at our hotel and for a flight to Cleveland Monday morning. We wouldn't play until Tuesday. I arrived at 3rd Coast to find Darlene waiting for me, sipping a glass of wine poured from a bottle of Paradigm Cabernet Estate.

"Well," I said as I sat down across from her, "this is a first for me, finding a woman waiting for me. I think I understand the allure for your gender in making a gent wait."

"You're fortunate to find me here at all," she said much too harshly; the progress I'd made earlier, at her shop, seemed lost. "I almost changed my mind."

"Really?" I said, admiring her hair, which shone in the dim lighting; she had untied it, letting it fall down around her shoulders. The result was a softening of her features and a lessening of her businesswoman mien. I refrained from saying as much, deducing she might not find the comment complimentary. "I had you pegged as a woman of your word."

"You know that much about me," she confessed as I poured myself a glass of wine. "It didn't help that you arranged for another night in Chicago and a separate flight to Cleveland."

I frowned as the waitress came to list the specials.

After she left with our orders, I said, "So you did it for me, not because you had any real desire to see me again." When she didn't refute me, I added, "Is it so hard to admit, to me as well as to yourself, that you like me?"

She seemed to soften. "I know you well enough only to say I don't *not* like you."

I thought about that for a moment. "Fair enough, and I'll accept that. But if you found you did, after a few dates and phone conversations?"

"I don't want to get attached to you only to find you have a girlfriend in Detroit. Worse, in every city you visit."

"Look," I said. "You're right to have your doubts, but you're wrong to distrust me on the premise of what I am. I admit to having a fling last spring, in Lakeland. I was guilty of using my newfound status as a major leaguer, but in the end it was she who played me, and I found that that was not what I was looking for. I don't have a woman in Detroit, save for my mother, or in any other city. That's not what I'm about. At the risk of scaring you off, I'd venture to say I'm looking for the same thing you seek."

"What makes you think I'm seeking anything?"

"You're here, aren't you? And no, I don't think it's just because I arranged to stay another night in Chicago. You've already admitted to not *dis*liking me. The next step is to see if you like me and whether there might be a future for us."

"And if there isn't?"

"Then we go our separate ways, hopefully enriched by what we shared."

"Fair enough," she said after a moment. And then: "I'm not a Cubs fan even if I am from the north side. And yes, I've been to a handful of Cubs and Sox games ..." She trailed off.

"That sounds like a preamble—I know what that word means," I added for humor.

Darlene smiled and said: "I have to admit, I find the fact you play baseball intriguing."

"That's a start, sharing your feelings. Do you find me attractive?"

Darlene looked at me a moment and said, "Let's just say you're interesting-looking with character."

"Ouch."

"That wasn't intended as an insult. Women are much less visual than are men. To tell you the truth, I was put off by you standing there on the sidewalk checking me out, like I was an item on display in my window. As if I didn't know that was what you were doing."

I nodded. "And maybe also amused by my effort to appear discrete?" When Darlene neither replied nor smiled, I added, "And when I chose to move on down the street?"

"No comment."

"Ah, pleading the fifth, eh?" When she again withheld a reply, I added, "And a little sore when I came back, as if it were only a second thought."

Darlene softened. "Am I that transparent?"

"Not really. I don't know you well enough to read you. But I found it easy to put myself in your place. It's to my credit, wouldn't you say, that I came back? So there was something about you I wasn't willing to discount without exploring further."

She seemed to think about that for a moment, and I thought perhaps my empathy had earned me some points. "You have a delightful sense of humor," she said, "which is important."

"That comes from playing a kid's game, although I don't imagine you'd find amusing the types of pranks ballplayers play on one another. The night I hit my first homerun, I returned to the dugout feeling as if I really belonged in the majors to find my teammates ignoring me. Later, in the clubhouse, I wound up with a face full of shaving cream."

"You're right, I don't find those things funny, but I understand male bonding rituals, even if they are at times childish. I've been told I can't tell a joke, but I love to laugh. And this," she said, pulling the tiny globe from her purse. "Even though I was initially angry, your reasoning touched me."

"I'm glad," I said. "Which reminds me, here's something I picked up for you after I left your shop." I pulled from a bag a copy of *You Know Me Al* by Ring Lardner. "I had to go to three bookstores, finally finding it at a used bookstore."

"Thank you," she said, I thought a little uneasily. "I'm afraid I don't have much of an appetite for fiction. My preference is for self-improvement and books on business. I see fiction as mere escapism."

"What a shame," I said. "Fictional characters are usually based on real people. I read fiction to learn something of the author—characters are but an extension of who he or she is." Darlene looked as if I'd just said something insightful. "If you like to laugh, you'll love *You Know Me Al.* The protagonist, Jack Keefe, is a naïve bush league pitcher getting his chance to play in the majors. The character is purportedly based on a real life player from the early twentieth century. I think you'll find Lardner a wonderful storyteller. He has a wonderful ear for dialogue and characterization. Just don't relate Keefe's bumbling immaturity too closely to me."

"If I thought that I wouldn't have agreed to have dinner

with you." Looking up from the book, she asked, "But who's Al?"

I laughed. "You'll find out."

Changing topics, Darlene said, "You said something back at the shop—about dreams."

I nodded, recalling the moment. "That I was living one."

"The same as a research scientist seeking a cure for Parkinson's."

I nodded again.

"The more cliché reference is cancer."

"My mother was diagnosed with Parkinson's a few years ago, just before my father passed away from colon cancer."

"I'm sorry."

"Nasty disease, Parkinson's. Not that cancer isn't, but cancer gets the lion's share of research funding. My mother's prognosis isn't good—she's lost her driving privilege, but she's still relatively self-sufficient around the house and doesn't yet require a lot of care. Yet even if they find a cure tomorrow, it won't undo the damage already done to her."

"So you've made Parkinson's your cause?"

I nodded. "This is only my second year in the majors, but I hope to be able to donate to research for many years."

"Do you have other family?"

"A kid sister."

"Are you close with her?"

I felt as if I was under interrogation, but I understood Darlene's reasons for her questions. She wasn't throwing me any curveballs in an effort to send me down swinging, and I expected to have her in the batting cage shortly with some of my own questions.

"Sadly, no," I said. "Which is a source of pain to my mother. She feels as if she is a failure in that respect. My sister tends to be a male-basher, and last time I checked, I found I'm still one of them. I'm guessing her dislike of my gender is the result of my father, whom she blames for my mother's sickness—Parkinson's can be the result of stress, and life with Dad was stressful. Theirs was not a good or happy marriage, but rest assured, despite the role models I had growing up, I have no desire to repeat their mistakes."

"Do *you* blame your father?"

"If I did it wouldn't undo anything, and I try not to let bother me things over which I have no control. Wherever Dad is, he's accountable to a higher authority. My sister, Karin, resents that I play ball. I'm around to care for Mom during the winter months, but obviously not so much during the baseball season. Fortunately, as her symptoms progress, I'll be able to afford to provide for better care—professional care—than either my sister or I could provide ourselves."

"And if you were to move to Chicago?" Darlene asked, and I understood her questions had all along been designed to reach this climax. While I could grasp her concern for a potential future as a couple, I couldn't help but feel she had maneuvered me to this point. Already she seemed to be asking me to make a choice.

"It's not the obstacle you might think," I said. "Mom doesn't want to be a burden to me or my sister. She wants me to be happy, and if I find happiness in Chicago, she'll be happy for me. I'm finding baseball to be lucrative, and so caring for her when she needs it won't be the load it might be for someone with more limited financial means."

Darlene seemed to weigh my answer before adding: "I know my questions must sound cold, clinical, selfish."

"I understand your apprehension, but I hope you won't let it stand in your way of following your heart."

"That," she said with a smile, and my heart fluttered, "is something with which I've always struggled. I have a good head for business, but I have trouble going with my feelings."

"Then it seems we're well-suited for one another. Although I have a good mind for baseball—contrary to what you might think, it's a thinking man's game—my love for literature means I'm right-brained. If you believe the experts, that means I'm creative, focus on aesthetics, and find it easy to go with my feelings. On the flip side I'm less logical." Darlene was smiling, so I asked, with feigned chagrin, what she found amusing regarding a man's feelings.

"I've been wondering about your perceptivity. You have no way of knowing that I spent three years as a lawyer, specializing in contract negotiations."

"Really, a lawyer? Well now that you've confessed, I can admit without fear of repercussions—there's that four-syllable word again—that I felt you seemed a little out of place in that arts and crafts shop."

"Why on earth would you think that would offend me?"

"To be honest, after our initial exchange I got the impression you were a woman who resented being evaluated for her beauty."

"You can't know what it's like to be a woman, to be undressed by someone's eyes."

"No, but I imagine less attractive women long to be noticed and perhaps even resent that some women find it offensive, to be appreciated for their beauty."

"Being appreciated is one thing," Darlene said. "Ogled, leered at, undressed, are quite other matters."

"Agreed," I said. "As a man, I can't possibly understand what that's like. Still, physical appeal, or in scientific terms, pheromones, play a part, don't they?"

"More so for men, I suspect, than for women."

"Perhaps. But what woman doesn't wish to be seen as beautiful in the eyes of her lover?"

"You and I are a long way from that, if ever," she said.

"I was speaking only in general terms," I said. "But I like what I see when I look at you, and I don't try to hide that."

"You don't ogle me, no, so I like that you show me that much respect."

"Thank you," I said. "But getting back to your question, it wasn't that I thought you weren't suited to being a business owner, I just questioned the type of business you own—arts and crafts. Now that you've admitted to practicing law in a past life, I wonder if you might be more creative than you think."

"Past life," she repeated with a smile. "I'm only twenty-eight and that was only a couple years ago, yet it does seem a lifetime ago. But no, I'm not so predisposed to art, although I wish I were. I chose that business because there is a market for it in this town. I really don't have an eye for product, so I rely on a buyer."

"Yet if I thought you not well-suited as a business owner, I would think you less suited as a lawyer."

"Not at all," she said. "I'm very well-suited for law. My father, with whom I'm very close, is a lawyer. Contract negotiations especially appeal to my business creativity. It's just that—" she broke off.

"Office politics?" I guessed.

She nodded. "You're right about my feelings over not only being judged by my appearance, but also the expectation that I should use it to the advantage of the firm. Even in the eighties it's difficult for a woman to be taken seriously, especially in a law firm. That's not the kind of power I want to wield."

"It would be easier for them to see you as a good lawyer if you were unattractive and overweight?"

Darlene shook her head. "Attractiveness on a woman or a man in a law firm is considered an asset—we do, after all, represent not only our firm but also our clients. However, there is a difference between presenting a professional appearance and using my sexuality."

"Understood. So you didn't get out of law to start a business, you started a business to get out of law. How did your father take it?"

"He was disappointed but he understood. He offered me a job at his firm, but I couldn't do that. If I couldn't be taken seriously at the firm for which I worked, how could I hope to be taken seriously at my father's firm?"

"Daddy's little girl. A Catch-22 to be sure. It's still a man's world, eh?"

"That it is."

I nodded. "So you appreciate art if only with the eye of the left-brained."

"I may not be able to create it," she said, "but I know

what I like, even if it isn't always popular with my customers."

"Then you should like baseball," I said. "It's artistic even if you don't understand the finer intricacies of the game."

"You sound as if you want me to like what you do."

"I do."

"Baseball is hardly what I'd call artistic."

"Then you've never seen a pretty swing—the balance, the shifting of weight and rotation of hips, the extension of arms—or a center fielder stretch out to rob a batter of an extra base hit in one of the alleys, or a batter, running like a deer, turn a double into a triple with a perfect hook slide. It's all poetry in motion."

"I don't see it the way you do, no. To me they're all sweaty athletes, mostly brawn with little between the ears, but I've seen my share of bloopers on the sports segment of the late night news."

I laughed. "Which is also part of the game's beauty—last night's hero can be tonight's heel. As for your brawn and no brains assessment, I can't deny its accuracy, but I would warn you against generalities."

"You're right," she said. "That was rather elitist of me, wasn't it?"

I said nothing, enjoying the moment, the warmth of the wine washing over me, Darlene's presence. If she felt uncomfortable with the silence she didn't show it, but she did break it: "I forgot to ask you, did you win this afternoon?"

"Is it important? When I asked you earlier whether the Sox had won last night, you said you didn't know or care."

"Tell me!"

"No, we lost, but even if we *had* won, dinner here tonight, with you, is the highlight of my day."

Darlene blushed and I wondered whether her reaction was to my compliment, the product of her reticence to acknowledge it, or the wine. "Did you score any runs?"

"No," I said, "nor did I drive in any." Darlene said nothing, so I ventured, "You really don't want to like me, do you?"

"That's the paradox, isn't it?" she said, avoiding a direct answer. "My logical mind tells me, 'no, you shouldn't like him—there are a hundred reasons why you shouldn't.'"

"I can think of but one and that is really no reason at all. Fear is no reason to avoid risk. If I had trusted my parents' fear, I wouldn't be sitting here today."

"They didn't approve of you playing baseball?"

I shook my head. "They felt I was setting myself up for failure and the disappointment that goes along with it. But I felt a much greater disappointment would've resulted had I not tried, given it my best. Their hearts were in the right place; I know they were only trying to protect me. Dad didn't live to see me make it to the show, but Mom, who knows a thing or two about dreams left unlived, is proud of me."

"I'm sure your father is, too."

I chuckled. "Well if he is I'm sure he wouldn't tell me. That's just the way he is—or was. His reluctance to pay me a compliment is part of what drove me to succeed. Still, I envy you your relationship with your father."

"He is very supportive of me. It probably doesn't hurt that I'm an only child."

"And your mother?"

"She's a middle child—older brother, younger sister."

"That's good to know," I said with a laugh, "but what I meant was, is she supportive of you?"

"Oh! I always seem to be on another page."

"That's okay. I have that effect on people, including my teammates."

"I imagine you do. But my mother is supportive of me, too, although she keeps after me about settling down with someone and giving her grandbabies."

"Which brings up my next question: How come a very attractive and successful business owner doesn't have a special guy in her life?"

"Because guys are intimidated by business owners, and my business is as yet anything but successful. What about you? You should have your pick of countless women."

"My story is not so different than yours. Meeting a woman of substance around the ballpark is not so easy. Miss Lakeland taught me that."

"What was her name?"

"Now that's a loaded question," I said.

"How so?"

"If I tell you I don't recall it you'll accuse me of a meaningless sexual encounter, which it was; yet if I tell you her name you may think I'm still hung up on her, which I'm not. Her name is unimportant; the experience, however, was a valuable lesson to a young rookie—that lovin' can easily be found around a ballpark, but love might only be found at a small arts and crafts store in Chicago."

"Now who's getting ahead of the game?" she said with a smile but little conviction.

"Not me. I have a good feeling about you, and us."

"I just don't want to be disappointed."

"I suspect you will be if you walk away from this table without agreeing to see me again." Darlene rolled her eyes. "What?"

"You're leaving for Cleveland in the morning."

"Translation: When will I see you again?"

Darlene smiled and blushed, and I imagined she might be wishing what I was wishing—that the evening didn't have to end.

"Don't think of my leaving for Cleveland as an ending; think of it as a beginning."

"Spoken with a true poet's heart. But that doesn't answer the question."

"Well," I said. "How do you feel about coming to Detroit after the Cleveland series?"

I ASKED THE CAB DRIVER TO WAIT AND WALKED DARLENE to her front door. After she unlocked it, she turned to me and thanked me for a pleasant evening.

"It takes two," I said.

With her purse slung over her shoulder, she held the

copy of *You Know Me Al* in both hands as a sort of barrier between us. "I hope you'll read it," I said, "from cover to cover."

"I promise," she said.

I got the feeling she was waiting for something more, so I took the initiative and bent to kiss her, holding her face in my hands. She responded and, feeling her resolve begin to waver, I took my lead from her, letting the kiss linger and transition into something sensuous. After our lips parted, she rested her hand on my shoulder a moment, and then abruptly turned and went into the house without a word, leaving me to wonder whether the kiss had blown it for me.

WHEN I GOT BACK TO THE HOTEL I PICKED UP THE PHONE and started to dial Darlene to say goodnight, to see if maybe she'd tip her hand about her abrupt departure, but it was late—after midnight according to the alarm clock on the end table—so instead I put the phone down and took a tepid shower. Afterward, I climbed into bed game tired, hoping my choice not to call wouldn't be misconstrued.

❧

HERNANDEZ LEADS OFF OUR HALF OF THE SECOND INNING with a screaming liner to third base for our first out, and Jones leaves it up to me to get something going after he flies out to the warning track in left.

Fernando has been attacking the strike zone early, and even though I typically take the first pitch, I resolve to swing at the first fastball he serves up. I get the heat, but it's elevated, and I foul it straight back over the umpire's right shoulder. The next pitch is a slider in the dirt. The next is a curve that misses outside. Fernando comes with a changeup that misses up high and I find myself ahead in the count, three and one. Anticipating the fastball, I'm ahead of the next pitch and pull it foul past our third base coach. After that, Fernando feeds me a series of fastballs—up, down, in and out—and I manage to get my bat on all of them but fail to put the ball in play.

Eventually Evans goes out to the mound to talk over the situation with Fernando, leaving me just enough time to think of Darlene in Chicago, to wonder if she's watching the game.

When Evans returns, I reach down for a handful of dirt, adjust my batting helmet and step back up to the plate looking for the fastball to drive someplace hard. A moment later, Fernando delivers a slider out of the strike zone at which I swing and miss.

I'm a better hitter with runners on because I focus on advancing the runner, thereby taking what the pitcher gives me, just trying to put the ball in play, usually behind the runner. In this situation, with two out and nobody on, I tried to do too much, hitting for power instead of just trying to make contact. It didn't help that I'd allowed my concentration to wander.

I walk back to the dugout cursing to myself, but I'm careful not to show my self-disgust. I'm always wary not to let my emotion show when someone bests me. Instead, I resolve to show them up next time.

After two innings, the game remains scoreless.

Third Inning

"YOU LOOKED GOOD DURING YOUR AT-BAT," Evans, my counterpart behind the plate, tells me as he steps into the batter's box, "corkscrewing yourself into the dirt."

"Not the first time it's happened and it won't be the last," I say. "I'll have another chance."

"Fernando has good stuff tonight."

"That he does. But it's a long game."

"Bring it," Welke calls out to Stewart from behind me.

We get Evans on three pitches, the last one a swinging strike.

"You looked good," I call to his back as he trudges back to the dugout.

Evans mutters something under his breath that I can't make out.

"I'M SORRY," Darlene's voice said into my ear. I'd called her after I'd had breakfast; my bags sat at the door, packed and ready for departure. I knew not calling until after I'd gotten to Cleveland would've spelled doom. I sat on the edge of the bed waiting for her to finish her apology. We'd had one date and already I was being blown off, and I was surprised by the weight of my disappointment. "I'm not good at this," she finished.

"Good at what?"

"It's not that I haven't dated, been in a relationship or two. But never have I considered a long-distance relationship."

"Oh," I said, trying for levity, "is that what this is, a relationship—already?"

"Of course not, not yet—"

"But your practical side won't let you get to know me just for kicks, consider that, at worst, you might make a new friend, sample a different lifestyle. At best that you might come to like me and that we could be good together."

Silence. I worried that Darlene had mistaken the passion behind my argument as anger, or worse, desperation. Neither sex finds desperation in the opposite gender a thing of beauty.

"You still there?" I asked.

"Yes, I'm here." And then: "It's just, well, every time I resolve to go for it, take a chance, to go with my heart, my head argues me out of it."

I said nothing; Darlene offered: "I guess there's safety in distance."

"Don't think of it as safety or you'll never consider this a risk-gain proposition. Think of it as forcing us to go slowly. I understand you're risking your heart. I am, too. I don't know you any better than you know me, but what I do know of you—that you're intelligent, love to laugh, independent and want to succeed on your own merit—I admire. I'm drawn to you and I see a lot of potential for us. I hope you don't mind me saying that it doesn't hurt that I also find you very attractive."

"I don't mind you saying that." A pause. "What I know of you I don't dislike. But sometimes bad things happen as a result of risk."

I nodded, realized she couldn't see me, decided it was unimportant, and said, "Little of value is ever gained by avoiding it. What did you risk by giving up practicing law to start a business? And what have you gained?" Without waiting for a reply, I continued. "I risked disappointment by playing baseball; look what I've gained. I'm living my dream. Maybe in some alternate reality I'd be writing a sports column for the *Freep* but wondering, *What if?* When I came into your shop yesterday it was because I'd asked myself that same question: *What if ... she's the one?*"

"But how can you be sure?"

"I can't, not without taking a chance to find out."

"But ..."

"Look," I said. "No match is made in heaven. I can't

promise we won't have our differences. Life with a ballplayer, from what I've heard in the clubhouse, can be trying. But it has its rewards—financial and otherwise. A career in baseball, well, barring a career-ending injury, I don't expect to play beyond thirty-eight. You may look back at these as the good old days, when I was rarely around."

"I don't think so," she argued.

I thought about her comment, said, "I can only hope you're right on that count. You mentioned a previous relationship—what was the attraction?"

"He was a lawyer."

"So you thought you had something in common."

"We did," she said. "He had a fine legal mind, and I admired him for it. But like everyone else in the firm ..."

"He didn't take you seriously."

"No."

"How did it end?"

"I found out he was sleeping with his administrative assistant. She was pretty, sexy, but when I found out, he told me she meant nothing to him, was just a plaything. Like that was supposed to make it okay, make me feel better."

"Ouch." And then: "He was a fool." When Darlene said nothing, I added, "Thanks. I know that wasn't easy for you to share, having known me but a day."

"We not only lived in the same city but worked for the same firm. If he couldn't be faithful to me, how can I expect that you would be, in Detroit, New York, Boston, Los Angeles ... *Cleveland*?"

"I understand your concern. Absence, under extreme conditions, doesn't make the heart grow fonder; but maybe working for the same firm was too much togetherness. Under the best of circumstances it takes time for a couple to build trust. We haven't yet consummated a physical relationship, and I won't ask you to do anything you're not yet ready for—"

"But you've asked me to come to Detroit next weekend."

"As commitments go that's minor. You can sleep in my

sister's old room at my mother's house, or I can put you up in a hotel. I don't want to screw this up, Darlene. Maybe after a few more phone calls, a trip to Detroit for you and a few more visits from me to Chicago we'll decide to take a pass and move on—and there's nothing wrong with that. We'll have invested nothing but time. Right now, I just feel the potential is too great to risk screwing up."

"It is?"

"For me it is."

A moment passed during which I wondered what she might be thinking even as I pictured her in a nightgown, hair tousled about her shoulders, sitting on the edge of her bed as I sat on this one, miles apart at opposite ends of the same city.

"I'll have to see if Marsha is available to work Saturday. She's the only one I trust to open and close the shop." I heard her sigh and then, "I'm not sure I'm ready to meet your mother."

"That's fine. I'll put you up in a hotel. The Yankees are in town for the weekend. You can sit with the wives of my teammates. What better way to get to know me?" Darlene laughed and I added, "I can show you some sights. Ever been to Greenfield Village?"

"No."

"Great little town. You'll see the birthplaces or homes of Henry Ford, Thomas Edison, the Wright Brothers, Noah Webster, Robert Frost—can you believe all those notables were either born or lived in the same village?" Darlene laughed and I thought, not for the first time, that she had a very sensuous laugh. "What? What did I say?"

"You can't be serious," she said, thinking I was.

"Gotcha."

"Oh, getting to know you is going to be interesting."

"If not fun."

"Promise?"

"You have my word."

Darlene was silent a moment, and I recalled last night's kiss, Darlene's soft cheek against my baseball-calloused hand. I ventured: "I can't wait to see you this weekend."

"I haven't yet agreed to come."

"No, but you haven't yet said you won't. Think about it. I'll call you every night during the week. We can get to know each other by phone, and if by Friday you don't feel comfortable with coming, we can make it another weekend."

"Thank you," she said, "for giving me that option. And thanks, too, for the book."

"You've started reading it?"

"Yes, last night. I waited for you to call, but you didn't."

"I wanted to, but it was late, and I was confused by your hasty retreat after we kissed. I thought maybe I'd blown it."

"I'm sorry about that," she said. "And no, you didn't blow it—far from it. It was delicious—you're a wonderful kisser."

"Like a good date, it takes two."

"I could very easily have asked you in."

"But the cab was waiting."

Darlene laughed. "That I ran was actually a good thing."

"A woman's logic." When Darlene said nothing, I added, "I'm pleased you didn't ask me in." I waited a moment; Darlene said:

"That's one of the things I like about you. Most guys would've been frustrated, maybe even angry."

"Well, I won't deny I was the former," I said, "but angry? Nah. I started to dial your number, but opted instead for a cold shower."

She laughed and said, "You *do* know how to make me laugh. And the book is funny, too. I've never read a novel with the idea of getting to know the author. It definitely puts a different spin on reading. Most people put the inscription at the beginning."

"And most people read from the beginning," I said. "Although I suppose if something were to happen to you before you finished reading it, you'd at least know how the story ends."

"A man's logic," she said, and I laughed and said:

"But that's why I said I hoped you'd read it from cover

to cover, so you wouldn't miss the inscription."

"From one baseball lover to another?" she read from what I'd written on the last page.

"It comes with the package—if you come to love me, you'll love the game."

Two beats: "Are you? My Backstop?" Also from the inscription.

"If you want me to be."

Three beats, then: "I think I might like to see you again."

"Great," I said. "Be sure to pack your sunscreen."

DARLENE STEPPED OUT OF THE TUNNEL THAT LED FROM THE aircraft looking touristy in a straw hat, print sleeveless blouse and a yellow skirt that flattered her legs and complemented her olive skin tone. The unseasonably warm weather for April, in the high seventies, was expected to hold through the middle of next week. I strode over to her and gave her an embrace followed by quick kiss on the mouth. She looked up at me smiling warmly, and something in her smile invited me to kiss her again. I did, recalling our first kiss from the previous Sunday. I was dimly aware of other passengers but didn't care. Darlene stepped back and said, "That's much better."

"You look great," I said. "Almost as if you want to be here."

"Who could pass up a chance to take in their first baseball game at Tiger Stadium?"

"Where the likes of Cobb, Gehringer, Greenburg and Kaline all once played."

"Never heard of any of them, but I know by name one Tiger who's playing today."

"You should know Cobb, at least," I said. "He's a prominent character in *You Know Me Al*."

"Oh, that Cobb."

I laughed. "Only the greatest ballplayer to ever play the game—one of baseball's nine immortals, the first ever enshrined in the Hall of Fame."

"Greatness is largely overrated and transitory." My face

must've betrayed its surprise. "You don't agree?" she asked.

"I don't know," I said. "I guess I never thought about it that way. Certainly it's transitory—Heraclitus wrote, 'All things flow, nothing abides.' What we are never changes; who we are never stops changing."

"Change is real, stability illusory."

"You're familiar with his beliefs?"

"He's Greek, I'm Greek."

"I love this part of a budding relationship," I said. "Nearly everything is a surprise, even if it seemingly fits with certain assumptions. I figured you for a Mediterranean heritage, but maybe Italian."

"Hardly," she said with a touch of indignity. "We boast the origin of democracy, western philosophy and political science."

"Which explains your highly logical mind. But the Greeks are also noted for their contributions to literature, including drama, as well as sports—you're familiar with the Olympics?"

"Darn," she said, smiling. "One-upping you is going to be a challenge."

"This shouldn't be a competition," I said. "We should be looking at becoming a team."

"I like the way you think," she said; I noted the warmth in her voice and hoped she'd not spent an inordinate amount of time during the week considering reasons to give in to her fear of risk.

"But really," I said, taking her by the hand, "we've been in stasis here ourselves for too long. I've a big day planned for us, so let's claim your baggage and get us some lunch."

Darlene laughed and said, "If this were a novel I'd say no one talks like that—'been in stasis too long' and 'claim your baggage.'"

"'In stasis' is a term that can be easily found in many science fiction novels—and isn't that why they call it 'baggage claim'?"

Darlene laughed again. "But that's exactly the way you talk."

"No sweating athlete, me, all brawn and nothing between the ears."

Darlene stopped and, as I turned to face her, took my other hand. "It really *is* good to see you. I'm glad I came."

"I hope you'll still feel that way come Monday morning."

"I'm sure I will."

"You know," I said, "I really believe you mean that. I wasn't sure, even after we spoke on the phone this morning, that I'd see you walk off that plane."

"Most of the time you're so sure of yourself, without being arrogant, but every once in a while you betray a touch of insecurity, and I find that charming, too."

I cupped her chin in my hand and kissed her again, enjoying the taste of her soft and moist lips. Afterward, I noticed Darlene's complexion had flushed, perhaps the result of her own passion.

AS WE WAITED FOR DARLENE'S BAGGAGE TO APPEAR ON the carousel, I brought up her belief that greatness was overrated.

"Really," she explained, "there are few truly great men. Name one?"

"Abraham Lincoln."

Darlene nodded. "Regarded by many as our greatest president—but he was assassinated."

"That should do nothing to detract from his greatness any more than Christ's crucifixion should detract from his," I said. "Like Christ, Lincoln was assassinated largely for his beliefs. He could've held the middle ground, played both sides the way many politicians today talk out of both sides of their mouths. He could've left the slavery issue for his successor to deal with, but he did what was right for right's sake, despite it resulting in the four bloodiest years in this country's history."

"Would you say that Hitler was a great leader?"

"He was a lot of things," I said, "including a mass murderer. He was also dynamic, but he let power corrupt him, and so he became this century's greatest tyrant. Greatness is largely based on perception. Casanova was known for his great prowess in the art of seduction, but I wonder if the many women he bedded and subsequently disappointed would view him as a great man. That Hitler pulled Germany out of the depths of a depression is largely forgotten, the result of his endgame."

"Which does not, nor should it, make him a great man."

"In light of where it took him and the world, I agree. But that he was a great orator, charismatic, can't be argued either. He won't be forgotten, nor should he, if we are to learn anything from his great tyranny."

"I agree with you," she said, "in that greatness is almost always based on perspective. In Lincoln's time, for every American who thought him great, another held a contrary opinion."

I thought about that for a moment, then offered: "Perhaps that is a prerequisite for greatness, that a man takes initiative in the face of opposition. Lincoln was a humble man with humble origins, and I imagine he thought of his actions not in terms of greatness but instead morality."

"So greatness is a term affixed to an individual by others, in Lincoln's case by historians?"

I nodded. "I imagine he'd be embarrassed by the memorial in Washington that bears his likeness."

"I won't argue that, but greatness in our culture I think is generally overrated."

"How so?"

"Our society is full of actors, and sports figures, idols who not only self-profess greatness but also manage to contrive large followings of the general public who help perpetuate that image."

"An idol is an object of worship. Something visible but lacking substance. Self-professed greatness is often a cover for insecurity. Greatness is a term best left to others to attach, although the Academy tends to be political in awarding best actor awards. To make it into baseball's Hall of Fame, one has to amass Hall-of-Fame-worthy statistics."

"And you?" she asked. "Do you aspire to the Hall of Fame?"

"No," I said. "I'm not arrogant enough to think I'll make it into the Hall. And I would imagine most inductees never played with the thought of making it. I love to play baseball, and I love the thrill of competition and winning. I play to the best of my abilities. After my playing days are over, if I've managed to attain the necessary statistics, I can only hope to be so honored, but that's not why I play. Anyone who does is not, in my mind, a ballplayer, but a statistician."

Darlene said nothing, so I added: "I've resolved to enjoy my on-field accomplishments after my playing days are over. If I think too much about yesterday's four-for-four day at the plate, I'm likely to go oh-for-four today, just as dwelling on an alternate yesterday's poor plate performance will likely end up in a prolonged slump."

Darlene nodded. "And this Cobb? I didn't realize he was a real persona, but from what I read of him in Lardner's book, he was not a nice man."

"That's an understatement," I said. "He was a despicable human being—arrogant, mean, nasty, a racist, a philanderer, a wife-beater."

"And so why is he in the Hall of Fame?"

"I see your point," I said. "Yet the Hall of Fame is about contributions to the game. Cobb forever changed the way the game is played. He still holds the record for highest career batting average, most batting titles—neither may ever be topped—most career runs, and several other records. He's the only player ever to reach first base and steal second, third and home on consecutive attempts. And he did that more than once."

"But how can you separate the essential man from his accomplishments?"

"Put that way it's difficult. I admit when I take the field at Tiger Stadium and look out to center field—the same center field in which Cobb played—I'm somewhat awed by his ghost. My own brush with greatness, I suppose."

"If he were alive today, would you want to meet him?"

"No. Having read his biography, I know enough about him to dislike him as a human being, and still I can set aside his life outside the chalk lines in deference to what he accomplished between them. Meeting him I think would only blend the myth and the legend with the man. He would become too human, and I fear the boy inside me would be greatly disappointed."

Darlene said nothing, and I sensed my answer had surprised her. I continued: "I admit, as a society we are preoccupied with greatness; second only to our satisfaction when greatness stumbles, which no doubt says a lot about our way of life."

"You're right about that," she said. "Sports hold a place in any society, but we've taken it to extreme, paying outrageous salaries for play acting and playing games, while teachers and social workers eke out a living. Hitler was responsible for the deaths of six million Jews and countless others during the war—yet he was a great leader who pulled Germany out of the depths of economic depression?"

I could say nothing to refute her wisdom; she went on: "I'm not comparing Cobb to Hitler. One played at politics, the other at a kid's game. Yet Cobb is but one sports figure. I'm sure there were others, are others and will always be others, who receive accolades for playing a game, but leave much to be desired as people."

"I can't argue that, but that's true in any walk of life. Your ex-lover was a fine lawyer, but he couldn't be true to you. Does his infidelity take away from his lawyer skills?"

"I suppose not," she said. "Fortunately I'm beyond judging him and, hopefully, all men, but that doesn't mean I'm not carrying around baggage as a result of what he did."

"Well, I lay no claim to that baggage," I said to lighten up the somber moment, "but I promise to be understanding and patient of it." Darlene smiled and I added, "I'm sorry to bring that up, if it's still a sore spot. Heavy conversation for a second date."

"That it is," she said. "I'll let you know when I'm sensitive to something."

"We haven't even breached the topics of politics, religion or sex," I said, and Darlene laughed. "But I suppose this is to be expected in a long-distance relationship. Everything will tend to get compressed. The highs will be high, the lows ..."

"Remind me again why we're doing this?"

"Because we like each other."

"Do we, really?" she asked, her tone again serious. "It occurred to me along about Wednesday, after we spoke on the phone, that we don't really know each other well enough to like one another."

"But we know each other well enough to know we don't dislike one another."

"A *dis*like for someone most assuredly will keep two people from ever becoming a couple. But 'like' isn't what brings a couple together. Like is something that comes after love, isn't it, when the heat of lust and passion simmers?"

"Maybe," I said. "It *is* what keeps a couple together. Yet there is something between us—some reason I asked you to come to Detroit and some reason you agreed to it. A physical attraction, yes, but intellectual, too, yes?"

"I admit I find our discussions stimulating."

"Which is good for the long haul."

Darlene nodded.

"And our kisses?"

Darlene blushed and said nothing, but she couldn't refrain from smiling.

"I love it when you do that."

"What?"

"Blush."

She reddened more and said, "I hate it."

"Well I find it endearing."

"I suppose I should say thank you."

"You're welcome. I hope it's something you will do only for me."

"I'd better warn you, it's something I do when I get angry, too."

"I can't promise I won't make you angry from time to

time," I said. "But you wouldn't want me to be agreeable all the time, would you?"

"Of course not."

"Without the occasional disagreement, we'd be robbed of the opportunity to make up."

"I admire that in you. You're outspoken and passionate in your beliefs. You're not afraid to debate with me, to voice your opinion. That you were willing to risk, in defiance of your parents, to pursue your dream is very appealing."

"Ah, the bad-boy syndrome."

"Not at all," she said. "But I realized last night, as I was packing my bag and feeling my doubt creep in again, that I want someone in my life who can push me to take more and greater risks."

"I'll certainly do that," I said, "But rest assured you won't be alone. I won't ask you to risk anything I'm not willing to chance myself." I laughed.

"What?"

"Now I know we're meant to be together. I always pack the night before, too."

STEWART HAS REALLY SETTLED IN. After getting Evans on three pitches, he needs only nine more to strike out the side—home plate umpire Tim Welke is still giving us a generous outside corner. Nearly as important, Stewart doesn't shake me off once, trusting me to call the pitches.

As he sits down next to me in the dugout I notice he's in a zone, nearly a trance, as he stares straight ahead, not even taking in the action on the field. I've seen him in this state only a few times during the regular season and learned not to intrude. When he's like this, good things happen for us: his slider is vicious. Opposing batters swing at and miss pitches that look like cheese only to end up well out of the strike zone—and true to my nickname, I have to be on my toes ready to block those that end up in the dirt—while his curveball entices them to do little more than hit ground balls to our infielders.

If he can go three more innings, through the sixth, we'll be in good shape. Seven would be better, then we can turn it over to Cantrell, our set-up man, for the eighth and our closer, Brooks, for the ninth. Still, we need to generate some offense of our own and get into the visitor's bullpen, which has been shaky all series long.

"LOOK AT THIS," I said, pushing the morning sports section across the table between us. Darlene had, after ordering lunch, gone to the restroom. During her absence, I'd had a chance to glance over what was written about the game last night with the Yankees in the morning edition of the *Free Press*. While she read where I pointed, I added, "Mike O'Hare thinks the Tigers should send me back down to Triple-A for more seasoning. He doesn't think I'm yet ready for the majors. Usually he's spot-on and I agree with what he writes."

"Except when he writes something like this about you?"

"This isn't about me," I argued.

"Oh, now, Backstop, isn't it?"

"Well of course it is, but that's not what I meant. Does he think Ted Williams managed to drive home every runner that was in scoring position when he stepped to the plate?"

"But you're not Ted Williams."

"Of course not—no one will ever be the hitter Williams was. I struck out in the sixth with a runner at second, which is the basis for O'Hare's reasoning. But Collins brought him home, so really, no harm done. I'm not the only ballplayer who's ever failed to deliver in that situation, and I won't be the last. I admit, I'm struggling right now, but it's not like I'm being carved up at the plate. I'm hitting the ball hard but not getting rewarded. Often a bloop single or a seeing-eye ground ball is all it takes to get a hot streak going."

"So you think this O'Hare has it in for you?"

"No. I don't know," I said. "Maybe he's just being contentious. Notice how he writes that I struck out in a six-three loss to the Yankees, which leads the reader to infer the game was on the line and I failed to deliver."

"So in this instance the pen is mightier than the bat," she said, referencing my quip from the previous weekend.

"I've gotten some good press, too," I said. "Before the season started, Joe Falls wrote in *The Detroit News* that he thinks I'm going to be good for a long time."

"But you seem upset about what O'Hare wrote. Do you think maybe he's right, that you could benefit from some time in the minors?"

"No, I don't think he's right. I spent a year in the minors, and it was good for me, taught me a lot about the game, in addition to teaching me what I needed to work on if I wanted to play and stay in the bigs. But that was then and this is now. I belong here, I've proven that. It's not going to help me playing Triple-A. I can learn more, improve more, by playing against major leaguers."

"Well, just who is Mike O'Hare?"

"A columnist for the *Freep*."

"That's not what I meant, but you answered my question just the same. He's just a journalist, Backstop, with a job to do, which includes increasing readership, often by stirring up controversy. He doesn't make decisions for the Tigers."

"No, he doesn't. But that doesn't mean that somebody in the front office won't be swayed by what he writes and pressure our skipper into sending me down."

"So you think he's a good writer?"

I thought about Darlene's question. "He has skills. Personally, I think he, and all sportswriters, could be a little more objective. But more and more the sports page is becoming an op-ed forum to, as you said, sell copy."

"Could it be you're a little jealous of him?"

"Hardly," I said. "It's not like I had to fall back on playing baseball because I couldn't cut it as a sportswriter."

"Well, that he has pull with the Tigers' management, either through his skills as a writer or knowledge of the game, is an assumption on your part, and betrays insecurity. You can't control whether you get sent down for playing poorly. You *can* control, however, how you play. You shouldn't let it bother you, what O'Hare writes, any more than you should let what that other writer—"

"Joe Falls."

"You shouldn't let what Joe Falls writes about you inflate your ego."

"You're right," I said. "I can't walk on the field tonight thinking about what the press wrote about me, for good or bad, or for sure I'll lay an egg."

The waitress brought our lunch, and I folded the paper and set it down in the booth beside me, resolved not to let it influence the remainder of the afternoon.

"Thanks," I said to Darlene. "I needed someone to put that into perspective for me."

"You're welcome," she said. "I'm glad I could help."

"You more than helped," I said, putting my hand on hers.

"How's that?"

"You're level-headed, which is not one of my strengths when it comes to criticism. I often let things like that get to me. I know I need to work on that if I'm to succeed at this level. So you see, darlin' Darlene, we *are* good for each other."

Darlene rolled her eyes.

"What?" I said.

"Time will tell," she said, and I couldn't be certain the seriousness with which she spoke was contrived to ensure against moving ahead too quickly. Then she changed the subject: "You mentioned writing a baseball journal for the *Free Press*. Do I get to read it?"

"I'll be sure to send some back issues home with you."

"I WOULDN'T HAVE THOUGHT YOU TO BE A LOVER OF poetry," Darlene said as we exited the house in which Robert Frost once lived. Built in Ann Arbor, Michigan, in the mid-1830s, Frost, who is said to have invited students from the University of Michigan to share tea and talk about poetry in this house, also wrote many of his poems in it, including *Spring Pools*, which was written over a three-day period during which he reminisced about springtime in New England.

"Because I'm an athlete?" I said.

"You warned me once about generalities, but yes, I guess because you play baseball. I sometimes forget you also write. I imagine once I've read some of your work I'll find it easier to find the balance between the two."

"To answer your question, I'm not a lover of poetry," I said. "But I appreciate good writing, and Frost certainly produced good writing. I took a course in college as part of my study in journalism, and what poetry course isn't going to discuss and dissect Frost? I freely admit, a poet I'm not; but I certainly appreciate, from my own failed attempts to write verse, the talent it requires. More than any other literary genre, in poetry it is more difficult to avoid sounding contrived, to circumvent the cliché. I have a copy of Frost's work, and I'm making my way through it. Not something one reads from cover to cover in one sitting."

"I admit to not reading the sports pages, but the sports recaps on the late night news come across as cliché."

"True," I said, "and it's the same in the newspapers, but it's almost a requirement. Sports are tailor-made for euphemism. Still, as a kid growing up I resented the interviewer who stuck a microphone in some ballplayer's face and asked him what it felt like to lose the big game."

"What drew you to journalism in college?"

"My love of baseball. I figured if I didn't make it in the major leagues I could pursue a career writing about it."

"So you had a plan B."

"Oh, yeah. That was part of the negotiation process I went through with Dad. I gave in to an education and he gave in to letting me play ball."

"I'm sorry he didn't live to see you play for the Tigers."

"So am I, but I often wonder if his death didn't remove a lot of the pressure for me to succeed. After he was gone, I had only to prove to myself I could compete at this level."

"I wish I could have met him."

"In a sense you have. He lives in me. I've been told I

sound like him, deliver punch lines to jokes the same way. I have his sense of humor, even his temper, although I'm more of a shouter than the door-slammer, glass-tosser he was. He could hold a grudge, but thankfully I got from my mother her ability to let go after my venom is spent."

"And your competitive spirit, from whom did you get that?"

I laughed. "That would be Dad. He taught me how to play Ping Pong and used to clean my clock until my game improved. After I started to beat him, he gave up playing."

"So that's why you feel you wouldn't be able to improve your baseball skills in the minors."

"I never thought about that, but you may be right. I also know that I want to play against the best players—not that there is a vast difference in the skill level. The game itself, although played on a much larger stage, is actually easier to play in the bigs. The fields are much better manicured, the lights brighter, so an uneven, poorly-lit field isn't something a major leaguer has to play against. The pitchers have better control. Even the umpires are better, more consistent."

"So what makes a major league player?"

"Promise you won't laugh?"

"I promise to try *not* to—with your sense of humor that can be difficult."

"It's what's between the ears," I said, and Darlene laughed at my thinly veiled reference to her assertion that athletes have little smarts. "You didn't try very hard," I said in a feigned woeful tone.

"I'm sorry," she said. "You're not going to hold it against me are you?"

"Not at all. If anything you score points for being on the same page."

"For once!"

"You're too hard on yourself. If we were ever to sit down and talk all things lawyerly, not only would I not be on the same page, I wouldn't even be in the same book."

Darlene laughed and said, "Now that's funny!"

We walked, holding hands, a half-dozen steps in silence,

neither of us uncomfortable with the momentary lapse in discussion.

"Thank you," Darlene said, "for bringing me here, to Detroit, for the weekend. Also for bringing me here, to Greenfield Village. I had no idea this place existed."

"You're welcome," I said. "I only wish we had more time to spend here. Maybe after the season ends we can come back and take in the museum."

"I'd like that." And then, a few steps later she ventured, "I like very much that you hold my hand." I thought she sounded embarrassed by her admission.

"Really?" I said. "Why wouldn't I want to? It's a connection with you."

"That's just it," she said. "It's a connection. One that all creatures great and small crave, but human beings, once they reach adulthood, seem to shun or deem it inappropriate."

I was curious about where she was going but refrained from asking, letting her decide how far to take this revelation. A moment later she went on:

"My ex-boyfriend never held my hand in public. He was always concerned about appearances."

"And apparently not enough about your needs."

"Given how it ended, that should've been an alert."

"Hindsight is wonderful." A few steps later it was my turn to break the silence: "You're not sorry are you? That it ended?"

Darlene took a moment to consider her reply before saying, "From love to hate to indifference, it took time for me to come to terms with it. When I realized the issue was his and not me, I was able to let it go. It was not a healthy situation and could not have ended with me getting from him what I needed, so no, I'm not sorry that it ended. But I'm still bruised by how it ended."

"I'm sorry for your hurt," I said, "but I'm glad you're here with me today, pleased you've given us a chance to get to know one another. I promise I won't hurt you."

"Woo-boy," she said. "I know you gave me the world last weekend, but that's a mighty big promise."

"I know," I said. "A promise all couples make early on during the courtship ritual. But I'm content to go slowly, take it one step at a time, until we're ready for the next one."

"And Monday morning, when you take me to the airport, or next month or six months from now, if I can't take that next step or don't want to, what then?"

"First, I would hope that's a decision we would make together. Second, I don't think it'll take us six months to decide, and third, if you took it upon yourself to decide as early as Monday morning, I would be disappointed and would certainly try to convince you otherwise using my logic, my sense of humor, and as a last resort, I'd try to appeal to your sense of romance, with which you have been blessed in abundance, even if you don't recognize it."

"Wow," she said. "You really take no prisoners, do you?"

"I play to win," I said. "Baseball is a team sport. The nine players who take the field thinking of their personal stats won't win. Contrary to popular belief, love does not conquer all—not if one partner isn't committed to making it work. But you know that already."

"Well," Darlene said, "that's about as serious as I've yet heard you."

"Love is a serious business—it doesn't just happen. Getting to know someone can and should be fun, and if it's not, then yes, move on and cut your losses before you get too attached. But commitment to love requires work and dedication on the parts of both interested parties. Loving, too, can and should be fun, and rewarding. If I commit to you you'll get my best as well as my worst, along with my sacrifice, but I would expect the same from you. I can't do it alone."

"The worst?"

"You know, bedhead and morning breath, stubble. General crankiness when I'm slumping."

"I don't know that I can share you with baseball," she said, "the days and weeks that you're away—and if we decide to try this, I won't share you with other women."

"You won't have to," I said. This conversation was

serious, so far ahead in the game, like a manager making early moves to set up the late innings. Darlene was right: we hadn't known each other long enough for us to even consider whether we liked one another, only that each of us didn't dislike the other. Yet I liked her well enough to have flown her to Detroit to spend the weekend.

"Look," I added. "I understand your trepidation, your reasoning for not wanting to chance this, really, I do. Trust comes slowly, through time spent together. Yet until we come to a mutual trust, don't you think it might cross my mind with whom you might be keeping company while I'm on the road?"

"That would never happen," she said with marked indignation, and then, "but I see your point."

"You said it yourself—you and your ex-boyfriend worked for the same firm and lived in the same city and he wasn't faithful. If someone wants to cheat, they'll cheat."

"But playing baseball," she said. "You're a celebrity. Aren't you putting yourself in harm's way?"

"If by 'in harm's way' you mean setting myself up for temptation, no, I'm not like that. I'm a one-woman man. I know you have only my word on that, which is why I think it's important that we spend time together in order to build trust. I've already told you I don't expect to find a quality woman around the ballpark. You had the mettle to go through law school, pass the bar exam, endure a broken heart and choose to heal from it rather than beat your head against a brick wall, subjecting yourself to more torment. On top of all that, you've decided to start a business of your own. That's quality." I took a deep breath and punctuated all I'd said with, "Jeesh."

"What?"

"If this were a novel, the reader undoubtedly would think I was sounding mighty desperate about now."

"No," Darlene said. "Not desperate. Passionate."

"Which is one of the things about me you told me you found appealing."

"I do," she said, and seemed to consider saying something more; when she decided not to, I said:

"Well then give me a chance. Give *us* a chance, beyond Monday. You can't make an informed decision to go forward without all the information. If you decide Monday to bail on this, you could be missing out on something really special—that's the real risk, don't you think?"

"I know that, logically, in my head."

"Really?" I said with a chuckle, trying to lighten up the discussion. "I thought it was your heart you had difficulty following."

"They get mixed up sometimes."

"Understood. So try following your heart but using your head at the same time. Remember hindsight? It's little different than foresight except that it comes after the fact and you end up kicking yourself and asking, 'Why didn't I see that coming?' when all along you saw it but just chose to ignore it, as was the case with your old boyfriend."

"How old are you?" Darlene asked, startling me.

"I'll be twenty-five in September, why?"

"You're so much wiser than your years."

"You think?" I said, laughing. "You haven't seen some of the pranks I've pulled in the clubhouse."

"No, really," she said. "You seem much longer in the tooth than some of the young men I knew in law."

"Well, I always hung with older kids when I was younger—they were the better ballplayers and even then I wanted to prove my skills against the best—and I was always told I was mature for my age. But really, watching my dad die from cancer and watching my mother succumb a little more each day to Parkinson's, well, it forced me to come to grips with mortality, that life really is shorter than any of us realizes, and to understand what's important."

"And what is important to you?"

"How I play the game of baseball—to the best of my ability. That I don't give in to the celebrity that comes with being a major leaguer ... to not get caught up in material possessions and to give something back for all that baseball provides me—in this case to Parkinson's research. And to find and share my love and my life with someone who wants to share their love and life with me."

EVANS IS RIGHT: Fernando has brought his "A" game to the mound. Like Stewart, he's settled in. McCandles quickly falls behind 0 and 2 and hits a come-backer to Fernando, who casually tosses him out at first. Radford, our number nine hitter, goes down swinging during a four-pitch at-bat, and Trexler pops out to second, swinging at the first pitch.

After three innings, Fernando has faced one more than the minimum and the game remains scoreless.

Fourth Inning

I'M STANDING AT HOME PLATE WAITING FOR STEWART TO finish manicuring the mound before taking his warm-up tosses. I gaze around at the throng of Tigers' fans around me, and my eyes alight on a spot about halfway up the lower deck behind the visitor's dugout where, nearly thirty years ago as a young boy, I sat alongside my dad and watched Mickey Mantle launch a Denny McLain blooper into the right field seats. Dad had voiced his discontent at McLain's audacity, but it was an eclectic moment for me—one that I hadn't asked Dad, as he lay in hospice awaiting death, if he'd recalled, fearing that he might admit the contrary. I'd dreamed then of playing major league baseball, but I wonder now if I ever really believed I could make that dream come true. Tonight I'm on the baseball world's biggest stage—game seven of the World Series, scoreless—and I'm trying to enjoy the moment, creating memories that will last the rest of my life, wondering how I'll feel after it's over, win or lose. This is what we work for during the off-season, what we play for, beginning in spring training. My first World Series and I'm thrilled to be here, where so many other major league players—Hall of Famers and others with greater skills than mine—fell short; but my emotions are subdued, not what I'd thought they'd be, and I know why. I think of Darlene, who I still love and adore. I look over at the wives' box painfully aware of her absence, and I wonder again if she's watching from her home in Chicago, if she cares enough to share, from a distance, my joy in achieving this dream, to see us win or lose the championship. My eyes tear and I choke back a sob.

Welke says, "Hey, Backstop. You okay?" and I'm grateful for the catcher's mask behind which I can hide my emotion. I nod and tell him, "Yeah. Yeah, I'm fine."

I look out to Stewart, a blur anxiously waiting on me to drop into my crouch. I blink away the moisture and squat, ignoring the protest from my aging knees. Six more innings and I'll have the entire off-season to worry about the aches and pains that go with playing this demanding position and that come with advancing age, to consider whether I want to put my body through this rigor for another season. At thirty-eight, I'm old to play this kid's game and I know it; but to-night I have six more innings to pretend at being the kid I am at heart.

Stewart has faced the minimum through the first three innings and is due to face the top of the lineup again. We'd started Gallegos off with a fastball his previous trip to the dish, so this time I call for a curveball; Gallegos, sitting on the heater, is unable to pull the trigger, his knees buckling as Welke calls strike one. Gallegos glares at Welke, sure the pitch missed outside. I flash one finger and indicate up in the strike zone and set up inside; Stewart's pitch is right where I called for it, and Gallegos watches it go by for another called strike. I figure that Gallegos is convinced we'll expand the strike zone with something soft, so I call for another heater. Gallegos is late with his swing and lines the ball into the visitor's dugout, sending his teammates scurrying.

Gallegos grunts, a sign to me that he's unsure what I might call for Stewart to serve up next. I signal for the change and I see Stewart consider shaking me off, but he thinks better of it; he nods and goes into his delivery. His arm motion is good, indicative of the fastball, but the pitch is up and in and Gallegos, although ahead, manages to get his bat on the ball, near his fists, and send it straight up. I leap to my feet pulling off my mask and, after locating the ball, fling the mask behind me, race back calling for it several times and snatch the ball from out of the first row of seats. After the putout, I look at the kid, maybe five or six years old, sitting next to his dad in the front row with his own glove on his left hand.

"What's your name, kid?" I ask.

"Bobby," he tells me, his eyes big as baseballs.

I hand him the ball and tell him, "What do you say you hang on to that for me, Bobby? After the game, win or lose, I'll be back to autograph it for you."

"Thanks, Backstop," the kid says, grinning from ear-to-ear. I trot back to home plate thinking about how much I love this game, how much I'll miss playing it after I step away from it, and how I'll miss, most of all, moments like this—giving a kid a memory that'll last a lifetime.

WE TOOK THE FIELD SHORTLY AFTER SEVEN; I was acutely aware of Darlene's presence in the wives' box. It was important I do well, my male ego wanting to impress her; but I was also haunted by O'Hare's article in the morning *Freep*. I knew it was vital that I clear my mind of both their presences if I was to play up to my expectations.

McGillicuddy sent down the first six Yankees he faced, while we managed to get the leadoff man on in our half of the second and move him to third, when I came to the plate with two out. I struck out swinging on the third pitch to end the threat. As I headed back to the dugout I couldn't help but think my job was on the line and that I'd end up in Toledo if I didn't start producing. Strapping on my gear in the dugout, I cursed myself for trying to do too much at the plate and promptly made a Herculean effort to kick O'Hare's ass out of my head.

We headed into the fifth inning still scoreless in what had turned into a good old-fashioned pitching duel, and with one out, I hit a hard grounder just inside third base that ended up in the corner in left field and left me standing at second base without having to dirty my uniform with a slide. Unfortunately, the inning ended with me still at second as Gibbons struck out and North popped up to second base.

Gutierrez, the Yankees' shortstop, laid down a perfect bunt toward first base for a single in the top of the seventh; then, using his speed, he tried to get into scoring position by stealing second. Fortunately, I smelled him out—no mean feat since, given the circumstance of a scoreless game heading into the late innings, everyone in the ballpark knew he was going—and called for a pitchout, firing a frozen rope to Gibbons to nail Gutierrez in a play that wasn't close.

I led off our half of the seventh with another double, this one deep into the gap in left center, and scored two outs later when Owens singled the opposite way to right field.

McGillicuddy was tiring but managed to persuade the skipper to let him go out for the eighth with a one run lead. This was, after all, the Yankees against whom he was pitching, the most storied franchise in major league baseball. He walked the first batter but got the next two, both on deep fly balls after taking the counts to full—the first to the wall in left and the second nearly to the warning track in center, the deepest part of Tiger Stadium. He was leaving the ball up in the strike zone, evidence that he was nearly out of gas. I met the skipper at the mound convinced McGillicuddy was done, but true to form, McGillicuddy, our ace, managed to convince the skipper he had enough left in the tank to get the next batter. I told him we could get Martinez with soft stuff and McGillicuddy didn't argue; yet when I got behind the dish and called for the curve, he shook me off. As a second-year catcher I knew enough not to argue, so after he also shook off the changeup, I looked over to our dugout, shook my head and proceeded to call for the fastball, setting up outside. McGillicuddy came right down the middle, belt high, and Martinez, sitting on it, drove it deep into the upper deck in right field. McGillicuddy was done for the night with no chance to pick up the win. Hart came in to get the next batter.

McGillicuddy glared at me when I came to the dugout for the bottom of the eighth, pissed off that I'd shown him up by looking toward our dugout, my own show of exasperation. But he knew not to say a word, not after I'd told him we should go after Martinez with soft stuff. Second-year catcher or not, he knew I wouldn't back down from a confrontation. Despite being our ace, McGillicuddy wasn't ever going to make it to the Hall of Fame. He'd had a penchant for blowing big games throughout his ten-year career, which was now entering the twilight stage. He also had an ego that was larger than his talent pool. I ignored his glare, knowing it was pointless to discuss the homerun he'd given up, disappointed that the skipper hadn't pulled rank and put in Hart one batter sooner, and knowing, too, that we still had two innings in which to pull out a win.

We went down in order in our half of the eighth, but Hart sent the Yankees down one, two, three in the ninth, and so we found ourselves down to our final three outs.

Reese, the Yankees' closer, retired our first two batters, but Myers managed to beat out a slow roller to third base for an infield single, which left it up to me. I stepped into the batter's box resolved to look for a fastball that I could drive somewhere.

Reese started me off with a slow curve that missed outside and Meyers went down to second base uncontested. He wouldn't record a steal the result of defensive indifference, which rankled me. The Yankees were apparently confident that they'd be able to get me out to end the threat and the game.

Reese came after me with another curveball that I watched go by for strike one. My own indifference told the Yankees battery I was looking for the heat, so they proceeded to throw soft stuff, the next pitch a change that landed in the dirt for ball two. After that, another curve that I pulled foul just outside the bag at third—a few inches to the right and I'd have had myself my third double of the game and, more importantly, brought home the tying run. Now that he'd gotten me thinking off-speed stuff, Reese came at me with a rising fastball; behind on it, I slapped it hard down past first base but foul.

After that, Reese resorted to the soft stuff, expanding the strike zone, forcing me to stay alive by fouling off pitches as I continued to look for the fastball I knew would eventually come.

I had an eleven-pitch at-bat going, the count still at two-two, when Reese again tried to sneak the heat past me; unfortunately, he overthrew it and it sailed way high to send the count to full. Reese was tiring, and he looked frustrated as he walked to the back of the mound to pick up the rosin bag and catch his breath. Manson, the Yankees' catcher, called time to go out to chat with Reese and give him a chance to catch his breath.

When he returned, I stepped back into the box and, tapping the dish with my lumber, found Mike O'Hare peeking in to tell me I'd do well to be sent down to the minors for more seasoning. I immediately called time and stepped back out of the batter's box to focus my thoughts. "Get outta here," I muttered to O'Hare.

Manson must've thought I was playing at being Ruth by calling my shot and so he told me, "Not a chance."

I chuckled and, O'Hare banished for the moment, dug back into the batter's box.

After taking a couple of practice swings, I squinted out at Reese who was looking in for the sign, and I guessed he'd come after me with another fastball. A moment later he rocked back and went into his motion. Reese wasn't very good at disguising his pitches; his curveballs all came at me with a slightly off-center arm slot, his fastball right over the top. When I saw his arm motion come forward I was locked and loaded. Without thinking mechanics, I kept my head down, rotated my hips out of the way and timed my swing perfectly, connecting with the ball on the sweet spot of my lumber, resulting in a resounding crack. I knew I'd hit it hard and that it was gone. It was just a matter of how far the ball would travel. I went into my homerun trot as the crowd erupted and I watched the ball carry, and carry and carry, until it glanced off the facing of the upper deck in left field. It was the first walk-off homerun of my young career.

By the time I got back to home, my teammates were all waiting for me in a mad melee of celebration. Even McGillicuddy offered me his somewhat subdued congratulations, although I questioned his sincerity—he much preferred being the center of such celebrations. With such an attitude, I wondered if the Tigers could ever hope to win the gonfalon with him in our starting rotation.

I STEPPED OUT OF THE CLUBHOUSE AND INTO THE PLAYERS' parking lot along with several of my teammates, where

Darlene greeted me warmly—a hug and a quick kiss on the lips.

"How exciting," she said. "You were wonderful!"

I muttered my thanks to her as several other wives voiced congratulations and then McGillicuddy, who'd followed me out of the clubhouse, said in a loud obnoxious voice, "What's this, Backstop, a new squeeze? You've been holding out on us." He gave Darlene the once over. "You going to introduce us?" The "us" was not intended to include the rest of the team, but instead to imply a personal introduction.

I glanced at Darlene, who barely managed to hide her disdain at McGillicuddy's pomposity, winked at her and said, "Guys, meet Darlene."

Most of the guys voiced variations of, "Nice to meet you," but McGillicuddy stuck out his hand and said loudly, "Hey, Darlin'."

Darlene's previous contempt turned to outward disgust, but for my sake she took his hand.

"That's Darlene to you and everyone else here, save for me," I said, trying to make light of McGillicuddy's overt come-on. He was the consummate buffoon to everyone present except himself. McGillicuddy ignored me.

"I'm McGillicuddy," he said, "but my teammates call me Mac. Are you going to be my teammate?"

Darlene was turning red, and I recalled how she'd blushed earlier out of shyness, but this time it was from anger. She glanced at me and I knew, buffoon or not, my previous diplomatic effort to put McGillicuddy in his place had come up short. I realized Darlene was keeping mum in deference to me, but that didn't mean she didn't expect me to put McGillicuddy in his place.

"Teammate?" I said. "You could learn a thing or two about team play after shaking me off twice only to give up that dinger to Martinez."

McGillicuddy looked over at me, the first time he'd taken his eyes off Darlene since we'd emerged from the clubhouse. I could see the anger in his eyes, but he was careful not to let it show to the others; to do so would be to betray I'd bested him. He looked around as the silence lingered uncomfortably, mirroring the looks of discomfort on the faces of the circle of Tigers and Tigers' wives.

"Relax, Backstop," he said. "I was only flirting."

"Try flirting with your wife for once," I said, "or anyone else who might welcome it for all I care. Darlene is off limits, understand?"

McGillicuddy's eyes told me to fuck off. What he said was, "Why don't we let Darlene decide what her limits are?"

I reddened with my own anger. I never had cared much for McGillicuddy. It wasn't enough he was a wrecker—he'd wrecked his own marriage and was prone to wreck his own fine pitching performances, as infrequent as they were, as he had tonight, nearly snatching defeat from the jaws of victory. Now he had to meddle in my off-the-field life. I drew in a breath, unsure of what I was going to say, but Darlene cut me off.

"Mr. McGillicuddy," she said. "Let me make my limits clear. Your flirtations are most *un*welcome."

I watched McGillicuddy's eyebrows rise; a moment later he said: "Well, far be it from me to force my affections on the damsel who doesn't welcome them, not when there are so many others who will."

With that, McGillicuddy stepped out of the circle and made his way toward his car; after a half-dozen steps he turned around to address me: "Just remember what I told you a year ago in spring training, Backstop. Don't let it affect your play."

Never had I wanted to hit someone so much. I had no comeback, but thankfully Hart came to my rescue: "Hey, Mac, if she's responsible for his heroics tonight, I say bring it on."

McGillicuddy, perhaps without a comeback of his own, only chuckled and walked off to find his car.

"Thanks, Hart," I said as the group started to break up.

"No problem, Backstop," he said, and then to Darlene he added, "Don't let Mac get to you. He's bigheaded but rather harmless. You just need to set boundaries and boy, did you ever set your boundaries. Trust me, was he ever irked."

ONCE IN THE CAR, I turned to Darlene and said, "I'm sorry about that."

"Whatever for?" she said. "You weren't the ass."

"I should've been able to put him in his place."

"You tried," she said. "But he's arrogant and obstinate. You'd only have ended up hitting him."

"You have no idea."

"Oh, you're mistaken there."

"Were my intentions that transparent?" When Darlene said nothing, I added, "It really riled me that he called you Darlin'."

"Well, I hope you won't let it deter you from calling me that in the future. From you, I like it."

I was surprised that she'd recalled from earlier in the day that I'd applied that term of endearment to her name.

Darlene continued: "I appreciate your attempts to defuse the situation with humor and your restraint in resorting to violence, but understand I can handle myself."

"I know that," I said. "You handled him very well. But I feel as if somehow I failed."

"You didn't fail," she said. "He was right in that I needed to set the boundaries." A moment, and then, "I'd have had less respect for you had you hit him, even if he deserved it."

"Sometimes the fist is mightier than the word," I said. "Although Hart managed to put him in his place."

"Well, I'm glad it didn't come to that. After all, you have to play alongside him."

"I wish I didn't have to," I said. "If he finishes his career with the Tigers or gets traded, it won't be too soon for me. His presence in the clubhouse is a cancer."

WHEN WE GOT TO DARLENE'S ROOM I ASKED HER HOW SHE got along with the other wives.

"They were all very nice to me and complimentary of

you, but honestly … I don't know quite how to say this …"

"What?"

"I think I understand what you mean about women at the ballpark."

I nodded to show I understood.

"And Trish?" she added. "I suspect she has a bit of a crush on you."

"Hart's wife?"

"She would never act on it, and I'm sure you would never take advantage, but yes, it was rather obvious to me."

I didn't know quite what to say. Hart was a highly principled man, deeply religious, as was Trish, so he'd told me. Darlene seemed to be looking at me expectantly, so I stepped over to her and kissed her. I let the kiss linger, taking my cue from her, until it turned opulent. When we parted, I stroked her cheek, marveling at its softness and noting its crimson flush from our afternoon in the sun at Greenfield Village, but I thought I detected her own passion, too, not only in her complexion but in her eyes. Darlene sighed as I let my eyes fall to the plunging neckline of her blouse, where the sun had left the olive tone of her cleavage tinged pink.

"Thanks," I said, resisting my desire, "for coming out this weekend."

"It's been more fun than I could've imagined," she whispered. She seemed to be waiting.

"I know it's too early for me to tell you I like you," I said, reluctant to change the mood but knowing I must. "But I'm very drawn to you."

Darlene only looked up at me and I, nearly drowning in the depths of her brown eyes, resisted the urge to kiss her again. Instead I said, "I should leave you to get ready for bed. I'll pick you up for breakfast at 9:30."

A moment later, looking back at her from the open door, standing in the middle of the room—her dark and voluminous hair, sumptuous features and bare shapely legs all screaming at my desire—I said, "Goodnight."

"Goodnight," she replied, and then, "Thank you, Backstop."

It wasn't until the elevator doors opened on the hotel lobby that I understood why she'd thanked me.

AFTER WE RETIRED GALLEGOS, Richards doubles into the gap in right center. With one out, I look into our dugout where the skipper relays the sign to give Reese the intentional pass, playing for the double play off Porter's bat, who is batting only .198 in the series. Unfortunately, after the intentional walk, Stewart loses his rhythm and walks Porter on four straight pitches. With the bases now loaded, I trot out to the mound to settle him down. I see a glazed look in Stewart's eyes, as if he is carrying the weight of this World Series game seven on his shoulders, which in a sense, he is.

"Relax," I tell him, putting my gloved hand on his shoulder. "You're throwing, not pitching. We're one ground ball away from getting out of this. Forget the runners, focus on the batter. Keep the ball down and pitch to the target."

"Okay," he says.

"We can get Higgins with your heat. It's still your bread and butter," I tell him to bolster his confidence, "but we'll need to set him up with the curveball." Then I pat him on his behind and say, "No pressure. Good luck, we're all counting on you."

Stewart chuckles and I see the doe in the headlights demeanor disappear.

When I get back to the plate, I check our defensive alignment; satisfied, I drop into my crouch and go through a series of signs designed to mask from the runner at second base the curveball intended to set up the heat. Stewart misses with it down and in, with Higgins checking his swing, telling me he's looking for the soft stuff. When Welke denies my appeal, I stand and fire the ball back to Stewart, nodding to reassure him in the aftermath of our purpose pitch. I crouch and signal for the fastball, and Stewart overthrows it in the dirt but I manage to block it, preventing the runners from advancing. Stewart misses with another fastball, sending the count to three balls and no strikes. Everyone in the park knows another fastball is on the way, so I signal for the changeup and, hoping to put some doubt into his head, mutter to Higgins that Stewart won't miss with another fastball. Stewart throws the change in a perfect location—down and in—and Higgins rolls over on it and hits it to the shortstop for a tailor-made double play to end the top half of the fourth, keeping the game scoreless.

In the dugout, Stewart sits next to me and thanks me. At twenty-three years old, I was playing minor league ball, and here, after losing games five and six in this series, Stewart, at age twenty-three, is being asked to play the role of stopper in the biggest game of his short career. In that moment I realize what I am to him, in part the result of building trust by having called games for him all season long: part role model, part voice of reason, part shrink. But for that last out, perhaps most importantly, I had showed confidence in him. I think of Dad, who'd expressed doubt in me, and of my first few years in this league. I'd had no one who took me under their tutelage, no veteran player who helped acclimate me to the big leagues; and Tom Anders, our manager at that time, was a throwback to some bygone era who lacked the ability to handle young players.

I nod to Stewart and say, "You've a long career ahead of you, Stew. You've good stuff, maybe the best I've seen on this staff." Then, thinking of my old nemesis, McGillicuddy, I add, "Don't let it go to your head. Ever. Enjoy this night, whether or not you go the distance, whether or not we win, because you might not ever get this chance again."

I think again of my dad, who, in trying to protect me, strove to prevent my chance at this chance. Stewart says nothing and I wonder if, at twenty-three, he understands.

❧

THE NEXT MORNING, AS WAS MY CUSTOM DURING HOME stands, I checked the morning sports section in *The News* to see what had been written about the previous night's game and read that Joe Falls had again written approvingly about my performance, lavishing great praise on my last inning heroics. "Take that, O'Hare," I muttered. Then I recalled what Darlene had said the previous day, that I shouldn't let negative press affect me any more than I should let good press inflate my ego. I folded the paper and dropped it on my coffee table, making sure to bring along several copies of my sports journal, as I'd promised Darlene I would.

"MMM," I moaned after I kissed Darlene. "Just as sweet as I remember from last night."

Darlene demurely said nothing, but her blush spoke volumes.

"You look great," I said, holding her by the hips at arm's length to look at her delightful figure beneath the floral sundress she wore. "I thought maybe you'd gotten too much sun yesterday."

"Someone reminded me to bring sunscreen. I'm Greek and don't burn easily, but I'd be a fool to think the sun doesn't damage my skin."

I kissed her again and, in response to her response, asked her if she was sure she didn't like me.

"I like how you make me feel," she said, and I thought she was avoiding my question. She embraced me warmly. "I had a hard time falling asleep last night."

"Yeah," I said, chuckling. "I don't sleep well in strange beds either."

"That's not what I meant," she said, smiling.

"Well if it's any consolation, I struggled to find the Sandman, too. I feared he'd opted to spend the night with you."

Darlene laughed and said, "So, Backstop. What does the morning paper say about your performance in last night's game?"

Grinning, I said, "See how well you already know me?"

"I thought you'd be pleased," she said, indicating the sports section on the table in the corner of her room.

"So you were curious, too."

"Of course."

"You're right, though, what you said yesterday. I can't get caught up in what the press writes about me. The media is fickle. Had I struck out last night to end the game they surely would've forgotten the two doubles I hit, as well as the homerun McGillicuddy served up, and focused on how I failed to come through in the clutch."

"You have a minor in journalism and only now understand that?"

"An easier lesson to learn when you're a disinterested third party. Still, I think I'd do well to cancel my subscription to *The Freep*."

"Really?" she said. "I had you pegged for a scrapbook."

"The funny thing about scrapbooks," I said, "they tend to tell a one-sided story—all good."

"There's nothing wrong with that."

"No, but I don't need a scrapbook to recall my moments of success. I'm sure that when my playing days are over I'll recall with fondness the highlights of my career."

Darlene seemed to consider a reply but refrained.

"Well," I said, "What do you say we get breakfast?"

"I'll be right back," she said, and departed for the bathroom, leaving me to admire her lovely legs, and I recalled last night's fantasy as I'd waited for sleep's mercy.

"DID YOU REMEMBER TO BRING COPIES OF YOUR BASEBALL journal?"

"I did," I said. "They're in the backseat of the car. I'll warn you now they're not nearly as entertaining as Lardner's novel, but they'll at least give you some insight into the life of a major league ballplayer."

"I'm hoping they'll allow me a glimpse into who you are, too, as a person."

I thought a moment as I took a sip of coffee, then said, "I doubt they will. I'm really a very private person and prefer keeping my private life out of the paper."

"Someone told me recently that one of the reasons they read fiction is to get a glimpse inside the author's head."

I laughed. "Now I understand why you were such a good

lawyer—not much escapes your notice and you've a very good memory."

"And it's not always what you say, but how you say it that reveals a person's nature, their personality."

"You're right about that, too," I said. "The editor at the *Free Press* and I agreed that we didn't want a dry third-person narrative, but instead a colorful account by someone in the game. Not just a report of what happens on the field, but a narrative of what takes place in the locker room, during batting practice, between teammates, coaches, the manager. We want to bring to the reader much of what goes on behind the game. My take on every piece is that of a retired ballplayer telling a story to his grandchildren. I can be as cranky as I like—the curmudgeon relating how I got tossed out of a game for arguing balls and strikes with the ump, or the clown telling how the new rookie was initiated in the locker room."

"That's a wonderful approach," Darlene said. "I imagine there are a host of people, like me, who are disinterested in sports because the players are just so many names with a number on their backs. Yesterday's game was meaningful to me because I know you personally."

I laughed and said, "And now you know McGillicuddy personally, too."

Darlene rolled her eyes. "He represents everything negative I ever thought about athletes: shameless superiority and ignorance of the real world, and the misconception of how the real world views them."

"He is all of those things," I agreed, "shameless, arrogant and ignorant. Not to defend him—I dislike him as much as you do—but athletes in general have to believe in themselves, their talent, in order to succeed. Baseball players especially have to deal with the mental toughness of this game. You strand a runner in scoring position but have to go out to your position and not let it affect your defense, and then sit on the bench and watch eight other batters go to the plate until you have another chance to prove yourself. McGillicuddy used to have pretty good stuff; he was one of the premier pitchers in the game a few years ago, before I joined the Tigers. Unfortunately, he's better in his own mind than he really is. He refuses to adjust his game to his aging arm, bringing his "A" game to the mound less and less frequently than he used to, refusing to relinquish his reliance on his diminished fastball in preference for his command and control. And of course his ego prevents him from listening to anyone, least of all a second-year catcher."

"Sounds like an entry from your journal."

"I wish it could be," I said, "but I would be committing career suicide if I went public with my opinion of a teammate. You said it yesterday—I have to share a locker room with these guys, and if I wrote something disparaging of McGillicuddy, every one of them would ostracize me, wondering when I might single one of them out for having a bad day at the plate."

"I see your point."

"Maybe after I hang up my spikes, should I write an autobiography, but even that carries with it certain risks. I wouldn't want to sound like the disgruntled former player pointing fingers at former teammates to maintain my own place in the spotlight, seeking to sell copies by being controversial."

"Is that what you intend to do after you retire, write a book?"

"Maybe," I said. "But that's a long way off. Right now I just want to play baseball. I'll worry about whether my career is interesting enough to write about after I hang up my spikes."

AT THE BALLPARK, after my pre-game stretches, I took batting practice. After yesterday's good day at the plate, and with the knowledge that Darlene was looking on, I felt loose and saw the ball well, hitting it hard—line drives, finding the gap in left center, and three times hitting it over the wall; then I worked on hitting it the opposite way. After taking my cuts, I headed for the dugout, feeling good about the upcoming game. A moment after finding a spot on the bench,

McGillicuddy sat down next to me.

"That Darlene of yours sure is one hot tamale," he said.

"That she is," I said, wondering if McGillicuddy was trying to get inside my head, to ruin my day at the plate. "She's also got a good head on her shoulders. She's smart, compassionate and a lot of other things I imagine mean nothing to you."

McGillicuddy ignored me. "You wouldn't mind if I had another go at her, would you?"

So he was trying to ruin my day. After Darlene told him last night that his advances were unwelcome, I was pretty certain McGillicuddy had no intention of putting his ego in the path of her rejection, and I was adamant about not letting him get inside my head.

"Look," I told him, "I don't like you McGillicuddy, not as a person, not as a teammate. I think your best playing days are long past. I'll call games for you, and you can shake me off like you did last night if you feel like serving cheese, and if you want to make a fool of yourself throwing yourself at a woman who thinks even less of you than I do, be my guest." McGillicuddy said nothing as I got up and found another spot on the bench.

Stanley, our third-year southpaw who I envisioned one day becoming the ace of our staff after McGillicuddy was gone, had a good day on the mound, limiting the Yankee batters to four hits and a lone run in an eight to one romp. I hit for the cycle, the first Tiger to achieve that feat since Hoot Evers did it in 1950. In the bottom of the second, I hit a first pitch fastball deep into the lower deck in left, followed up that with a double in the fifth, scoring on a single, singled in the seventh, and finished the day with a triple on a long fly ball to the flagpole in center in the ninth, chugging into third base standing up. The game was stopped momentarily while Higgins, our third base coach, retrieved the ball for me.

In the clubhouse after the game, after I'd showered, Hart came by to hand me the baseball I'd hit for the triple. After ruffling my hair he told me, "Great game, Backstop."

"Thanks," I said, dimly aware of McGillicuddy getting dressed at the locker across from mine; he'd said nothing to me since our exchange before the game. I looked at the ball where Hart had written, *Hit for the cycle ... what a Hoot!* — the last a tribute to Evers. "Thanks, Hart, but with my speed, that'll likely be the only triple I ever hit."

Hart laughed and said: "If you can continue to find the flagpole, I imagine you'll have plenty more." And then: "Your friend, Darlene, is she staying for the Boston series?"

"Alas, no," I said. "She's heading back to Chicago tomorrow morning. She has a business to run."

"Too bad," he said. "I hope her good luck stays with you. Maybe you ought to let her touch all your bats."

I laughed. Baseball players are a superstitious lot. "That may not be a bad idea." And then, "But that's not like you, Hart. You always put your trust in a higher authority."

Hart laughed, said: "It's good to have friends in high places."

McGillicuddy was gone and I hadn't seen him depart. In that moment I realized he'd become a non-entity to me.

I TOOK DARLENE TO GREEKTOWN FOR DINNER AT Pizzapopolis.

"I don't normally indulge in pizza during the season, preferring to eat healthier," I said. "But it's one of my favorite foods, and I figured we should celebrate your first visit to the Motor City. Hopefully the first of many."

"And a Tigers' win," Darlene reminded me, holding up her glass of Heineken, "as well as you hitting for the cycle. I had no idea what that was until Trish told me."

I laughed, touched her glass with mine, and said, "Baseball is a game made for statistics. Sometimes they go too far, though, when they calculate a switch hitter's average against left-handed pitching on Tuesday night games played in the month of August on artificial turf, indoors, with runners in scoring position with two out and the count full."

Darlene smiled and told me again that she thought my sense of humor delightful. "I have no idea what all that means, but if you write as colorfully as you talk, I imagine your journal will be just as entertaining as Lardner's novel."

"Thanks," I said sheepishly, abashed by her praise.

"Why do you have such a difficult time accepting a compliment?"

"I don't know," I said, surprised by my transparency. "I suspect it might have something to do with not receiving much approval from my dad while I was growing up."

"That may also be why it's important to you what the press writes about you."

"It's something with which I continually struggle," I said. "I play the game because I love it, and I don't need the press to tell me when I've had a good game or a bad one, but somewhere inside of me must be a kid seeking approval whether from a cheering crowd or a sportswriter."

"It's human nature to seek approval from others, especially in professional sports, I imagine, where the stakes are high and the stage so visible. But I suspect the best athletes are those who are able to shun the outside criticism, as well as the accolades, and compete for their own enjoyment and personal satisfaction."

"You're a wise woman, Darlin'," I said. "Is it any wonder I'm drawn to you?"

At that moment our pizza was brought to us.

"Ah, I love a good pizza," I said.

"And it's not as unhealthy as you think—it contains ingredients from the four basic food groups. And there's something to be said, too, for liquid carbohydrates," she added before taking a sip of her beer.

"I like the way you think," I said. "A good stuffed pizza is hard to find in this town, and this is the best I've found outside of Chicago."

"I'll be the judge of that," Darlene said. "It looks delicious, but remind me to take you to one or two of my favorite places in Chicago. What?" she said to my chuckle.

"It does my heart good to hear you making plans for our future."

"I suppose I am, aren't I?" she said, smiling. And then,

to guide the conversation into safer waters, she added, "You really are a good baseball player."

"Thanks," I said, determined to accept her praise with grace rather than embarrassment. "Not to deflect your compliment, but baseball is a very humbling game. You happened to catch a series during which I played well, and I have you to thank for that. It felt good knowing you were watching. But this game is filled with ups and downs. Make no mistake: luck plays its part. Baseball is often a game of inches—a ground ball down the line can seem to have a mind of its own when it rolls foul, or a hard-hit ball right at someone continues a slump, just as the seeing-eye ground ball can extend a hitting streak. Every hitting streak eventually ends, as does every slump. The key is to keep the slumps to a minimum and ride the streaks with humility."

"Well, thank you, too," she said, "but you have skills, that's obvious. If you didn't, you wouldn't be playing for the Tigers, and my watching would matter little more than if your dad was watching."

"Maybe so, but every successful man boasts of a good woman who stirs him to achieve greatness. Don't downplay your role this weekend in inspiring me to play well."

Darlene smiled and said, "I'm glad I could be here for you."

"So am I."

"This is good," Darlene said after her first bite, "But it's not as good as Nancy's back home."

"I'm glad you like it, and I look forward to sampling Nancy's next time I'm in Chicago."

We ate in silence for a few minutes, and then I said: "I've been thinking about a business proposition. How would you feel about becoming my agent? My contract is up at the end of the season."

"But I know nothing of the baseball fraternity."

"You don't have to," I said. "You specialized in contract negotiation, and I'm not looking to hold the Tigers for ransom. Hell, I'd play this game for meal money."

"Well," she said with a grin, "I think it prudent you

don't let management know that."

"See?" I said jokingly. "I'm already benefiting from your sage advice. But really, I just need you to ensure no one is taking advantage of me."

"Don't you think we may be getting ahead of ourselves?"

"Maybe. But you don't have to decide now. We've got until the end of the season. By then we should know where we stand with each other, and even if we decide against continuing our budding romance, there's no reason why I shouldn't pay you fifteen percent of what you negotiate. We'd both benefit. Just give it some thought."

❧

REYNOLDS SWINGS AT THE FIRST PITCH AND HITS A SOFT fly to the left fielder to lead off our half of the fourth. Lott follows with a five-three groundout. When Miller works the count to three-two, the home crowd, which has grown uneasy in this pitchers' duel, begins to voice its support. Miller sends Fernando's tenth offering, a fastball, deep into the gap in left center; the crowd erupts in anticipation of a homerun and our entire bench leaps to the railing of the dugout to follow the ball's trajectory, but Simon, the center fielder, runs it down for the putout on the warning track. We head to the fifth inning still deadlocked at zero.

Fifth Inning

STEWART TAKES THE MOUND WITH HIS CUSTOMARY swagger, and I wonder whether my advice to him in the dugout might in part be responsible for it. As he finishes his warm-up tosses, my mind drifts to Darlene in Chicago, and I imagine her watching the game, wondering whether she has any regrets over our separation. The longer we remain apart, I fear, the greater the chance that we will make the separation permanent. No, absence does not make the heart grow fonder. It simmers passion, cools the heart—closes doors. Her trust was broken, shattered. I shattered it. Perhaps it is foolish pride that prevents her from reconciling. She once professed to not holding a grudge; but after nearly a year, I'd have thought she would've forgiven me, invited me to move back home to work on rebuilding what we had, so much of it good—too much, in my mind, from which to walk away.

❧

WE SAUNTERED THROUGH THE HOTEL LOBBY TOWARD THE elevator hand-in-hand, neither of us looking forward to saying goodnight.

Once in her room, I set the bag containing copies of my journal on the bed as a sort of deterrent, noting with chagrin that the maid had turned it down for the night. I took Darlene in my arms and kissed her, something I'd been looking forward to doing since the game ended. I felt my desire and was pleased when she didn't pull away.

"I like the way you make me feel, too," I whispered, echoing her sentiment from earlier in the day. We stood a moment in each other's arms, enjoying the danger, and then I added, "Thanks again for coming. It was great having you here, seeing you, getting to know more about you."

Darlene looked up at me. "Thank you, Backstop, for

your chivalry. It goes a long way toward building trust. It's difficult, knowing I'll be going back home without—without knowing when I'll see you again."

"I'll call you every day."

"Not the same as being with you, having your arms around me."

"No," I said. "I suppose we may never know, beyond a shadow of doubt, when the time is right to hand our hearts completely over to each other. When the time comes, it'll require a certain amount of risk. But waiting will help us to do this the right way."

"I know, and I keep telling myself that, but after ... after the last time, I doubted I'd ever again feel desire for another man."

"Understandable."

"And now I'm wondering if it would be so wrong to give in to that longing."

"You have no idea how easy it would be for me to take advantage of that admission."

"I appreciate and admire you for your restraint." She paused a moment before adding, "I'm going to hate getting on that plane tomorrow."

"As will I having to watch you walk down that tunnel alone. But really, would—"

"No," she said, cutting me off. "I'm sure it would make it even more difficult."

"Already finishing my thoughts for me?" I said; Darlene wasn't smiling. I sighed. I don't want to risk all of those tomorrow nights by giving in to my need for one night, no matter how pleasurable I imagine it would be. "We've a whole lifetime of tonights ahead of us."

"Knowing that is not going to make watching you walk through that door a second time any easier."

"Doors," I said. "They can be closed behind you, sealing off the distant past, even as others wait to be opened to a promising future."

Darlene seemed to consider how many more doors she'd have to watch me walk through before I no longer had to; a moment later she put her arms around me again and held me tightly.

AT BREAKFAST THE NEXT MORNING DARLENE TOLD ME she'd stayed up too late reading my journal entries.

"You're a wonderful storyteller," she said. "More, you're a gifted writer."

"You're very kind."

"I mean it. Your very colorful character shows through. Your voice is playful and knowledgeable. I can see these collected into a book one day, not so unlike *You Know Me Al.*"

"When the time is right," I said. "When you can negotiate for me a contract with a major publisher."

"We might make a pretty good team at that," she said, and then, "What?"

"I'm glad to hear you say that. It shows you've been thinking about tomorrows spent together."

"After this weekend, after last night—I think we're doing this the right way, and that I at least want to explore the possibility."

"Once again we're on the same page," I said, grinning.

"I dreamt about you last night," she said, blushing.

"I hope I can one day live up to the fantasy," I said, guessing at what she may have dreamed.

WE SAT IN THE BOARDING AREA, waiting for the announcement to board.

"After the Boston series," I said, "we travel to Milwaukee for a weekend series with the Brewers before heading to the west coast for a two-city tour, and then we'll be home again."

Darlene said nothing; she seemed to be calculating the number of days I'd be gone.

"Hey," I said. "Milwaukee is near to Chicago, so why don't you start making plans for next weekend?"

"I'm sorry," she said, brightening. "Of course, I'd love to see you next weekend."

"Then stop thinking about my trip west. That's a week away, and it's not as long as it sounds, even if the distance seems insurmountable. Remember, you've a business to run, which should keep you busy, distracted and out of trouble, and I'll bring you to Detroit the following weekend."

"It'll take more than the mundane aspects of running a business to distract me." Then she sighed and said, "I feel like a schoolgirl fretting over when I'll see you again, and I like that feeling, but it's unsettling, too. I loved getting off the plane Saturday and seeing you waiting for me. I had a wonderful time watching you play."

"Even that twelve-pitch at-bat?"

"Normally I'd find that boring, but knowing it was you, wondering what you were thinking, what was going through your head ..."

"Was like reading a novel to learn something of the author?"

Darlene laughed. "Something like that. And that you won the game single-handedly—it was exciting."

"It was a team effort," I said. "Hart gave us a chance."

"And spending the weekend with you. You've treated me very well, given me hope at ..."

"Finding love?"

Darlene ignored my question, but she didn't correct my conclusion. "There is something to be said about a condensed courtship, spending time with you like this, but I know I'm going to hate boarding this plane. Can a future relationship survive, let alone thrive, on such extremes?"

"Time will tell," I said. "But I think it can, if we want it to, for the short-term at least. Even if that short-term is several months. After the season, we can revisit my moving to Chicago."

Darlene said nothing, but I could see what she was thinking.

"I know," I said. "September seems so far away. There's frustration in the distance, along with safety, even as we take small steps toward the ultimate risk/reward venture. But this can be fun, too, the courtship ritual. I can bring you to some of our road games—to New York, Boston—if your business responsibilities allow it."

"That won't be easy, but I'd like that very much. It will be fun, going to cities I've never been, and seeing you play, getting to know the life you lead, on and off the field."

"Nothing so glamorous there," I said, "but having you along will make it so." Darlene smiled. "And next winter I'll enjoy being a part of your life in Chicago, assuming you can stand having me around for four months."

Darlene turned to me, put her hand on my knee. "Tell me we're doing the right thing, risking this."

"Of course we are," I said without pause. "Whatever we decide in the fall, at worst I expect I'll have a new agent and a good friend, at best a lover and potential life mate. If we give up now, refusing to risk the reward, we'll be left forever wondering *what if?*"

At that moment, all too soon, the boarding announcement sounded. We stood and embraced, and I kissed her, warmly, passionately, and I realized my desire from last night had never really left me.

"I miss you already," I whispered when our lips parted, enjoying the firmness of her body against me.

Darlene sighed, turned and made her way to the tunnel, without looking back, and I felt the ache of my desire change to a different kind of ache.

WE DROPPED TWO OF THREE GAMES TO THE RED SOX AND my hot bat cooled. Although I was still seeing the ball well and hitting it hard, I had only four hits and a single RBI to show for the three games, proving once again that baseball is a game of inches and that hitting is a streaky business. I took solace in that I was at least continuing to hit the ball well, if directly at someone. I told Darlene on the phone Wednesday night, after dropping the second game by a single run, that I'd gladly have gone hitless in exchange for winning both games, which had each been one-run losses.

"You'll come around again," she said, sounding confident. Still, I couldn't help but think she sounded more distant than the three hundred miles that separated us.

"You okay?" I asked.

"I miss you," she said after a pause. "These two days seem like two years. Every time the bells jingle and someone walks into my shop, I look up expecting, wanting, to see you coming through the door."

"I miss you like crazy, too," I said. And then, to change the somber moment, "So does the team. They're all convinced you're good luck for me."

Darlene said nothing.

"This will get easier," I offered, not wanting to ask the question that was on my mind, whether she was having second thoughts.

"I don't want it to get easier," she said. "I just want to be able to see you whenever I want. I don't want to spend my life counting down the days before I see you next."

"I know," I said. "I feel the same way. But it doesn't have to be a lifetime. Only a few months." Darlene was silent. "I enjoy feeling your presence in my life even while we're apart. It makes me feel good, thinking about you, and knowing I'll be seeing you in a few days. I've always enjoyed going to the ballpark, but now I really love it—I love feeling your presence during the game."

"I wish I could say the same. Coming to the shop is anything but a pleasure. I've taken to reading the box scores in the morning, but that's hardly a substitute for seeing you. And these phone calls ..."

"I understand," I said. And then I voiced my concern from a moment ago: "You're not having second thoughts, are you?"

"No," she said quickly, adamantly.

"Thanks. I feared maybe you would."

"It's too late for that. I've gotten too attached already."

"Then hold on to that attachment, Darlin'. It can only grow, and while these separations may not ever become easier—and you're right, we shouldn't ever allow them to become easier—they can go a long way toward focusing us on what lies ahead."

I waited for Darlene to say something. Finally, she complied: "I feel so foolish, selfish, like a little girl who wants something she can't have—her heart's desire."

"There's nothing foolish about wanting your heart's desire. And I'd like nothing more than to be your heart's desire." When Darlene said nothing, I added, "What's more, I like that little girl in you. I don't want you to ever lose her."

"This isn't the type of relationship I dreamed of having."

"Oh but it is, isn't it?" I asked. "If it wasn't, you wouldn't have come to Detroit last weekend. The circumstances surrounding it—my career—might not be something you ever envisioned, but there must be something you see and hope for, or we wouldn't be on the phone right now."

"I know that, but I can't help but feel there's something unnatural about this, that we're somehow setting ourselves up for failure."

"Focus on that and chances are we'll manifest that outcome. The average hitter fails three out of four trips to the plate, but if he steps into the batter's box thinking *out*, he likely will hit into one."

"I love that about you," she said. "You're ability to not think failure."

"It's contagious," I said.

"Is it?"

"Just like winning," I said. "The team that goes out expecting to lose usually does; the team that takes the field with swagger expecting to win often finds a way to do so. If we expect happiness, it can be ours."

Darlene laughed and said, her voice rife with the warmth to which I'd become accustomed, "Do you ever stop thinking in terms of baseball?"

"I do," I said. "Whenever I think of you in my arms, and whenever I think about kissing you and of my life with you."

"You say the sweetest things."

"And you? Besides my not being there, what do you think of when we're apart?"

"Your soft kisses, your arms around me, of—"

"Maybe waking up beside me?"

Darlene said nothing, only let a soft sigh escape her lips, and I imagined her lovely complexion blushing, which was all the answer I needed.

"Then hold on to those thoughts," I said, "and let's make them a reality."

IN THE CLUBHOUSE FRIDAY NIGHT, before our game with the Brewers, I was in particularly good spirits, laughing and joking with my teammates. Hart asked me if Darlene was making the drive up from Chicago.

"No," I said, watching McGillicuddy lacing up his spikes across the aisle from me; he was tonight's starter. "She's coming up for tomorrow's game."

"Great," Hart said. "I expect another good game from you at the plate."

I laughed. "Like you don't expect that every night. But really, aren't you putting too much pressure on her?"

"You can't deny that good things happen when she's at the game. She's a keeper, Backstop, so treat her right."

"She is that," I agreed. "And I don't deny she makes me want to play well. I give you my word I'll treat her well."

Hart put his hand on my shoulder and told me he wished us much happiness. Across the aisle, McGillicuddy, having taken a long swallow from a bottle of Coke, punctuated Hart's blessing with a loud belch.

MCGILLICUDDY GOT HIT FOR THREE RUNS IN THE FIRST BUT settled down after that, going six innings before being pulled for the seventh with a pitch count over one hundred and the score deadlocked at three.

Clayton led off our half of the seventh with a single to center and moved to second on a fielder's choice. Cooper struck out swinging, which left it up to me. I'd gone hitless in my previous two trips, in part because I'd tried to pull the ball. Maxwell, the Brewer's starter, had good stuff and had pitched me outside all night. With a runner in scoring position, I resolved to look for something I could take the opposite way. Maxwell started me off with an inside fastball that bent me backward, but went back outside with his next fastball and I was ready, lacing a soft liner over the second baseman into right field to score Clayton.

Hart came on to pitch the eighth. I'd always enjoyed catching for Hart because we were more often than not on the same page; he rarely shook me off. But I also liked Hart. We roomed together on road trips, and I'd found he was easy to room with. Like me, and unlike many of the other guys who stayed out late, Hart retired early, after a call to his wife and kid. He also liked to sleep late, so being an early riser, I had the bathroom to myself and was able to complete my morning ablutions and head to breakfast and off to see the sights of whichever city we were visiting before he stirred. A highly principled and religious man, Hart reads the Bible every night. I'd never read it, so I suggested we read it together, which had thus far prompted many interesting discussions on its text.

Hart goes through a little ritual each time he takes the mound: after his warm-up tosses he walks to the back of the mound and, head bowed, says a little prayer, finishing with a quick sign of the cross. During one of our discussions I asked him, respectfully, whether he didn't think that God might not have more important concerns on His mind than baseball. Hart patiently explained that we all, each and every day and in our own way, give glory to God, whether by planting a garden, being a good husband and father, by choosing integrity over dishonesty in the business world, by not giving in to temptation, yes, even by playing baseball—in short, by using the gifts with which He has blessed us. His brief prayer on the mound wasn't an appeal for God's help in pitching but instead an acknowledgement of God's presence in his life, and a thanks for the blessings He bestowed on him, his wife and child and his baseball skills, which he used, in his own way, to bring glory to God. While I didn't fully understand his explanation, his beliefs certainly seemed to work for him—a happier, more contented man I don't believe I've ever met. Reading the Bible, as well as my thought-provoking discussions with Hart, has given me pause for thought regarding my own spirituality.

Hart got an occasional spot start but was most effective out of the pen, having only two good pitches: a fastball that had good movement and a wicked changeup. Hart made short work of the Brewers in the eighth inning, retiring all three batters he faced on a dozen pitches, the third batter on a called third strike. Heath, our closer, pitched the ninth and retired all three batters he faced, and we took the first game of the series 4 to 3.

❧

STEWART DISPATCHES THE FIRST TWO BATTERS ON SIX pitches, Smith on a shallow fly ball to left and Evans on strikes, but Fellows takes first base on a seeing-eye ground ball between third and short on a one-two count. Stewart made a good pitch, but Fellows did well to get his bat on the ball and beat our alignment, which was playing him to pull. I've seen Stewart upset at similar circumstances, but to his credit, I watch him march to the back of the mound for the rosin bag, shake off the weak hit, and focus on the next batter, who hits a first-pitch soft liner to second base to end the top half of the fifth and keep the score at zero.

❧

SATURDAY MORNING AND I AWOKE BRIGHT AND EARLY TO Hart's soft snoring in the next bed. After my shower and shave, I called Darlene at her shop as we'd arranged; it was just after nine. Darlene sounded distraught.

"My morning help called off work," she told me. "I'm trying to reach someone else, but so far I've had no luck."

"Hey," I said quietly so as not to disturb Hart. "That's okay, don't worry about it. Do what you can. I'm heading down for breakfast. I'll call you when I get back. If you can't make it up, I'll rent a car and drive down after the game and we can have dinner."

The sound of Darlene's sigh came through the handset,

and I wondered if maybe she expected that I'd be upset at this sudden change in plans. "I'm so disappointed," she said.

"It's okay, really. It's not a show-stopper. Life happens. All does not always go according to our wishes."

"I was worried you'd be angry."

"That's not who I am. After five days, what are a few more hours? It'll make seeing you that much more gratifying."

"Thanks for understanding." She sounded relieved.

"Good help is hard to come by, eh?" I said.

"You get what you pay for. People go into business thinking they'll have the freedom to come and go as they please, that they're not responsible to a boss. But worse, they're responsible to the business. When the hired help fails to show up, it's up to the owner to fill in."

"I understand. Tomorrow you're closed and you can come up for the matinee finale, just like we planned."

"Thanks," she breathed into the phone.

"Not a problem. Now I'll let you get back to what you need to do and call you back in an hour or so."

After we hung up, Hart rolled over and said, "Darlene's not coming to the game?"

"Doesn't look like it."

"That's too bad," he mumbled groggily. "It's good you weren't angry with her."

"How can I be angry over circumstances?"

"A more selfish man would be. She seems like a good woman. Trish likes her. She seems good for you, and if she doesn't know it yet, she's lucky she found you."

"Well, it was me who found her," I said, "but I'm hoping my good fortune will become our good fortune."

"God willing," he said. "Now let me go back to sleep."

I grinned and left to Hart the onerous task of sawing his wood while I headed for breakfast.

"I WAS WORRIED YOU'D BE UPSET THAT I COULDN'T MAKE the game tonight," Darlene said from across the table. We were dining at a tiny bistro that specialized in seafood.

"How could I be upset over something you had no control over?"

"I once knew someone who would've been very irate over just such a circumstance."

"I'm not him."

Darlene smiled and shook her head.

"What?" I asked.

"You really are too good to be true."

I laughed and said, "Well before you go pinching yourself, you should know I'm not without fault."

"Name some."

"Well, I'm a morning person."

"So am I. Try again."

I thought a moment. "I have to sleep on the right side of the bed."

"That sounds more like superstition, one with which I can live."

"I worry too much about what other people think—namely the media."

"That's not a fault, merely a weakness, one which you are endeavoring to overcome."

"With your patience and tutelage."

"Come on," she urged. "Hit me with your worst. You leave your dirty socks on the floor?"

"Nope. You won't have to pick up after me."

"Ouch," she said, hitting the table with her knee.

"You shouldn't pinch yourself so hard," I said, and Darlene laughed, pleased that I was on the same page.

"Some people accuse me of immaturity—of never having grown up," I said.

"That comes with playing a kid's game, I imagine. You have your grownup moments, and besides, I like your youthful outlook on life."

"Okay," I said. "This should wake you up: I'm obsessive compulsive—"

"Ah, control issues! Finally, a chink in the armor!"

"No glass or dish gets left in the sink unwashed. I squeeze the toothpaste from the bottom of the tube."

Darlene laughed. “That’s your worst?”

“You know what they say: It’s the little things that break up a marriage.”

“Whoever ‘they’ are, but I share your kitchen and bathroom habits.”

“I can be stubborn and bull-headed. I don’t find it easy to admit when I’m wrong, but I rarely hold a grudge, unless the person is deserving of it.”

“Well, I can be stubborn, too, so that’s something we’ll have to work on together.”

“I suspect that can work to my advantage when it comes to you negotiating my new contract.”

“One of the first things I learned in law school: the first person to blink loses. But tell me, morning person that you are, what do you do with your morning hours?”

“Breakfast, coffee, the morning paper—Mike O’Hare, the box scores, the crossword puzzle. When I’m on the road I like to window shop—but you already know that.”

“I hope you don’t make a habit of window shopping for women.”

“A one-time endeavor that was unintentional, one that I suspect resulted in finding a treasure greater than I could ever hope to bargain for.”

“Good answer,” she said.

“You sound like a jealous type,” I said, and immediately regretted my jest. I could see I’d struck a nerve.

“Not by nature I’m not, but I have good reason to not trust.”

How quickly I’d jumped from the same page to a different page in another chapter in some other book—from comedy to tragedy. “I’m sorry, Darlene. I wasn’t thinking. Another flaw of mine: I sometimes speak before thinking.”

“Which sometimes reveals the truth about what a person is thinking.”

“In this case I wasn’t thinking. Truly, I didn’t mean to open that wound.”

“I know you didn’t,” she said. “I’m not angry.”

“But I’ve hurt you.”

"No, you didn't. Someone else did that."

"I should've been more sensitive."

"Maybe so," she said after a moment, placing a hand on top of mine, "but you can't yet know my boundaries any more than I can know yours. Apology accepted and let's move on."

I took a deep breath and frantically tried to find that previous page. "What do you like to do with your mornings?"

"There's a park near my home. It's quiet, and other than the occasional jogger, I enjoy the solitude."

"Mornings are special. The birth of a new day. I do the park thing, too."

"With so many others still in bed, I feel a beautiful sunrise is for my eyes alone. It gives me a chance to reflect on the previous day and focus on events of the day to come."

"I find it's especially good for my creativity, when I'm writing my sports journal."

"But you enjoy the cheering fans, too."

"In the park? No. I find them annoying."

Darlene laughed and gave my hand a squeeze; her previous demeanor seemed banished. "I hope you won't mind my coming along sometime."

"I'd love to share my mornings with you. As much as I enjoy them alone, I've always felt they could be much more if I could share them with someone special."

DARLENE INVITED ME IN AND I WAS DELIGHTED TO FIND her home modest and tastefully decorated. On the mantle of a wood-burning corner fireplace sat a photograph of Darlene between two elders who I took to be her parents; to either side of the photograph stood two ceramic candelabras, ornate but refined. Above the fireplace hung a magnificent oil painting I would later learn was a representation of Kamini port on Hydra Island, painted by Yannis Stavrou in vivid colors of blue and green, its buildings in white and subdued shades of orange and burnt red. Located in the Argosaronic Gulf, Darlene would tell me that Hydra Island is one of the few places in the world where cars, motorcycles, even bicycles are not allowed. The carpeting was off-white, with two walls painted to match while the other two were painted a soft pastel green. A large bookshelf covered much of one of the white walls; most of its shelves held books, but one bore a collection of tiny vases bearing images of, among other Greek personae, Zeus, Hera and Europa, as well as other reproductions of Greek sculptures, including Winged Victory of Samothrace. Other furniture, more contemporary, included a loveseat before which resided a low coffee table, two other high-backed chairs, and a rocking chair in one of the room's corners.

"Can I get you something to drink?" Darlene asked.

"A glass of wine would be great."

"Burgundy?"

"Whatever you're having."

While Darlene left for the kitchen I took a moment to light the candle on her coffee table and proceeded to check out the books in her bookcase—no fiction, but volumes of books on law and many others on business.

"Disappointed?" she said, handing me a glass of wine.

"Why should I be disappointed?" I said. "It's who you are, and I like who you are. Which reminds me, have you finished Lardner's book?"

"Yes. You already know I read little fiction, but I enjoyed it for the opportunity it gave me to glimpse into the game of baseball, even if Lardner's depiction of Jack Keefe's naiveté was a little over the top."

"Another of my flaws," I said. "I love parody."

"Not a flaw," she said in my defense. "What a boring relationship it would be if we mirrored each other's taste one hundred percent."

"So opposites attract?"

"Not to an extreme, no. But some differences, small ones, cause people to stretch and grow. Without growth, stagnation results."

"Well, I hope you'll take no offense if I tell you I have little desire to read any of your books on law."

Darlene laughed. "I forgive you. I expect they'd be

rather dry to the uninitiated."

I felt the wine begin to warm me. I looked at Darlene's features in the dim candlelight and felt my desire begin to assert itself. To head it off, I turned and indicated the bookcase with my wine glass and said, "I don't see *Al* here."

"I keep it on my nightstand in my bedroom," she said softly, "along with the world you gave me when we first met. They comfort me at night."

I nodded, not knowing what to say, how to proceed, what Darlene expected of me. "I'm sorry, Darlin,'" I managed, "about my carelessness earlier. I wouldn't hurt you for the world."

"It's forgotten," she said, and the sincerity with which she said the two words convinced me it was so.

I took her glass from her and set it down on the coffee table with my own; then I took her in my arms and kissed her, tasting the wine on her lips and feeling her melt against me. When our lips parted I looked into her dark eyes where I saw my own desire reflected. I wondered a moment if it had been a mistake to accept her invitation to come in; by doing so I'd put us both at risk. Yet I could see in her eyes that my saying good night and letting myself out would be a bigger mistake—bigger, perhaps, than my earlier jest gone awry. *What reward is there to be had without risk?* I asked myself.

"I'd like to stay the night," I whispered, "if you'll have me."

Without a word, Darlene took my hand and led me to her bedroom.

IN THE AFTERGLOW WE LAY SPOONING, but I sensed something not quite right.

"You're not sorry, are you?" I asked.

"No, God, no," Darlene said. "I wanted you to stay, and I don't know that my ego could've withstood you walking out my front door to go back to your hotel to spend the night with John Hart."

More talk of doors, I thought; yet I couldn't be sure whether the humor in the image with which her statement left me was intended, so I held back my laugh. Darlene continued.

"This was ever so sweet and I'm not sorry. I'm glad you asked to stay. I wanted you to ask because I couldn't."

"And I didn't want to put you into the position of saying no," I said. "Something my own ego feared."

"Had you left I'd have thought there was something wrong with me. That you didn't want me."

"I've wanted you since the moment I saw you."

A moment later, Darlene said, "So I guess this is what we both wanted."

"I'd say so, yes. But something is troubling you."

Darlene broke free of my embrace to roll over to face me. Propped up by an elbow, she told me, "Backstop, you have to believe me when I tell you I no longer have feelings for ..."

"You can say his name."

"David. The love is gone, as is the hate. But the hurt ..."

"I imagine will linger for quite some time, if not forever," I said. Then I asked, "I'm your first lover since David?" I wanted, perhaps needed, to say his name. Somehow, saying it made him real even if I had no image to which to pin the name.

"Yes."

Darlene's eyes welled up with tears. In my confusion, I couldn't know what question to ask, but she went on.

"I love how you loved me tonight, and it *was* you I wanted, your mouth on mine, your hands on my body, you inside me, believe me. But there was a moment, the fleetest of moments, when my old anger reared its ugly head, and I felt, for a moment, that I'd gotten revenge." When I didn't say anything, Darlene prompted me, "Say something, Backstop."

"I believe you when you say the love and the hate are gone, and I suppose one can heal only so much alone, that there comes a time when to move forward with healing one must take a new lover."

"I'm sorry it had to be you, Backstop."

"I'm not," I said, trying to sound positive, surprised by my possessiveness. "I don't like the idea of you having had another lover other than David, who I've had time to build up in my mind as a total shit."

Darlene tried to smile through her tears, gave up and said, "I'm not on the rebound."

"I didn't say you were," I said, but with little conviction.

Darlene apologized again: "I'm sorry I hurt you."

"Not that we're keeping score, but I suppose that makes us even tonight. I could've been happy going to my grave ignorant of this, but then, I asked, didn't I?"

"I'd have told you anyway, Backstop, in the morning, after breakfast. Honesty builds trust."

"But was your honesty in this for us, moving forward, or only to assuage your own guilt?"

"Both," she said. "Although I can certainly understand your doubt of the former. You were very tender tonight, but you didn't get my best and you need to know that and the reason why."

"I don't know about that," I said, reaching over to caress her cheek. "You were everything I fantasized you'd be."

"You're very kind, but fantasy aside, first time love-making can at worst be disastrous, at best be very sweet. I'm pleased you stayed and I don't regret it—it was you I brought to my bed, even if I had a momentary lapse of mis-placed passion. You certainly know your way around a woman's body, but we don't yet know our way around each other's body. Trust me when I tell you I'm going to enjoy getting to know yours."

With that, she leaned over to me and kissed me. I let my hand slide down her flank to her hip and pulled her on top of me; with her breasts crushed against me I felt a resurgence of my earlier passion. "You know what they say," I breathed into her ear, inhaling the fragrance of her hair.

"I don't even know who 'they' are," she whispered play-fully into the dark.

"Baseball statisticians."

"What are they doing in my bed and what is it they say?"

"Baseball is a game of inches."

"Mmm," she moaned as she stroked me. "I do believe they're right ..."

FERNANDO HAS ONE-HIT US THROUGH FOUR INNINGS. When Hernandez starts off our half of the fifth with a strikeout, the crowd proceeds to sit on its hands. It had been that type of season for us: in winning ninety-six games we'd had two win streaks of ten games and several others of six or more; but when we slumped, we slumped badly—once losing seven of ten, another where we dropped six of ten, and finishing the season with four straight losses. I feel the crowd senses we're mired in one of those slumps and will finish the series, and our season, with a 1 to 0 loss. With four and two-thirds innings left, I know there is still a lot of baseball left to play; and with the way Stewart is pitching, we, too, are but one hit away from winning the championship. I climb the dugout steps and head to the on-deck circle as Jones steps into the batter's box.

Fernando has been keeping our hitters off-balance all night with his changeup, which he is unafraid to serve up no matter the count; his control as well as his command have been nearly as good as Stewart's. He's been extremely sharp with his curve ball, which he has been throwing at a variety of speeds. His second time through our lineup I've noticed he's mixing up his first pitch and so, having started me off with a fastball my first at-bat, I resolve to look for something soft that I can maybe slap the other way.

Fernando had started off Jones his first trip with a slow curve and this time comes with the fastball, which Jones watches go by for strike one. Jonesy has not had a good series at the plate, and he looks nervous to me. Jones, now looking for something soft, swings behind another fastball that's low and away. He steps out to regain his composure. He stretches, stoops to get a handful of dirt, steps back into the box and looks out to Fernando in an effort to try to guess what's coming. "Look for the heat, Jonesy," I mutter to myself; but Jones, convinced he won't see a third straight fastball stands there like the house by the side of the road and watches go by another fastball, right down Michigan Avenue—the same Michigan Avenue on which, fifteen or so miles west of here, I learned how to drive a stick-shift so many years before—belt high, for a called third strike.

"Next time, Jonesy," I tell him as we pass each other, him for the dugout, me to the plate. Jones says nothing, which tells me he's befuddled.

I dig into the batter's box still thinking soft, certain Fernando won't come at me with heat, knowing I'd just watched him dispose of Jones with three straight; but that's exactly what he throws—at the knees and away.

"Strike one," Welke calls from over my right shoulder.

"Fooled ya," Evans tells me.

I ignore him and take a couple steps away to clear my head. "What, you don't like me no more?" Evans says.

I take a deep breath, another, before stepping back in. I look out to Fernando who shakes off the first sign, then the second, before nodding. *Fastball,* I think to myself, and sure enough Fernando comes with a fifth straight heater, but I'm ready for it and lace it to left field just over the outstretched glove of the leaping third baseman.

From first base I watch Evans go out to the mound to discuss with Fernando how he wants to pitch to left-handed hitting McCandles. I'm guessing they won't start him off with a fastball. Preston, our third base coach, is probably telling McCandles the same thing as they converse halfway between home and third.

I'm aware of how quiet the home fans are, despite this game seven, winner take all setting. To them a two-out single is hardly a rally. *How quickly they forget,* I think, *the number of two-out rallies during the regular season that put a "W" in the win column for us.* Fans are fickle. They love you when you win and boo you when you don't. Detroit fans are knowledgeable. A blue collar town, they appreciate a good work ethic, root for the underdog. Still, they expect us to win this game seven; indeed, we were the favored team among the statisticians as well as the media, expected to win in five games. When we dropped game five away and game six here, within the friendly confines of Tiger Stadium, the so-called experts accused us of playing down to the competition, of letting them hang around, and that we were ripe to lose three straight.

Evans is back behind the plate. I step off first and note that Fellows, the first baseman, is playing behind me to fill the gap between first and second. Having stolen maybe twenty bases in my entire career, I'm no threat to steal in this situation, and the entire stadium knows it. Fernando doesn't have a good move to first, so I get a healthy lead, but not too healthy. I don't want to invite too much attention.

Fernando gives me a perfunctory glance as he goes into his delivery—no slide-step but his customary high leg kick—and misses in the dirt with a slow curve. His next pitch, without a glance at me, is a hard slider that breaks down and in on McCandles, who whiffs on it to send the count even. On his third offering, Fernandez turns to bluff me back toward first, and serves up a change at which McCandles, ahead of the pitch, swings and fouls off.

I look to our dugout but see no sign forthcoming. With the count at 1 and 2 and two out, I resolve to steal second if Fernando looks my way; if I'm thrown out McCandles at least will start the sixth inning with a fresh count. Fernando shakes off the first sign, nods at the second, looks my way and goes into his windup. I break for second base; a third of the way down the line I sneak a peek toward home to see if the ball is in play. Evans has the ball, is up but off-balance, double-pumps because the shortstop is late getting to the bag, and the ball sails on him, allowing me to slide under the tag. The crowd, sensing a rally in the making, maybe in approval of the size of my gonads, roars its approval. I've been a crowd favorite in Detroit. Two years ago, when trade rumors were flying—the aging catcher for a young stud middle reliever—the media, as well as the fans, voiced their combined discontent. Not wanting to wear another uniform, I was ready to hang up my spikes if the rumors turned out to be true. Of course I now regret those two years, for what happened in New York at the end of last season.

With the go-ahead run now in scoring position, the full house stadium crowd is abuzz. The middle infielders are back, unmindful of holding me close. After fouling off two pitches, McCandles hits a soft liner to right on which I get a good break. As I near third base, Preston's left arm is pin wheeling frantically and so I step on the inside corner of the bag and chug toward home, ignoring my barking knees. Six feet from home I see Evans, blocking the plate, come up with the ball and turn toward me; my only chance is to knock the ball loose, so I opt against a slide. I brace myself and collide with Evans, left shoulder first, knocking him back and onto his ass, but he holds onto the ball as I hear Welke call, "Out!"

The stadium is silent as I make my way to the dugout. I imagine tomorrow's lead sports story, should we go on to lose this game, deriding Preston for making the wrong call, sending me against a gold glove right fielder with a cannon for an arm. Yet had I scored, those same sportswriters would call the decision the right one. Such is the nature of sports. In the heat of battle split-second decisions are made; in hindsight it's easy to second guess. In my mind Preston made the right decision, given the circumstances: a tight game in the middle innings, you have to make the opposition throw you out.

In the dugout, as I strap on my gear, many of the bench players walk past me, pat my shoulder and praise my audacity in stealing second base.

After five full innings, the score remains tied at zero.

Sixth Inning

AFTER STEWART FINISHES HIS WARM UP TOSSES, I trot out to ask him how he feels. "I'm going the distance," he tells me. "That's all I wanted to hear," I say, patting him on the behind.

Stewart looks toward home, where Gallegos waits to step into the box. "I want to strike him out, for throwing you out at home, Backstop."

I nod, tell him, "You're my Tiger. Let's strike out the side."

Behind the plate, I squat and tell Gallegos, "The kid wants to strike you out, for being so discourteous to this aging veteran."

"That ain't never gonna happen," he retorts, swinging his lumber menacingly at Stewart.

I chuckle at Gallegos's use of the double negative and think about how that might look on the printed page should I ever decide to write an autobiography.

We start off Gallegos with a fastball low and away for a called strike. Welke, God bless him, is still giving us a generous outside corner. Then we climb the ladder with more heat for a called second strike, and higher still, this one inside and letter high, at which Gallegos swings awkwardly for strike three. Disgusted, Gallegos takes a two-handed swing at the ground with his bat and heads for the dugout.

"Thank goodness the ground has less movement on it than Stewart's fastball, eh?" I say.

Gallegos mutters something under his breath that sounds like, "Kiss my ass, Backstop." "Never say never," I call to his back.

We start off Richards with a curveball and, unsure what to expect, he shortens his swing to protect the plate and fouls the pitch off my right ankle. I hobble around the plate area in an effort to walk it off while Phillips, our trainer, comes out to check on me.

"You okay, Backstop?" he asks. "Yeah, I'm fine," I tell

him. "Takes my mind off my knees."

He chuckles and tells me to hang in there. "Only three and two-thirds' innings to go," Phillips assures me. "Go on, get out of here," I tell him. "Nothing short of a fracture will keep me from finishing." And then, "Have some ice ready for me in the dugout."

Phillips heads off, leaving me to ponder over my last two seasons, playing mostly at first base. That roster move had saved my knees, allowing me to play these last two seasons and in this World Series behind the plate, where the skipper wanted my experience; but if I hadn't played the last two years I'd still be with Darlene. Not *an equitable tradeoff,* I reason, feeling the ache of her loss, *even if we win the World Series.* Nothing will take away that sting, least of all the pain of a foul tip off my ankle. I continue to test my ankle, thinking back to the discussion Darlene and I once had about my faults. We'd had fun with it, but I'd neglected to tell her of my weakness for a beautiful pair of legs. "I'm a one-woman man," I'd told her in another discussion. At the time it was the truth, even as she accused me of its untruth in the aftermath of my sin.

"You ready to go, Backstop?" Welke asks me. He's been generous in giving me time to walk off the pain in my ankle. "Yeah, I'm ready," I say as I settle into the catcher's box. "Damn," I mutter to myself, not from the discomfort in my knees competing with my ankle. *You're a fool, Backstop,* I think, recalling the pain I'd caused Darlene and myself. "Was she worth it?" she'd asked me the night she found out. "Of course not," I told her, despising myself for being the cause of the hurt etched into her tear-streaked face. My reply did nothing to allay her pain and only made me sound a bigger fool. She wasn't worth it then and she certainly isn't now.

Richards steps back into the batter's box and, glancing down, I see that his back foot is a good three inches out of the batter's box. I learned long ago to keep batters honest about their stance. Once the chalk line is obliterated, they cheat back to give themselves a longer look at the pitch and a better chance of hitting the outside breaking ball as it breaks across the plate. It also increases the chance that their swing might clip my glove and they'll be awarded first base for catcher interference. "Hey, Tim," I say, pointing to Richards's back foot, "he's out of the batter's box." Welke advises Richards to move up and I hope that Richards will be unsettled—a batter's head is a fragile thing.

We get Richards on two more pitches: a changeup that he beats into the ground foul to the right of the plate and a rising fastball that is called a third strike.

WE AROSE EARLY THE NEXT MORNING BECAUSE OF OUR early game in Milwaukee. I made breakfast while Darlene showered and got dressed. Omelets were the order of the day—ham, feta cheese and mushrooms, the latter I'd already learned was one of Darlene's favorite foods. After we ate, I showered and dressed while Darlene cleared the dishes, and we then took a walk to Seward Park, which was within walking distance of Darlene's home in the Old Town district.

We sat on the grass to watch the sun climb over Lake Michigan, which was obscured by the cityscape. Breakfast had been quiet, with each of us enjoying the presence of the other, the comfort of last night's lovemaking, and small talk. I took Darlene's hand and asked:

"How are you?"

"Very content, thank you."

"Me, too." And then, "Still no regrets?"

"Not a one." Then she held my hand in both of hers, palm up, to kiss it. "I love your hands. Large and calloused. Yet your fingers are long and graceful. Fingers I would imagine would make for a fine pianist."

"Or a typist," I said, grinning. "I take batting practice without gloves to toughen them up so they won't blister."

"One of the nuances of baseball," she said, smiling. "So much I want to learn about you."

"It'll come in time, for both of us. We should enjoy the

process rather than try to learn everything at once."

"Sage advice."

"Coming from a ballplayer."

We fell silent for a few moments, the sounds of the Sunday morning traffic soothing. Then Darlene said, "You make a delicious omelet."

"It was the mushrooms," I said. "Would you say the same thing had I used garlic and onions instead?"

"Garlic," she said, wrinkling her nose. "Good for keeping werewolves at bay."

"And me?"

"Not a chance," she said, leaning over to kiss me.

"Woof," I said after we broke.

"Good boy," she told me, mussing my hair.

"Funny you should mention the piano," I said. "My mother wanted me to play, and my father paid for lessons when I was very young."

"You hated it, I imagine, because it took you away from playing baseball."

"Not at all," I said. "I love music. Good old-fashioned, straight-ahead, no-brainer rock and roll, and jazz particularly. Thelonious Monk, who passed away a couple years ago, is my favorite jazz pianist and composer. Brubeck is another favorite, for his odd sense of timing. I had a lousy tutor though. Gave me a sheet of music and told me to practice it, but he taught me little of how to play." *Like my father*, I thought, *who showed me how to throw a ball and swing a bat, but taught me little of the game of baseball.*

"Do you still play?"

"Not seriously, no, although I own a piano. After I'm done playing baseball, I want to take it up again. As an adult I have a greater appreciation of music."

Darlene looked pensive, as if perhaps she were looking back, through a door still ajar, thinking of someone who had once taken her for granted, shown her a lack of appreciation. I wondered how long it might be before she would be able to close that door forever. I leaned over to kiss her.

"Just wanted to show my appreciation," I said. "For last

night, for you, your company. For your beauty."

Darlene smiled but said nothing; I changed the subject.

"You lived here in the city all your life?"

Darlene nodded. "I grew up in the Gold Coast district, not far from here. One of the more affluent neighborhoods. My father is a very good lawyer."

"Have you told your parents about me?"

"Yes. Mother was less than pleased that you play baseball. She wants me to marry a lawyer, but after David, she just wants me to be happy. She felt better about you when I told her you also write for a newspaper."

"And Dad?"

"Dad was intrigued. He grew up a Cubs fan, took me to a few games when I was a girl, and occasionally takes a client to Wrigley."

"When will I get to meet them?"

"There's no hurry, really."

"Not even after last night?"

"Especially not after last night," she said. "I'm nearly thirty years old and I don't need their approval where affairs of the heart are concerned, but I'm still their little girl. They were thrilled when I met David, who is from the south side and a Sox fan, but you know how that ended."

"So am I what you want?"

"I know I want to find out."

"Good answer," I said. "I'm still committed to finding that out, too."

"I'm glad." And then, with a smile she said, "I'm sure they'll take to you. What's not to like?"

"That's just what I was thinking," I said with a grin.

"Mom is more concerned about social order, but you're well-spoken. You'll find Dad easily approachable. Bring him a good Cuban seed cigar, share a glass of good single malt with him, treat me right and he'll be your friend for life."

"I like him already."

"You smoke cigars?" she asked tentatively.

"Occasionally. Not so much during the season, when I'm more concerned about what I put into my body, especially where my lungs are concerned. But I find a cigar soothing, one of the nicer pleasures in life, although I prefer bourbon to scotch."

"I agree," she said, "about cigars," and I thought I detected no small amount of relief in her tone, and then I realized what she was telling me.

"You mean ...?"

Darlene nodded. "I'm an only child, remember? To Dad I'm both his daughter and the son he never had. You've seen me in business attire and dresses, but I was a bit of a tomboy in my youth."

"I like you in dresses."

"I've noticed," she said. "I think my legs are too muscular, and ..." She glanced away, seeming to recall some past memory, and then looked back at me to say, "I'm glad you like my legs."

"I also like that they're attached to you," I said, well aware of what she'd left unsaid.

"You're sweet."

"After the season is over and I can spend more than a few days at a time in Chicago, we'll share a good smoke as we move forward and discuss my new contract."

"Are you sure that's what you want, for me to represent you? Surely you'd rather have someone more familiar with the baseball world."

"I'd rather have someone more familiar with me and my wants and needs," I said. "I told you before—I don't want to hold the Tigers for ransom. My current agent was a referral. He resides in New York, and I've never even met him. He did right by me with my current contract, but as a rookie there was little to negotiate, and I'm not his only client. With you as my agent, I'd say you'd have my interests, and only my interests, at heart. Are you going to tell me you wouldn't benefit from fifteen percent of a three-year multi-million dollar deal?"

"I had no idea baseball salaries had risen so much."

"Pete Rose opened the door in '79 when he signed for four years with the Phillies for 3.2 million. My bat has been coming around, thanks to you, and if I finish strong, who knows what I might be able to get? We'll need to look at other third-year players with similar numbers, but that'll be easy. I'd like you to meet our general manager, Mr. Lajoie. He's a real gentleman, one of the more respected GMs in the league. I think you'll find him to be fair and easy to negotiate with. I'd say we could sign with one face-to-face meeting and a couple phone calls."

"Well," Darlene said, "The money sounds good, and I do miss that part of my former life. Let's do it."

"Great," I said. "Darlene the deipnosophist. Has a nice ring to it, wouldn't you say?"

Darlene laughed and shook her head.

"What?" I said. "Still having trouble getting past the sweaty athlete with little between his ears?"

"Are you going to tell me you were familiar with that word prior to meeting me?"

"I was," I said. "I love language—my third great love."

"I don't want to know your second."

"No? Remind me to tell you one day. But really, what good is learning a new word if you can't use it? Greek negotiator was a clue in a crossword puzzle I recently worked. That deipnosophist finds its origins in Greek I thought interesting."

"But are you familiar with *Deipnosophistai*, written by Athenaeus, a discussion of several Greeks around a dinner table around 225 AD?"

"I did not know that," I said. "But I'm delighted to learn something new. The guys in the clubhouse will be intrigued to say the least, when I share that with them."

Darlene laughed and I told her I thought her laugh wondrously canorous. She looked away but thanked me.

"Seems I'm not the only one who has trouble accepting a compliment," I said. When Darlene said nothing, I added, "I take it David wasn't very forthcoming with them."

"No," Darlene said uncomfortably.

"I'm sorry. I didn't mean to embarrass you. I was just making an observation."

"That's okay. I like that about you, that you're observant."

I glanced at my watch. The sun was getting warm and it was getting late. "Come on," I said, taking her hand. "We should probably head up to Milwaukee. We've a game to get to, remember?"

THE TEAM WAS LEAVING FOR THE COAST IMMEDIATELY after the game, so Darlene followed me up to Milwaukee in her car. Afterward, she'd drive back to Chicago.

In the clubhouse, Hart came by my locker as I was lacing up my spikes.

"You spent the night with Darlene?" he asked. His tone told me he didn't approve.

"Don't judge me, John," I said. "I know what the Bible says, but this is the twentieth century. Surely the rules and regulations that applied two thousand years ago are today a little out of date."

"God's Word never goes out of date."

"Look," I said, "you told me yesterday you thought she was a keeper, and I agree. I fully intend to marry Darlene."

"But you can't know that you love her, not after one night. And sleeping with her will cloud your judgment."

"So will not sleeping with her," I said. "You're right, it's too early for either of us to know whether we love each other, or even like each other, even if we both agree that we like how the other makes us feel."

"Building a relationship with you on the road is going to be difficult."

"You're right about that."

"And sleeping with her will not keep her faithful."

"I'm not foolish enough to think she might not meet someone else while I'm away, but the physical part is as important as the rest. We didn't plan it, but if it hadn't happened last night it would've happened eventually. I'd never marry someone without knowing whether we were compatible in bed."

"I did," Hart said.

"Are you happy?"

"I love Trisha."

"I know you do, John," I said. I'd always thought of Hart as happy, but that he hadn't directly answered my question gave me pause. Loving someone and being happy were, in my book, two different sports. In God's eyes, loving others brought glory to Him, as I'd learned from my discussions with Hart while reading the Bible. But loving someone solely for that purpose, to bring glory to God, without personal happiness ... well, surely that couldn't bring glory to God. "Time will tell if Darlene and I can cut it as man and wife, but I'm sure going to give it my best, and I think she is, too. Please don't judge us."

"I'm not judging you, Backstop. That is for God. But He expects us to hold each other accountable for our actions."

"I appreciate that, John. And I hope you'll continue to do just that—hold me accountable. But let me assure you I have the best of intentions where Darlene is concerned. It's a long season, and you of all people should know the stress being away from family brings. Believe me, once the season ends, I intend to spend as much time as I can in Chicago getting to know Darlene. Should we decide to marry, it'll be sooner rather than later."

"You have my blessing in that," he said, "and my prayer that, God willing, you will marry."

"Thanks, Hart," I said standing up and shaking his hand. I'd long ago determined that Hart was the closest I had to a best friend, both on and off the field.

WE HEADED INTO THE BOTTOM OF THE SECOND SCORELESS. With a runner at second and two out, I had a chance to drive in the game's first run but struck out swinging on a pitch out of the strike zone. In the dugout, as I strapped on my catcher's gear, I thought of McGillicuddy's advice: *Don't let it affect your play*. There was no doubt I was loose, the result of last night, but I was also distracted for the same reason, deeply conscious of Darlene's nude body against mine, her kisses, her soft caresses, her soft sighs as I discovered her secret places, as she moved against me. Then I thought of Hart's assessment that good things happened when Darlene attended our games. With that I resolved to put out of my mind last night's lovemaking and focus instead on Darlene's presence here at the game.

I felt much better at my next plate appearance in the fifth, leading off with a double, but was stranded at second; while in the eighth, I hit the ball hard but to the deepest part of the park in center for a long out. In the end, we lost 3 to 1 in a game during which the Brewer's pitching dominated our hitters.

AFTER I SHOWERED AND DRESSED, I had only a few minutes to say goodbye to Darlene before boarding the bus that would take the team to the airport.

"I'm sorry I didn't bring you good luck today," she said.

"Not your fault," I said.

"Well, gee, it's not right that I should get the credit when you do well and none of the blame when you lose."

I could see she was trying to keep the conversation light, not yet ready to say goodbye. I chuckled. "I'll never hold you accountable for a loss or a hitting slump. The Brewer's out-pitched us today, that's all there is to it." With that I took her in my arms, held her a moment, and then kissed her with all of last night's passion. When we stepped back, I could see her fighting back tears.

"I'm sorry," she said. "I promised myself I wouldn't cry when it came time to say goodbye."

"Hey," I said. "It's okay."

"No, it's not. All I can think of is last night and how much I want to take you home and—"

"I know," I said, well aware of what she wished to do once we were home.

"And next weekend seems so far away."

Unsure of what to say to assuage her grief, I took her in my arms again until her sniffles subsided. Then I kissed her again, softly this time, and wiped the tears from her cheeks.

"Hey," I said. "I miss you already, you know that,

Darlin'. And I thank you for last night, for giving so much of yourself. I can't promise the week will go by fast, but I can promise you'll see me again, and I promise you many more nights like last night."

Darlene said nothing, only held on to me like she didn't ever want to let me go.

DARLENE WAS RIGHT: the team's trip to the west coast seemed interminable. Our nightly phone calls were mostly perfunctory discussions, chit-chat that seemed to do little to keep us connected—small consolation during our week-long abstinence. We learned that the age-old adage that absence makes the heart grow fonder is erroneous. I wondered more than once, as I'm certain Darlene must have, whether we could survive let alone thrive during these long absences; yet neither of us brought it up. Perhaps we both feared that bringing that concern, or others, to the forefront of our calls would be a first step toward succumbing to our dread of what we were hazarding—disappointment, heartbreak—and that the potential reward was no longer worth the risk.

Our single night of intimacy left me ravenous for Darlene's company, and it affected my play at the plate. I had but two hits in our series against the Angels, and three against the A's, none of them contributing anything positive to our four losses in the seven games we played before we returned home. Nothing I tried could get McGillicuddy's advice out of my head: *Don't let it affect your play*. Something more for which I could despise him. That he seemed withdrawn from me on the bench, which suited me just fine, and never once shook me off during his start against the Angels, one of our two wins, only left me feeling that he was silently mocking me. Even Hart seemed to hold back from offering me encouragement, which I took as disapproval for my consummating a physical relationship with Darlene. Finally, somewhere over the Rocky Mountains during our flight from Oakland to Chicago, he ventured to ask about Darlene.

"She seemed upset," he said, "when you boarded the bus

last Sunday."

"She was," I said. "But not with me, only the circumstances." Hart seemed relieved but said nothing, so I added, "I miss her, that's all. I'll play through it."

After a moment, Hart said, "It's difficult, being away from loved ones." And then, "This game can be hard on relationships."

"And relationships can be hard on this game."

"Put your trust in God," he advised me.

I sighed. "You have more practice at that than I do, John. I'm a pragmatist. I tend to trust what I know and can see."

"And it's been seven days since you've seen Darlene."

"That's not what I meant," I said, although I'd sensed Darlene's aloofness on the phone, discarded it as uncertainty over whether she was doing the right thing by giving us a chance. I, too, sensed that September was a long way away. We'd known each other but a few weeks—not long enough to determine whether we even liked each other let alone loved one another. I'd walked into her life off Michigan Avenue, a busy thoroughfare in downtown Chicago. How many other would-be suitors had done the same before me, and how many others would do so before September? I wondered if I would feel this way had we not consummated our relationship in the manner we had. Probably not; by sharing our bodies we'd taken a major step, invested, committed to one another, risked our hearts. Hart was right in that it was clouding my judgment.

"I trust Darlene," I told Hart. "And I trust myself."

"Do you, really?" he asked. "Trust Darlene."

"I trust that she'll remain faithful to me."

"That is but a small part of trust. Perhaps, because of your absence, your faith in her, in a future with her, is being tested."

I thought a moment about what Hart had said, what he was intimating. He was right, I did have faith issues with Darlene, the result of our lone night of intimacy, which had manifested itself in our phone conversations as well as my batting slump. Darlene's coolness fed my own, which in turn fed hers; and so I began to fear that she might, at any time, tell me she could no longer afford to invest time and feelings in us, that life with a major league baseball player was not something she wanted. Darlene had told me that she'd gotten attached in the time we'd known each other; but somehow during the week, I'd lost my faith that she was as adamant about giving us a chance as she had been prior to my boarding the bus in Milwaukee. Perhaps she, too, feared that I might reach the same conclusion: that a part-time relationship would soon fail to meet my expectations, my requirements. Until last Saturday we'd invested little more than time in each other's company. By sharing our bodies, we'd invested something of much greater value, were risking much more. Abstaining until the end of the season—a perilously long five months away—would not have been the answer. I was certain Darlene would throw in the towel long before then. Hell, I couldn't be certain that I wouldn't. We'd have to arrive at a solution, commit to not bailing out for the wrong reasons, until we could conclude whether or not we liked each other well enough to make the commitment lifelong, and, together, make it work.

"Thanks, Hart," I said. "You're a wise man, for a late inning reliever."

When we got to Chicago and the rest of the team boarded our connecting flight to Detroit, I told the skipper I was laying over for a couple of nights and would catch a flight to Detroit Tuesday morning, arriving in time for our next game, the first of a three-game set with the Twins.

&

STEWART'S FASTBALL IS SIZZLING, and it has more movement on it than I've seen all year. We get Reese on three pitches, all fastballs, the last a called strike.

In the dugout, Stewart takes a seat next to me and asks, "How's your ankle, B.S.?"

I despise that shortened version of my moniker, for the reference to its more common usage. "You've got enough to think about, Stew," I tell him, holding a bag of ice against my ankle. "Leave my ankle to me."

&

MY HEART WAS HAMMERING AS I APPROACHED DARLENE'S front door. I'd told her I would call her when I got back to Detroit, and I was having second thoughts about dropping by unannounced. Would she be pleased or put out?

I knocked and a moment later Darlene's surprised face peeked out at me. But there was more than surprise on her features. Moreover there was no affectionate welcome, and so I determined it had been a mistake for me to surprise her like this; a moment longer and she swung the door wide and asked me to come in. As I stepped in I understood the reason for her coolness. On her divan sat a man.

"Oh," I said. "Am I intruding?"

"As a matter of fact," the man said, standing. He was short with dark hair, tightly permed, and rather nondescript features—neither handsome nor homely, they betrayed Jewish origins and a large quantity of haughty self-importance.

"No, you're not intruding, Backstop. I'm glad you're here. David was just leaving."

"Backstop?" he said. "What kind of name is that?"

"A good one," I said. "One I've earned and bear proudly."

"Darlene—" he said, ignoring me, and then he stopped. Perhaps he could tell from her demeanor that further debate would bear no fruit. As he stepped past me and into the open doorway, he seemed to measure me from his stature a full head below me, trying to gauge what Darlene saw in me, possibly trying to determine the depth of our intimacy. "I'll call you and we'll talk."

"There's nothing to discuss," Darlene said and closed the door. When we were alone she threw her arms around me with the warmth I'd recalled from last weekend, warmth that had been absent from our transcontinental phone calls. "I'm so glad you're here," she whispered.

"So am I," I said in return. "I think."

Darlene covered my mouth with hers, effectively cutting off further discussion. When I'd been properly welcomed, she looked up at me and said, "It's not what you're thinking."

"And just what is it you think I'm thinking?" I asked, cringing inwardly at my failed attempt at humor.

"Sit down," she said, leading me by my hand to the settee and sitting next to me. She didn't let go of my hand. "I know how it must've looked."

"It didn't look like anything I need to concern myself over," I said; and then after a moment I added, "It's my guess he wants you back."

Darlene sighed, perhaps trying to determine where to start. "One of his colleagues saw us at Seward Park last Sunday. Two years he waited," she said, jumping ahead and leaving me to infer that the colleague had ratted her out. "Two years!"

"Wait a minute," I said, wondering if I'd misjudged. "You sound as if you—"

"What? Oh, no, no, believe me, I have no interest whatsoever in reconciling. It's just that, before I saw him for what he is, I wanted him to fight for me. I'm embarrassed to say now that I could've forgiven him, even though it wasn't a one-time slipup but a long-term affair, had he fought for me."

"Fought for you?"

"He asked me to forgive him, but when I told him I needed time to reconsider, he just gave me the time. He didn't try to woo me, didn't try to make it up to me, promise it would never happen again. He just gave me the time."

"I'm sorry," I said.

"When I told him it was over between us he didn't fight for me, didn't try to convince me otherwise, to give him another chance. He just nodded and said he understood; but he told me he'd take me back if I should change my mind."

"Arrogant," I said. When Darlene didn't say anything, I ventured: "That was fine with him until you didn't change your mind, when he learned you were moving on with someone new."

"He told me he never stopped loving me, said he'd fired his assistant."

"Probably because, after she found out she was no longer the other woman, she feared someone else would become the other woman and so she dumped him."

"That's speculation," Darlene said, sounding ever so lawyerly. "But he didn't fire her until last week."

"You didn't think it strange that he didn't fire her immediately after you found out?"

"He feared a lawsuit for wrongful termination."

"And no doubt he claimed she was good at her job, didn't want to lose a good assistant."

"He said he needed to wait, to acquire professional reasons that she couldn't refute."

I waited a moment, asked, "Does he know who I am?"

"That you play baseball? Yes, I told him tonight. He sneered, told me I needed someone with intellect."

I laughed. "Baseball players: our intelligence precedes us, eh?"

"I told him he didn't know what he was talking about, and that he had no idea what my needs are, not now and certainly not while we were together."

When I said nothing, Darlene went on: "He was here for only a few minutes before you knocked. I let him in only because I wanted to make sure he understood that it was over between us."

"I believe you."

"He called several times during the week," she confessed. "After the first call I told him not to call anymore. When I wasn't expecting you, I let the answering machine take my calls. His calls I didn't return. I was going to tell you when next I saw you, but I didn't want to worry you while you were away."

"Not that I could've played much more poorly," I said with a grin. "I guess that explains your aloofness during the week."

"I missed you and, well, you seemed cool, too, and I

feared maybe you were having second thoughts about me, about us."

"Hardly. But I suppose we're like-minded. I feared you might be thinking the same thing."

"Hardly," she said, imitating me. She took the hand she'd not let go of since she'd dismissed David and kissed it; she then held its palm to her cheek, her eyes closed. Then, completely shifting gears, she said, "What are you doing here, in Chicago?"

"What, you don't like surprises?"

"Normally, no, I don't. But this one, yes!"

"I'm AWOL from the Tigers until Tuesday morning. I'm yours to entertain until then. What do you have in mind?"

DARLENE LAY WITH HER HEAD ON MY CHEST, her breathing thick with sleep's contentment commingled with the bliss of lovemaking. I thought of last Sunday, our first time making love, her confession afterward that I'd not gotten her best, the reason why. Some part of me had understood, during our passion, that she was not entirely present. Tonight she had given herself to me entirely, and I loved her for it. *Trust me when I tell you I'm going to enjoy getting to know your body*, she'd told me last weekend. Tonight she'd employed what she'd previously learned even as I made new discoveries of my own; the result had been more than sweet.

THE NEXT MORNING, in Seward Park again after breakfast, the rest of the world lost in its Monday morning business, I told Darlene that I never had told her the reason for my surprise visit.

"You mean it wasn't to see me?" she asked, feigning disappointment.

"Of course it was," I said, stroking her knee, sheathed in nylon.

"You sound serious."

"The last week," I said, "apart from you, was difficult. Too difficult to ignore."

"Last night made it worthwhile."

"Yes, it did. But tomorrow—"

"Is still a day away."

"Still, I'm going to hate leaving for Detroit."

Darlene was silent, perhaps fearing what I might say next. To put her mind at ease I said, "I imagine it will get easier, but I don't want to get comfortable with these departures and absences."

Darlene merely let out her breath, and I imagined her relief.

"Last night," I said, "and last weekend, were big steps. I want you to know how important they were for me in committing to you."

"Thank you," she said. "I feel the same way."

"I'm looking forward to the off-season."

Darlene smiled. "You make that sound novel."

"I guess it is. I'd play baseball all year long if I could. But I'm looking forward to spending my winter in Chicago with you, becoming a part of your life here."

"I'm glad," she said, placing her hand atop mine, which still rested on her knee.

"But getting to September is going to be trying. I hated that you cried last Sunday when I got on the bus."

"Backstop, it's okay," she said, surprising me. "Prepared as I was, I still wasn't prepared for that first time, but I know now what to expect. It's never going to be easy to see you off on a road trip, but it's not something I can't cope with—knowing your homecomings will be like last night. And that David tried to reconnect only made me more certain of that. Last Sunday, after I watched the bus drive off and I drove back to Chicago, I had plenty of time to consider my feelings." Darlene paused, continued: "You're right, sharing our bodies was a commitment, and I realized that if I hadn't grieved you leaving, I wouldn't care, nor would I be committed. You look relieved."

"I am. I came here thinking we needed a plan to get us through to the end of the season."

"A plan? I thought the plan was for you to see me when

you can, and to bring me to some of your road games."

"It is."

"After that, as your deipnosophist, the plan is to negotiate for you a new contract, and to see if we can stand the rigors of unlimited togetherness."

I laughed. "Unlimited togetherness?"

"I know, it's not a legal term."

"No, but it does denote a certain comfort."

"The only problem with the plan is how to get you playing well during those gaps when you're away. I don't want to be responsible for your slumps."

I grinned and said, "I suspect I'll now be able to play through them."

"Good. Now," she said, glancing at her watch, "some of us have to work for a living. Marsha is supposed to open the shop at ten but I don't like leaving her alone."

AS WE APPROACHED DARLENE'S SHOP, walking hand-in-hand, we saw David, leaning against his car. As we neared he seemed to consider the possibility that I'd spent the night with Darlene; my ego relished his uncertainty.

"Darlene," he said, ignoring me, "can I have a minute with you alone?"

"No, David, you can't," Darlene said. "Please don't come around or call anymore. If you do I'll consider it harassment, and I'll take the necessary measures to ensure you'll stop."

David waited a moment, considering saying something more; then he looked at me and decided against saying anything that might make him look weak in my eyes. Then, as he pushed himself off the side of his car, he said, "Very well. But I think you're making a mistake."

"My mistake," Darlene said, "was thinking you cared about me. I won't make the same mistake. I wish you well and I hope you find happiness. Now please leave me to find mine."

I held open the door and followed Darlene into her shop. Once inside, as I watched David's car depart, Darlene introduced me to Marsha, a tall reedy young woman in her early twenties and who seemed impressed that her boss was dating a Detroit Tiger. She giggled and confessed she was a White Sox fan.

"I forgive you," I said. "There are worse teams to root for—like the Yankees."

Marsha giggled again but said nothing, perhaps a product of youthful self-consciousness.

"I've some retail things to do," Darlene told me. "Nothing nearly as exciting as playing baseball before a throng of cheering fans."

"I'm cheering for you nevertheless," I said. "I've an errand I want to run and I'll be back in a couple of hours to take you to lunch, if you can spare some time for your number one fan."

"I'll make the time," Darlene said, smiling.

I refrained from kissing her in front of the hired help and left.

I RETURNED TO THE SHOP SHORTLY AFTER NOON AND handed Darlene a plastic bag with two Montecristo Cigare des Artes Belicosos Largos—a cigar that was one of my favorites. "For later," I said.

"But I thought you didn't smoke during the season."

"I'll make an exception tonight. You've earned it. Consider it a celebratory smoke in recognition of your independence and your commitment to the future."

"A good way to celebrate. I can't wait."

WE DINED THAT NIGHT AT THE GRECIAN TAVERNA IN THE Far North Side neighborhood, taking a cab from Darlene's house after she changed into more casual attire. The waitress had just cleared the remains of our dinner, and I'd clipped and lit one of the Montecristoes and handed it to Darlene.

"Thank you. You know it occurs to me that I've yet to cook for you, while you've made breakfast for me twice now."

"Breakfast doesn't count as cooking."

"Not if it's breakfast cereal out of a box it doesn't, but your omelets are nothing short of epicurean."

"Epicurean? Is that like a Herculean homerun?"

Darlene laughed. "Something like that. Your omelets always hit a homerun for me."

"I'm glad," I said, holding a flame to the foot of the second cigar. "I just assumed, you being a modern woman, that you disdained domestic chores like cooking."

Darlene drew smoke from the cigar, exhaled after a moment, and said, "On the contrary, I love to cook, although it's bothersome to cook for one. I'd have made dinner for you tonight but for an empty pantry. Had I known you were coming, I'd have been prepared."

"Another time," I said. "Tonight I just want to sit here and look at you. You look mighty sexy with that cigar."

"Thank you," Darlene said, smiling.

I watched the end of her cigar glow cherry red in the dim lighting as she inhaled from its head. "This is very nice, mild yet complex, perfect with the wine," she said.

THE NEXT MORNING, as I boarded my flight to Detroit, I recalled the images of Darlene's nude body, soft skin, the pleasure of the previous night's lovemaking as we continued to learn each other's body, her movements in counterpoint to mine, and I knew my recent batting slump was at an end.

FERNANDO MAKES SHORT WORK OF US IN THE BOTTOM OF the sixth, getting Radford on a hard grounder to short, Trexler on a fly to left, and Reynolds on a fly to the warning track in right. I detect that he is beginning to leave the ball up, evidence that he is beginning to tire. I make a note to tell our hitters in the seventh to be patient, to make him throw a lot of pitches.

I love the drama of a low-scoring pitching duel, but I sense the home fans are growing more restless. Fans are capricious; yet what would the game be without them?

The seventh will be a test for Stewart, who went the

distance only four times during the regular season. “Pace yourself, Stew,” I tell him as we head out to our positions, “if you want to be around for the ninth.” Stewart says nothing, more evidence that he’s focused.

Seventh Inning

WE START OFF PORTER WITH A FASTBALL RIGHT DOWN Michigan Avenue for a called strike, which sets the table for a slider out of the strike zone at which he lunges and misses. Porter curses himself before stepping back into the batter's box. He's unsure what might be coming next, and I imagine he'll shorten his swing to protect the plate, so I call for a fastball down and in. Porter tips the ball into my mitt for strike three—Stewart's fourth consecutive strikeout and tenth of the game—and Porter heads back to the dugout muttering a string of expletives.

I wait for Higgins to dig in and think of my father, whether, wherever he is, he is proud of my accomplishments in baseball, or whether he is merely ashamed of what I did to Darlene. I want to forgive him for so much—as I long desperately for Darlene's forgiveness—especially for handicapping me in so many ways. But in order to forgive him, I feel I must somehow elevate myself into a position of judge, and that's something I find I just can't do. I accepted long ago that I am who I am, the good and the bad, as a result of this man about whom I know so little and who left me before I could prove myself to him. If I could only resolve to stop staring at my past looking for answers, or to assign blame, I might finally be able to consign him to a less prominent place in my life, into a favorite corner to which I can go from time to time if only to dust off the cobwebs.

Somehow I found the courage to risk my dreams, even when they seemed to exceed my grasp, despite Dad's inability to succor me. Still, in failing Darlene, I failed to become the man I always wanted to become. The sin rests entirely with me. Yet in the aftermath of that sin I fought for Darlene. As I continue to fight for us. But it's a battle I can't win alone.

In my youth I once considered that my father, due to my mother's unhappiness, should not have married and, in my own unhappiness with my father, that he should not have fathered children. But what did that say of me, my self-image, my self-value? Indeed, what does Darlene's unwillingness to fight for what we once had say of me? Yet I'm unwilling to concede defeat—perhaps the result of the ballplayer in me—although my resolve, like my knees, weakens day by day.

DARLENE AND I MADE IT TO THE END OF THE SEASON, although it wasn't without its trials and tribulations, the normal frustrations associated with long absences. Yet those difficulties somehow bonded us, made us stronger as we focused on the next step in our commitment. The constant departures and the many days and sometimes weeks apart were never easy, but the homecomings were wonderful, making the rest of it bearable as the season wore on and October neared. We treasured the moments we spent together, despite them being all too short.

I brought her to New York for a series in July and to Boston in August, both cities to which she'd never been. In New York, I took her to Zabar's deli on the Upper West Side and McSorley's Old Ale House in the East Village—founded in 1854 and its floor unswept since—two of my favorite haunts in the Big Apple. Darlene loved Zabar's, but found McSorley's hardened and somewhat seedy ambience not to her liking. She also found offensive that female patrons were prohibited until the early 1960s. Not surprising, she found New York too glittery, preferring Boston's more historic and academic appeal. Her commitment to her business precluded her from traveling more often; but she never had cared much for living out of a suitcase. To the contrary, I enjoyed seeing the sights of the cities to which I traveled as a Tiger, although in time I, too, tired of it, eventually finding it a necessary evil to playing the game I so loved. When I reached the twilight of my playing days, I began to look forward to finally putting down roots.

My schedule precluded me from joining Darlene to celebrate Mother's Day with her and her mother or from spending the day with my own mother; but as luck would have it, we played the White Sox in Chicago on the weekend of Father's Day that year. After a 3 to 2 win over the Sox—a game which I'd arranged for Darlene and her parents to attend—we adjourned to the restaurant of her father's choice to celebrate both the win as well as Father's Day. A steak lover, he took us to Gene and Georgetti's, one of Chicago's last men's club steakhouses, an establishment that boasts an all-male wait staff, a maître d' who was on a first name basis with all of the regular patrons, including Darlene's father, and which Frank Sinatra frequented whenever he was in the Windy City.

"MOM, DAD," I said, taking each of their hands in turn after Darlene introduced me. Darlene had previously told me her parents' names—Aldora and Nestor—but I wasn't comfortable calling them by their first names, and Mr. and Mrs. Petropoulos seemed too proper. Her father's handshake was firm, and he held my hand a long time, an indication to me of his warmth and sincerity. He seemed taken by my reference to him as "Dad."

"It's nice to finally meet you," her mother said rather formally. Missing from the statement was the proverbial *what are your intentions toward my daughter*?

Her father was more outgoing and, despite his stature in the Chicago legal system, more taken than his wife with the notion his daughter was dating a major league ballplayer.

"I've been following the Tigers and you since Darlene told us she was seeing you," he said. "It seems you have a promising career ahead of you."

"Thanks," I said, basking a moment in the words I'd never heard from my own father. "I understand you're a Cubbies fan."

"Tried and true blue," he said, grinning. "But I can still root for the Tigers, at least until they meet the Cubs in the World Series."

"A good answer," I said, finding I liked this man.

Darlene had told me he would be easy to like. He might be all business, even ruthless, where legal matters were concerned, but outside his element he seemed down to earth. "If that should happen," I added with a nod to Darlene, "I hope that at least one member of the Petropoulos family will be rooting for the Tigers."

"Absolutely," Darlene said. "You're my Tiger."

"And you're my Darlin'," I said to her with a wink. Then, to Nestor, "The Cubs haven't won a championship since 1908, and their last pennant was in 1945. You think they'll do it in our lifetime?"

"They're overdue, don't you think?" Nestor asked.

I nodded.

"You think you might ever play at Wrigley as a Cub?"

"I'm from Detroit and a Tiger tried and true blue, but I love the game and will play anywhere if the Tigers don't want me. The Cubs are a storied franchise, one for which I'd gladly play. It would certainly make life for Darlene and me a lot easier," I added, glancing at Darlene, who smiled and said:

"I like the way you think."

"Hey, we're a team, aren't we?"

Her mother, perhaps feeling left out of the conversation, asked me what my real name was. I told her, explaining how I'd acquired my nickname; she merely nodded, and I took no offense at her cool demeanor. Darlene had warned me that her mother would likely be difficult to win over. She might be elitist by nature, or perhaps the result of the lifestyle with which her husband had provided her. I was glad that Darlene had gotten her warm and friendly nature from her father.

During dinner Darlene's father and I swapped baseball stories.

"Ernie Banks was the greatest shortstop I ever saw play," he told me. "He and Baker were the first two blacks to play for the Cubs—not as famous as the Tinker to Chance to Evers combination."

"*Baseball's Sad Lexicon*," I said. "As penned by Franklin Pierce Adams:

"These are the saddest of possible words:
'Tinker to Evers to Chance.'
Trio of bear cubs, and fleeter than birds,
Tinker and Evers and Chance.
Ruthlessly pricking our gonfalon bubble,
Making a Giant hit into a double—
Words that are heavy with nothing but trouble:
'Tinker to Evers to Chance.'"

Nestor nodded, seemingly impressed by my recitation. "Written from the perspective of a Giants' fan," he said, "and first published in the *New York Evening Mail* in the early part of the century. Tinker, Evers and Chance," he added for the benefit of the uninitiated, "were part of the Cubs' World Series winning teams in '07 and '08, and in large part responsible for the Giants' frustration at the hands of the Cubs."

"Many people misinterpret the reference to 'hit into a double' as a two-base hit."

"All three were inducted into the Hall of Fame, largely, I suspect, as a result of that poem," Nestor said. "Banks, at least, made it into the Hall on his performance."

"The first of only five Cubs to have his number retired," I said, adding that as a youth I had a voracious appetite for reading about baseball players of bygone eras.

"I grew up listening to Dizzy Dean pitch for the Cubs."

"Previously the ace of the St. Louis Gashouse Gang," I acknowledged.

"As a boy, I loved his bravado. In 1934, as a Cardinal, he boasted that he and his brother Daffy would combine to win forty-five games that season, a feat they completed as part of a doubleheader, with Dizzy winning the first game with a three-hit shutout and his brother tossing a no-hitter in the nightcap. In the clubhouse after the second game, Diz was purported to say to his brother, 'If I'd a-known you was gonna throw a no-hitter, I'd a-thrown one too!'"

I laughed, impressed by Nestor's impersonation of the Arkansas native Dean—he had a good ear for dialect—and said, "I understand he once predicted he'd strike out Vince DiMaggio four times in one game."

"He did, too! DiMaggio hit a popup behind the plate during his last at-bat, and Dizzy screamed at his catcher to drop the ball, which he did, allowing Dizzy to complete the prophecy."

I thought briefly of my father and of his derision of Denny McLain for purposely serving up a homerun to Mantle. Unlike my father, Nestor understood the game of baseball for what it was: entertainment, not so unlike professional wrestling, sans the scripted outcome.

"I detest such arrogance," Aldora announced in one of her few contributions to the dinner conversation. I recalled Darlene's confession that she often was on another page, and I understood from where Darlene got it. Strangely enough, her mother had just inadvertently endeared herself to me, even if she never completely took to me.

"It ain't braggin' if you can do it," Nestor said, again quoting Dizzy in his southern dialect. Aldora said nothing, but her complexion reddened.

I shared that I had idolized Denny McLain in my youth, also for his boasting, which he often backed up before his off-the-field behavior and arm troubles caught up with him. "I watched him serve up a blooper to Mantle to hit over the right field wall at Tiger Stadium the year before Mantle retired." I left out my father's scorn of McLain.

"I never cared much for Mantle," Nestor said.

"He was a Yankee," I said, feeling no need to add more. "Now, Kaline," I continued, "was the consummate ballplayer. Few players can play right field the way he did. He seemed to glide out there, easily getting to balls other fielders would run after, elbows flailing and caps flying off, only to play on one hop. And what an arm! Tailor-made for right field. He could hit, too, for average—winning the batting title in 1955 at age twenty-one, the youngest player to do so, breaking the record set by Cobb—as well as occasional pop. He became the thirteenth player in history to hit two homeruns in the same inning that same year. And he was a smart base runner, too. He stretched more singles into doubles than most other hitters with more speed. Ten Gold Gloves, fifteen All Star appearances, a World Series Championship." I shook my head. "A grand career and the first Tiger to have his number retired."

"You mean even before Cobb?" Darlene asked.

"They didn't wear numbers in Cobb's day," Nestor said.

"Fancy that," Darlene said. "Cobb is another favorite of Backstop's."

"I admire him for his baseball skills," I said, "not as a human being."

"A bad seed, Cobb," Nestor concurred, "from what I know of him."

"Quite the contrast to Kaline," I said, "who is beloved by Detroiters and quite possibly the most popular athlete ever to play in my town. He now works the Tigers telecasts with George Kell, another Tiger great. I see him in Lakeland during spring training. He offered me some batting tips. What a rush to have a Hall of Famer work with me."

"I saw Kaline play once at Comiskey, late in his career. A true professional," Nestor said. "Certainly deserving of his place in the Hall of Fame."

"I applauded him for turning down a hundred thousand dollars from the Tigers, even as I later learned his teammates eschewed him. I thought Rose signing for three-quarters of a million dollars a few years later was obscene, and then more than three million with the Phillies ..."

"Which opened the door for this modern era."

"Agreed," I said. "When I understood the fiscal discrepancy between what the owners made at the gate and from broadcast rights and what the players were paid, I consented that the players were owed a greater share. Still, I won't say it hasn't had a negative effect on players' attitudes."

Nestor said, "What would you say to a base salary with incentives for achieving certain milestones? Number of homeruns, runs batted in, bases stolen, games won?"

"Didn't I tell you my father had a fine legal mind?"

Darlene asked.

"It's how Corporate America functions I suppose," I said, placing a hand atop Darlene's; she caught me sneaking a peek at her exquisite features, and I smiled back at her. "But the players' union would never agree to it."

"A shame to be sure. I suspect we'd see greater production, perhaps more records broken, if contracts weren't guaranteed. Is it any wonder we see players coast through two years of a contract, content with their past performance, until the final year of their contract?"

"An imperfect system," I said, "but infinitely more fair than it once was."

The waiter arrived to clear the remains of our meals, and I ordered three single malts and a Baileys for Aldora, which Darlene had previously informed me her mother enjoyed. As the waiter departed, I broke out three cigars—Montecristo Whites, Cubans that I'd gotten during a recent trip to Toronto when we played the Blue Jays—and said: "In celebration of Father's Day, in honor of Darlene's dad."

"And to your own father, who can't be with us tonight," Nestor added.

"And may the Cuban embargo be lifted," I said.

Darlene puffed heartily at the cigar I'd clipped and lit for her, and her mother showed her disdain: "I wish you wouldn't smoke, Dasha. It's not ladylike."

"Oh, Mother," Darlene said.

"Would you think less of a man secure enough in his manhood to cry at a funeral?" I asked, and immediately kicked myself. This was not the way to win over Darlene's mother.

"Of course not," Aldora said.

"Then why should a predominately male custom like smoking cigars detract from a woman's femininity?" Darlene asked.

Aldora said nothing, and I realized Darlene had approved of my standing up for her.

"They're adults, Aldora," Nestor said, admiring the White. "What's between them is their business."

"I'm sorry, Mrs. Petropoulos," I said in keeping with her formality. "I didn't mean to offend you."

"Nonsense," Nestor said. "Aldora forgets that Dasha is old enough to live her own life."

Aldora flushed, so like Darlene I thought, but kept her umbrage to herself. I wondered if she might voice her displeasure to Nestor later, in privacy, at being patronized.

LATER, as we lay in bed and I stroked the inside of Darlene's thigh, I asked her why she'd never told me her Greek name.

"My parents are the only ones who still call me by my birth name," she whispered. "I took to Darlene as a child because it seemed more American," she rushed to finish, breathless.

"What's it mean?"

"Gift of God."

"I like that," I said. "You really are a gift."

Darlene moaned to my caress and effectively ended the discussion, rolling over to cover my mouth with her own.

THE NEXT MORNING, after my shower, I came into the kitchen to hear Darlene say into the phone, "I've got to go, Mom. I'll talk to you later."

After I kissed her, I said, "That sounded ominous."

Darlene sighed, rolled her eyes, and reminded me that her mother could be difficult but that she'd come around.

"So she doesn't like me."

"I'm not sure that I do yet, remember?" she said with a laugh.

"But I'm growing on you, right, like a fungus?"

"That's disgusting," she said, wrinkling her nose. "But yes, I'm getting kind of fond of you."

"Glad to hear it," I said and kissed her.

"She thought you presumptuous in calling her 'Mom.'"

"Mrs. Petropoulos it is," I said, grinning.

"Thank you," Darlene said, "for dinner last night, and the cigars. You most certainly won over my dad with your baseball lore. I should've warned you my mother hates that I smoke an occasional cigar."

"I suspected. But I didn't want to leave you out."

"Thank you for that. It was a good moment, one which I would not have wanted to miss. It was a wonderful way to end the evening, after a Tigers win."

"You're welcome. I'm glad you were a part of it, too. Wouldn't have been the same without you."

Darlene wrapped her arms around me. As I kissed her I cursed the flight awaiting me at O'Hare that would take me from Darlene's embrace, even as I looked forward to the next time we could be together.

❧

CONVINCED WE HAD GOTTEN THE OPPOSITION THINKING fastball, I call for a first pitch curveball, which Higgins hits softly for a four-three groundout. Three pitches later—all soft stuff—we get Smith to pop out to short to retire the side and head into the stretch.

In the dugout, as I take a seat next to Stewart, the skipper comes by to ask Stewart how he feels. "Don't even think about taking me out," he says. The skipper looks at me and I concur with a nod, and so he moves on to the other end of the dugout, nervously chewing on a sunflower seed. In that moment, his seriousness over the stakes of this game reminds me of my father.

I'm remiss to say anything that might intrude on Stewart's thoughts, so I remain mute, holding the icepack against my aching ankle, which is noticeably swollen. I picture Darlene curled up on her sofa in Chicago watching the game. Fourteen years I've played this game, and this is the culmination; yet the notion that Darlene might not be watching somehow makes it seem meaningless.

"Ah, Darlene," I mutter aloud, "why won't you fight for us?"

If Stewart hears my rumination over the din of the home crowd as Lott approaches the batter's box, he ignores it, says nothing, and lost in my own private torment, I'm grateful for his silence.

I never felt that by leaving on road trips I was, as Darlene once suggested, putting myself in harm's way. I certainly had chances to be unfaithful—opportunities abounded around the ballpark, such as the one that had presented itself to me in Lakeland my first year. I arrived for my first spring training eager to play baseball, a wide-eyed rookie naïve to all that went along with being a major league ballplayer. I won't deny those opportunities didn't do wonders for my ego, even assuring my desirability in Darlene's eyes. I credited Darlene for making me want to be a better man in ways my father, the result of the dynamics of his relationship with my mother, failed to teach me. The Lakeland experience, not to mention the callous disdain McGillicuddy had for his marriage, left me with the certainty that that lifestyle—risking love with Darlene for the empty lovin' that could be easily found around the diamond—was not what I wanted.

Over the years, Darlene watched me sign many an autograph for eager fans of both genders—at the ballpark, during the Tigers Winter Caravan, even during my personal appearances at Parkinson's groups, fundraisers and hospitals. She heard me exchange pleasantries with many young women enamored by a brush with fame. I never played the role of flirter, even in response to a flirt. If she ever viewed that as being in harm's way, she certainly never let on. By then perhaps her trust had reached the point of being rock solid.

DARLENE DIDN'T MEET MY MOTHER UNTIL AFTER THE season ended, when she came to Detroit the second week in October to meet Bill Lajoie to negotiate my new contract. I recalled my discussion with Nestor on Father's Day, about an incentive-based contract, and so on a whim and against Darlene's advice, I opted to go for a lower base salary laced with incentives for achieving certain milestones: thirty percent of runners thrown out attempting to steal, homeruns (twenty and thirty respectively), batting average (.300) and, in an effort to share in our pitching staff's numbers, staff earned run average, wins and strikeouts. Based on the season just past, I was certain I could match those numbers even as some would force me to stretch, which is what I wanted. Mr. Lajoie was more than happy to accept such an offer and expressed a desire that all his players be so accommodating. We were careful not to disclose the terms of my contract. I'm proud to say all of my contracts were similarly based on incentive. I also suspect, although there is no way to prove it, that my success in this game is the result of those incentives.

After I inked the paper, I took Darlene to meet my mother, to take her to dinner in celebration of my new contract.

Perhaps because of her own mother's unwillingness to accept me as her daughter's suitor, Darlene was nervous about meeting my mother.

"Relax," I told her. "What's not to like about you?"

"I said the same thing to you about my mother."

"You're not a ballplayer," I said, grinning.

"No, but I'm a woman and don't most mothers disapprove of the girl their sons bring home for them to meet?"

"Are you speaking from experience?"

"David's mother did not like me. I imagine she blames me for her son's infidelity."

"That's a supposition, probably based on anger."

"I don't imagine he ever brought her home to meet his mother."

"Which does little to assuage your hurt. But really, I urge you to check your preconceptions of my mother at the door. She really does want me to be happy, and I'm sure it will do her heart good to see our happiness."

MY MOTHER'S PARKINSON'S WAS ADVANCING QUICKLY. The slight tremors that had, a few years ago, been the warning that something was amiss, had advanced to affect her motor skills, speech and decision making. She could look forward to greater bouts of depression as well as rigidity and postural instability. At that point, she would need in-home care, and eventually she would need to be moved into a care facility.

Initially, her medication had left her with good days and bad days; but as her system acclimated itself to the medication, became less responsive to it, she had bad days and worse days. When she opened the door to Darlene and me, I was delighted to see that, as bad days went, she was enjoying a decidedly good one. I talked to her often when on the road and she nearly always seemed depressed. But her mood at least always seemed to improve when I visited, because a visit usually resulted in an escape from the confines of the house. I could sympathize with her being a prisoner in her own home, but I couldn't quite empathize entirely with all that that entailed.

"Mom," I said, giving her a hug. "Good to see you."

I introduced her to Darlene, who in turn gave her a hug and, taking a page from my script, said, "It's nice to meet you, Mom."

Her warm greeting elicited a smile from my mother, who, with a concerted effort to speak, said, "I've heard much about you."

"All of it good," I said with a grin for Darlene's benefit.

"Yes," Mom breathed.

"Mom," I said, "I hope your appetite is good, because today, thanks to Darlene's hard-nosed negotiation tactics, I signed a new contract with the Tigers."

Darlene laughed and said, "I had little to do with it. Your son had his own ideas about how the paper should read. All I did was go along with it."

"I got enough up front, guaranteed, to be comfortable. The rest I'm sure I can earn."

"I raised him to not be greedy," Mom said, adding that she had a taste for pizza. Unfortunately, she had quickly learned that too much protein in her diet set her tremors into motion. Still, although her steady diet of fruits, salads, fish, rice and couscous had caused her to lose weight at an alarming rate—she had never been more than ten pounds over her optimum, except during her pregnancies—she was not yet ready to give up the occasional pizza.

"Great," I said. "How does DeLuca's sound?" DeLuca's, I knew, was one of her favorites for pizza.

"That sounds good," she whispered, with considerable effort.

THE WAITRESS WHO CAME TO TAKE OUR ORDER BORE THE nametag, Terri, and I realized she was the kid who'd grown up down the street from our house. Maybe five years younger than I, she had blossomed into an attractive young woman. She recognized me and, calling me by my birth name, asked for my autograph in that star-struck way most of the women around the ballpark ask. I scrawled *Backstop, Detroit Tiger* across a blank check she'd offered me. After exchanging a few pleasantries about her working her way through college, I gave her our order, which included two shots of bourbon and beers for Darlene and me, a decaffeinated iced tea for Mom, who shied away from stimulants, and our pizza, with an order of anchovies on the side for me.

After Terri left, my mother said, "I don't know how you can stand those things."

"You and me both," Darlene said with a laugh and a wrinkled nose.

"A Greek who doesn't like anchovies," I said. "Go figure."

"You have a nice laugh," Mom said to Darlene.

"Thank you," Darlene said.

"Yes, she does," I said. Darlene's laugh always warms me; it was one of her many attributes that brought comfort to me when we were apart. "She withheld it when we first met, despite all my best efforts, but when she finally relented, I knew she was a keeper."

Darlene blushed slightly while Mom told me I was being silly.

When our pizza arrived, and while I was cutting up a slice into mouth-sized pieces for my mother, she apologized, for Darlene's sake. "I'm sorry," she said. "I have Parkinson's." Mom had never been able to stop herself from apologizing for her condition when in public.

"That's okay, Mom. Darlene knows."

After dinner, I offered to cut up the last slice for Mom to take home, but she told me to take it, saying she didn't care for cold pizza.

"That's why I bought you the microwave."

"I don't like that thing," she said, which was her way of saying it frightened her. I considered suggesting she use the toaster oven to warm it, but thought better of it. My childhood memories of my mother were of a woman with no small amount of confidence, who embraced new technology. But my father, ten years her senior, fearing anything that might liberate his wife, had managed to bully that out of her. And now Parkinson's was doing its best to finish what my father had started.

I sighed and saw a look of dismay on Darlene's face.

"Can you take me to Penney's?" Mom asked in an effort to cut off further discussion of pizza and microwave ovens.

I realized what had started out as an evening of celebration had turned into a night out for Mom. I knew it wouldn't be long before the pizza would start to cause the tremors, but I also knew I couldn't say no to her. She had had little freedom while Dad had been alive, even less now, the result of the Parkinson's.

"Sure, Mom," I said.

MOM MANAGED TO CLOSE J. C. PENNEY'S. By the time ten o'clock rolled around, we had purchased a pair of earrings at the jewelry counter, a purse in the handbag department, and a new pair of slacks with matching blouse from the clothing department. There had been a time when Mom could've done all this in thirty minutes or less, but thanks to her affliction, these purchases turned into a nearly two-hour ordeal as she fretted over which pair of earrings to buy, the size of the purse, and the colors and pattern of the blouse. I mourned the loss of the woman who once was able to unerringly pick out paint for the dining room without a piece of wallpaper and a carpet swatch to which to match it.

As we pulled out of Penney's parking lot and onto Warren Avenue, Mom told me she needed to stop at A&P to pick up a few grocery items. By now her tremors were in full swing and her voice was little more than a whisper, but I gave in to her wishes.

At A&P, we stood in front of a shelf of kitchen trash bags for several minutes while Mom, her tremors now uncontrollable shakes, agonized over which ones she wanted. A woman pushed her grocery cart past us and I heard her young son ask his mother, with no attempt to hide his curiosity, "What's wrong with that lady?" I resisted the urge to reprimand the kid, recalling my own father hissing at me not to stare when, at age five or six, he caught me gaping at a one-armed man in a restaurant. Kids just don't know any better.

AFTER WE GOT MOM SETTLED AT HOME, on the drive to my apartment, Darlene said, "I'm sorry, Backstop. I had no clue of her condition."

"That's okay. Most people, unless they have firsthand exposure, have no idea."

"You're very good to her."

"Thanks, but as often as I accommodate her, I also refuse her. Sometimes, especially after a road trip, the last thing I want is to chauffer her around town."

"You have a right to set boundaries."

"I know that," I said. "But with boundaries comes guilt. I can't imagine, traveling the country as I do, what it must be like for her, with no driving privileges, how small her world has become. You should know, too, that it's highly likely that next week my sister will take her back to Penney's to exchange the purchases she made tonight for others."

"That sounds symptomatic of her illness. Does she have any neighbor friends who can take her out?"

"She had two, but she managed to overstay her welcome with them."

"That's too bad."

"She's not their responsibility," I said. "It's funny how

people fear an illness like Parkinson's." I sighed.

"What?"

"Sometimes I feel as if she manipulates me. Which is probably how her friends felt, and why she lost them."

"You've been blessed with a good life, your future bright and full of hope, while hers must be unbearable."

I nodded. "You have no idea what she was like before the Parkinson's. I've been grieving her loss for years now. I suspect that when she's finally laid to rest, I'll have little left to grieve."

"Well, I hope you will bear no guilt over that," Darlene said. "I'm not saying you should find happiness in the death of a loved one, but you should at least take comfort that their suffering is at an end."

When I said nothing, Darlene added, "You're doing right by her, Backstop. You should have no regrets."

WE CULMINATED WHAT WE NEVER QUITE ACHIEVED IN OUR hoped for celebratory night out by making love—slowly, passionately—yet I couldn't help but feel a certain sadness in the aftermath. Hoping to distract me, or perchance for reasons of her own, Darlene, her head on my chest, intruded on my thoughts.

"Tell me about Terri."

"Our waitress? She grew up down the street from us. Skinny little kid was more an annoyance than anything. My mother often teased me that she had a crush on me. In retrospect, I imagine she was probably right. At fifteen, who wants a ten-year-old hanging around?"

"I think the crush is still there."

"Because she asked for an autograph?"

"But she called you by your name."

"Why wouldn't she? That's the name I grew up with."

Darlene said nothing, and in the moment of silence that ensued I realized something was amiss—in Darlene's tone of voice as well as her line of questions concerning what hadn't even been a childhood sweetheart. Conscious of the burn with which David had left her, I ventured, "No need to be concerned, Darlene. She's still just a kid to me."

"Can you deny you didn't like what you saw tonight?"

"I was surprised, yes, to see her these many years later. I won't deny she's blossomed into an attractive young woman, but rest assured, Darlene, I have no interest in her whatsoever."

"But you seemed—not quite present, here with me." Darlene's assertion wasn't an accusation, but one of uncertainty, a product of the insecurity for which I could thank David for leaving her.

"You're right," I said. "I was distracted, but not for the reasons you think. If I seemed not quite present it wasn't because of thoughts of our waitress."

A moment later, Darlene suggested, "Your mother?"

"Yes," I said. "Her marriage was not a happy one. My father was overbearing. He blamed her for the state of the family budget, yet her taking a job to help out was an affront to his self-image as breadwinner." I paused a moment, hoping Darlene would allow me to gather my thoughts without interruption. She accommodated me. "You talked earlier about finding comfort in the passing of a loved one's suffering. When Dad died, I took more comfort in that my mother's suffering at his hands was at an end than I did in the end to his suffering." Darlene must've known what was coming; still she said nothing, allowing me to tell my story in my own words. "And now Parkinson's has stepped in to finish the job my father started."

"Oh, Backstop, I'm sorry," Darlene said, unable to contain her own pain at my confession, which I hadn't yet begun.

"I want so much to be happy, Darlene."

"Aren't you, with baseball? You've achieved your life's dream."

"That and more," I said, cupping her cheek with my hand, aware, as I always was and forever would be, of its satiny texture. "But happiness, this happiness, seems to have a price. My father is gone, abandoning me before I could share my accomplishment with him."

"Is that so important, your need to prove yourself to him?"

"I suppose it is, although I can't explain why. I hope in time it won't be." I sighed and forged ahead: "And now my mother has, in her own way, abandoned me, too, the result of her affliction. She understands what baseball means to me. And while I can't really share the finer fruits of my life in baseball, beyond an occasional pizza from DeLuca's, I'll never be able to bring her to a ballgame. I can't imagine watching me on the tube brings her much joy."

"Oh, but you're wrong, Backstop. You're her son, and I'm sure she takes great joy in watching you play, even if it is only on TV. I'm sure she wishes she could attend a game, but I'm also sure that not being able to go doesn't in the least take away from her joy over what you've accomplished."

I said nothing, leaving Darlene time to consider the remainder of what I'd confessed. A moment later she added, "Backstop, it's not your mother who has abandoned you. I think it's you who fears that you are abandoning her."

I could say nothing in the face of Darlene's wisdom even as I felt my heart swell with love for her. She was right: I'd never considered that my guilt over my mother's illness while I went on living my life was the result of my feeling that I had abandoned her.

Eventually I ventured, "I envy you your relationship with your father. He is a dad in every sense of the word."

"Thank you. You took to him very easily, as I suspected you would. And he to you." Darlene considered a moment before adding, "I can't imagine what it will be like when I finally lose him."

"You will grieve your loss. Something I've not been able to do for my father."

"Perhaps you will finally grieve properly once you are able to forgive him for not being more nurturing to you, for abandoning you, and for making your mother unhappy."

I said nothing; Darlene went on. "You shouldn't let your parents' unhappiness stand in the way of your own, Backstop. You can be whatever you want, achieve everything you wish. You've said your mother wants you to be happy. Happiness is a choice. So choose to be happy."

My vision blurred; I blinked away the moisture, said, "Sage advice, Darlin' dear. Thank you."

"You know I'm happy to share my dad with you."

"You will?" I said, chuckling.

"Seriously. Maybe it was because they were both lawyers, but I could never see Dad being close to David. Dad didn't say much in the aftermath of that ruin, but I suspect he expected it to end poorly."

"Would you have listened had he warned you?"

"Probably not."

"A parent can't shield their child from all of life's disappointments."

"No. And I'd like to think I'm better off, wiser, more certain of my desires, better equipped to give love having gone through that heartache."

"I think you are."

"You didn't know me then."

"No," I said, "but I'm glad that I know you now."

"Aren't you sweet," Darlene said, kissing the palm of my hand. "You know, in you he may find the son he didn't have—you're more alike than you may think, despite your preference for bourbon," she added, laughing that softly melodic laugh that never failed to lift my spirits. "And you may find in him the dad you never had."

"Thank you," I said, "I love you for that." It occurred to me then that, over the five months we'd been together, we'd exchanged that sentiment many times—*I love you for that*—but neither of us had yet told the other that we loved them. Perhaps we feared that such an admission, like the lover who has the name of his or her loved one tattooed someplace on their anatomy finds it to be a precursor of doom, would spell disaster to our future.

I rolled over, kissed her softly on her shoulder, let my hand slide down to her velvet hip, and then kissed her lips, gently slipping my tongue into her mouth. When our lips parted I told her that I loved her. Darlene sighed, as if the weight of the world had been lifted from her.

"I've know that for months," she said. "You've showed me that you do many times and in many ways. But I've been waiting to hear you say the words. Thank you." And then, "Αγάπη μου αγάπη μου λίγο καιρό." It was the first time I'd heard her speak Greek and I immediately fell in love with the sound of the language. "Love me little, love me long," she translated. "I love you, too, Backstop. More than you can know."

We made love again—as love should be made, in celebration of our professed love, both of us fully present.

NOT TO BE SHOWED UP BY STEWART, Fernando brings his three-hitter into the seventh, coming after Lott with heat. Lott makes him work, however, before finally succumbing to an unassisted groundout to first base in an eight-pitch at-bat.

Fernando looks frustrated, perhaps wanting to duel with Stewart pitch for pitch, which should work to our advantage, if we show patience. Miller stands in and works the count to three and two before hitting the tenth pitch into the gap in left-center. Unfortunately he gets under the pitch, putting too much air under it, which gives the center fielder, much to the chagrin of our fans, enough time to camp under it for the second out.

As Hernandez digs in, I make a concerted effort not to think about Darlene's absence. Unfortunately that gives my dad a chance to intrude on my thoughts. *What if,* I ponder, *I'd chosen to listen to you, Dad, and had not pursued this dream of mine? How different my life would've been. Perhaps I'd be writing a sports column instead of being the subject of many a column. I'd never have met Darlene, would never have cheated on her, perhaps a subconscious attempt on my part to sabotage the happiness I sought. Yeah,* I admit to myself, *and at age thirty-eight, I'd still be asking myself,* "What if?"

Hernandez swings at a first pitch fastball and hits a

screaming grounder to third that Richards spears and, after picking himself up, throws to first to complete the out and send the game, still scoreless, into the eighth inning.

As I leave the dugout and head out to the center of my baseball world, I think: *So many what ifs.* I recall asking Dad, as he lay in hospice, if he had any regrets. "Hell yes," he told me. "No one gets out of this life without them." I never thought to ask him what some of his might've been—whether they included me and Karin, getting married. Dad was wrong about a lot of things, but concerning regrets he was right. I regret with my whole heart what I did to Darlene, and regret, too, that she won't let me make it right. The second regret would not exist without the first; yet in time, I suspect it will grow to rival the first. Darlene's forgiveness and willingness to fight for us won't undo the past, but it would at least help us to close the door to that unpleasant chapter of our life together, a door she is certain to close at some point, with or without me on the other side.

Eighth Inning

AS STEWART BEGINS HIS WARM-UP TOSSES, I realize I fear winning this game seven more than I fear losing it. I think back ten days to my visit with Dad at the cemetery before the series started. I finally realized that I no longer needed Dad's approval of my accomplishments. I'd cursed myself then, for allowing him to stand in the way of my happiness for so long. I left the cemetery having finally forgiven my father and secure in the knowledge that it was my last visit to ask questions of a man who, in death, is as resigned to withholding answers as he was in life. But I was accosted by the sadness that my mother, having succumbed ten months earlier to complications arising from her battle with Parkinson's, hadn't survived long enough to see me reach baseball's pinnacle. She, too, had grieved over what I'd done to Darlene, telling me I was a fool and that she was disappointed in me. And so there are two women in my life I'd let down. Even so, I resolved to play the World Series not for my father's approval or to take the sting out of my mother's displeasure in me, or even to help me forget the atrocity I'd committed against Darlene. I determined to play, win or lose, for myself.

I fire the ball down to second base and realize, not for the first time, that baseball is a business. But first and foremost it's a game, a game played by grown men—a privileged few, among whom I count myself—and because it is a game, I know I will not lament as a failure on my part should we lose.

But winning it without Darlene at my side I know will be a loss of unbearable magnitude.

As Evans digs into the box, I make a concerted effort to put thoughts of my parents, of winning and losing, out of my mind. Although I have a game to play, business to tend to, I take comfort in Darlene's invisible presence, which I've taken with me to every game I've played since we met.

Of all the major team sports, baseball is the only one not

governed by a clock. A regulation nine-inning game can be played in less than two hours or as many as four. In two innings, time indeterminate, I'll have plenty of time to consider the repercussions of its outcome.

Repercussions, I think as I put down the sign for Stewart. It's strange that I can still manage to associate that word with much happier times.

❧

THE FOLLOWING DAY, I put Darlene on a flight back to Chicago to shop for a ring, while I made arrangements to have my belongings put into storage and paid off the remaining three months of my apartment lease. By the end of the week I was in Chicago with my shaving kit and pretty much the shirt on my back. I was used to living out of a suitcase during the season, so it didn't bother me. Still, I spent a couple thousand dollars on a wardrobe that included a dark pinstripe suit, wingtips, a couple of dress shirts and ties for formal wear, and several pairs of casual slacks, along with some shirts and sweaters and an overcoat to get me through the Chicago winter. With so little in the way of wardrobe, Darlene had me put these items in the closet in the second bedroom. I joked to her that the husband's closet never seems to come with the house.

Darlene had picked out several rings but wanted my opinion on my preference. I told her the decision should be hers, price notwithstanding, but she insisted that my happiness with her choice was important to her. I had the jeweler withhold the prices and pointed out my favorite. Darlene said nothing, merely nodding to the jeweler that we'd take that set of rings. When I pressed her for her preference, Darlene refused to tell, relenting only on our wedding night, admitting to me that my choice had also been her first choice. "Honest?" I asked. "Honest," she replied. "A good omen," I said, kissing her, eager to make love to her for the first time as husband and wife.

Against her mother's wishes, we opted for a small wedding. The wedding Aldora wished for would've taken no fewer than six months to plan, which would've put me in spring training. Darlene and I didn't want baseball to interfere with the wedding or our honeymoon, and neither did we wish to wait another year for a fall wedding. We planned a January affair, shortly after New Year's, at a small chapel with only immediate family and close friends in attendance. A January wedding, we both agreed, was appropriately symbolic of our new life together.

John Hart was my best man, and he couldn't have made a more fitting toast at the reception, quoting *Proverbs:* "Whoso findeth a wife findeth a good thing."

His wedding gift to us was a check for five thousand dollars. When Darlene expressed shock over the amount, John downplayed his generosity: "The Tigers pay me well to throw baseballs. It is a small amount for me, but large enough to show the importance of the journey you are about to start." And then, to lighten the moment, he added: "In truth, I had no idea what to get you. Backstop has a long and potentially well-paid career ahead of him. What do I get for someone who can have whatever he wishes and knows what he and his new bride need? With my gift I hope you will purchase something you both want, whether foolish or sensible. I only ask in return that you think of me as the gift giver."

Darlene wept with happiness over John's generosity; I teared up, too, and after Trish concurred that the amount of their gift wasn't a financial burden to them, we both readily agreed to his simple request.

We made love that night as if for the first time: tenderly, passionately, with all the joy of the moment, unaware of the world and baseball, as well as with all the hope for our future. Afterward, as we held each other, Darlene wept. After her tears were spent, I propped myself up on my elbow to look at her and asked, jokingly, whether she was disappointed. She laughed and said, "Foolish man. No, of course not. I've never been happier."

"I'm glad," I said.

"You?"

"Never happier." While Darlene kissed the palm of my hand, I asked, "Did you ever think, nine months ago when we first met, that we'd end up married?"

"No," she replied rather sheepishly.

"I did."

"Men and their hormones," she said, laughing, and I joined her, my heart swelling from the music. "Actually," she added, "I began to think it was possible the night you took me and my parents to dinner on Father's Day."

"Really?" I asked, surprised by her admission that it was so early in our courtship. "Why didn't you tell me then?"

"I was afraid I'd scare you off."

"Nothing could've scared me off. And that's not my hormones talking," I added with a grin.

"You've always treated me well, Αγάπη." Αγάπη (agape) is Greek for love, and it was the pet name Darlene had given me last October, after we'd both professed our love for each other. "But I was taken by how you treated my parents. It was important to you that they like you."

"It wasn't important to you?"

Darlene looked pensive. "Not really," she finally said. "My mother liked David and you know how that ended. I realized one of the reasons I worked so hard to make that work was to please her, even at my own expense. I'm not sure even now how she feels about you. But the important thing is how I feel about you."

"Did you and David ever discuss marriage?"

"No. I guess at some level I knew he wasn't marriage material. But this is our wedding night and I don't want to talk about him."

"Agreed. I hope the door to that part of your past is closed forever," I said and bent to kiss her breast.

"It is," Darlene breathed, her chest rising to my moist kiss.

"You're a beautiful woman, Darlin', and I love everything about you." And then I added, "Did I tell you how beautiful you looked today, in your wedding gown?"

"Only six times," Darlene said, smiling. "But who's

keeping score?"

"Not me." And then, "Although it was Greek to me when you first said it, love me little love me long," and I bent to kiss her mouth.

WE RETURNED FROM OUR HONEYMOON IN NEW ZEALAND, and three weeks later I headed to Lakeland for spring training. My off-season in Chicago and the wedding had kept me from my usual workout routine, so I had a slow April, heating up in May and finishing the season well, achieving all of the milestones set down in my contract. That spring, McGillicuddy surprised me by congratulating me for getting married. I thanked him, and he told me baseball was hard on marriage. It was the closest he ever came to acknowledging that he had a problem. I found out later, from our bullpen coach, that McGillicuddy's wife had finally had enough of his philandering and had filed for divorce.

Darlene was good for me, and marriage was good for my career. During the off-season I hung around Darlene's shop serving as an unofficial buyer, at which I became very good. In time she came to trust me with some of her buying decisions. Eventually her shop became quite profitable.

Over the years that followed, I put up solid numbers. Maybe not good enough to make it to the Hall of Fame, but I was playing for love of the game and for love of Darlene, and I never considered my numbers above and beyond those milestones in my contract that served as incentive. As always, I focused on my play, resolved to enjoy my accomplishments after my playing days were over. Darlene continued to serve as my agent, and negotiations always went well. I always received a raise for my contributions to the team.

☙

STEWART IS AHEAD IN THE COUNT TO EVANS ONE BALL, two strikes, and he continues to work quickly. I throw the ball to him, he looks in for my sign, nods, but before he can go into his delivery Evans calls time out. Knowing Stewart is in a rhythm, Evans hopes to break it by calling time.

Stewart rocks back into an upright position and waits, seemingly indifferent, for Evans to step back in. A moment later, Stewart brings it: heat, high and tight, and Evans is unable to catch up to it, swinging and missing for strike three. Evans asks Welke if he'd just swung at ball two; Welke concurs that the pitch was high, and Evans heads back to the dugout in silent consternation.

We've managed to keep the opposition off-balance all night. When they've showed patience, we've attacked the strike zone; when they were aggressive, we came with off-speed stuff. Fellows tagged us his last trip with a groundball single to left. We'd come after him then with off-speed pitches, so in an effort to cross him up I call for a slow curve. Stewart nods—he hasn't shaken me off once these last three innings and I'm proud of him, for showing trust in me. He goes into his windup, and deposits the pitch into my mitt for a called strike. I throw the ball back out to Stewart and nod at him. That last pitch was probably the best one he's thrown all night, hitting the target right where I called for it and buckling Fellows's knees as he was thinking fastball. After fouling off a changeup, I call for the hard slider, which Fellows hits hard again into the hole between short and third; but Trexler is playing well over and manages to make the pick on a tough in-between hop, and he throws the ball across the diamond for Radford to scoop out of the dirt to beat Fellows by a step and a half for the second out. That leaves it up to Simon, their diminutive shortstop with good speed, to get something going.

Simon is young with plenty of promise, but he's also a free-swinger. He's been a thorn in our paws since game four, hitting over .400 since, stealing three bases and scoring three runs. We've done well tonight to get him once on strikes and again on a lineout to second. After getting ahead of him with a first-pitch fastball, I determine to expand the strike zone markedly to see if we can get him to go fishing. A hard slider in the dirt gets Simon to swing out of his shoes, and Stewart's changeup on our third offering drops at the last moment, leaving Simon to beat it into the dirt. Radford meets the ball a third of the way down the first base line, where he fields it easily and waits for Simon to meet him, and makes the tag to end the top of the eighth inning.

September 1995

FOR THE FIRST TIME IN MY CAREER THE TIGERS MADE THE playoffs.

I never went out with the guys after a game, not because I feared putting myself at risk but because, married, it just didn't seem right; but that night, in New York, I made an exception in celebration of clinching a playoff berth. We were scheduled to fly back to Detroit the next morning, Monday, to begin a three-game set with Kansas City after an off day. Radford, Trexler and Reynolds came by our room and invited John and me to go out with them. John begged off, not yet having spoken to Trish and his kid; but I consented. I'd already talked to Darlene on the phone, accepting her congratulations for winning the Division, exchanging "I love yous," when they enticed me with an evening at McSorley's. I hadn't been there since I'd taken Darlene the first year we'd known each other.

McSorley's was hopping with college kids from New York University and Cooper Union University when we got there a little after nine. Standing at the bar and half-finished with my second dark beer, I was put off by the noisy young crowd and ready to call it a night as soon as Reynolds and Radford returned from the loo when I was approached by a young blonde of maybe twenty-seven or twenty-eight.

"You're a Tiger, aren't you?" she asked me. I recalled noticing her when she came out of the restroom a few minutes ago. Pretty was an understatement—and the miniskirt she wore showed off a dazzling pair of legs.

"How can you recognize him without all of his catcher's gear on?" Trexler said from my left, laughing. The blonde gave no indication that she was aware Trexler and I were together.

"I saw the interview after the game," she said, moving a wisp of blond hair behind her ear without taking her eyes off me. I took a swallow from my glass of beer and seemed to notice, for the first time, all the rings on the bar's surface left by other wet beer glasses. "You're that catcher, aren't you?"

"Backstop," Trexler supplied.

"You're going to the World Series."

"Not yet, we're not," Trexler said. "We need to make it through the playoffs first."

"Oh," she said with no disappointment. She seemed to know as much about baseball as my kid sister did when we were growing up. With all the seriousness and wisdom acquired during her five-year tenure on the planet, she once referred to the Fall Classic as the World Serious.

At that moment, a young man, a year or two out of college, approached and said, "What are you hanging with these old guys for? Come on, let me buy you a beer and get to know each other."

"I told you I'm not interested, so leave me alone," the blonde said. Oily and unkempt, he was out of this girl's league, but she hadn't yet been able to convince him of that.

"You're a babe," he said, leering at her breasts.

"Go away!"

"I just ... I just wanna talk," he said, changing tacks and taking her by her elbow.

"Stop it!" she said, pulling away. The kid couldn't take his eyes from her breasts.

"Look," I said in my best Bogie impersonation. "Of all the gin joints in the East Village, you have to walk into this one. Why don't you train your sights on someone else?"

The kid looked at me glassy-eyed, evidence that he'd already had too much to drink. "Gin joints," he said with mustered condescension. "Only a pussy drinks gin. Are you a pussy, old timer?"

"Yeah, I'm a pussy," I said, discounting the insult and cognizant of the fact that McSorley's doesn't serve hard liquor.

"Yeah you are," the kid said, running the words together in his slurred speech. Then he turned to the blonde and, taking her again by her elbow, said, "Come on, hot stuff, let's go over to my table." Around "his" table sat a couple of other college-aged boys and two similarly-aged girls. This guy seemed to be the one unscuffed baseball in the bucket, and he didn't relish the notion that his buddies were already on-base, threatening to circle the bases and score without him. So here he was, caveboy that he appeared, lunging after this good-looking blonde with his club, like a batter behind in the count trying to connect with a split-finger fastball in the dirt.

"Take a hike," I said.

The kid looked at me a moment with squinted eyes and said, "You say somethin', old timer?"

"The girl obviously prefers company other than yours."

"Yeah? And what are you gonna do about it?" In his inebriation he was braver than he might be otherwise.

"I'll knock your block off," I said. "Now scram."

He looked at me, perhaps measuring me, before saying, "It wouldn't even be a fair fight."

"Sure it would," I said, pushing myself up from the bar against which I had been leaning to show I was a full head taller than he. Then I added, as Radford and Reynolds returned, "My buddies will ensure that."

The kid looked at my teammates, and perhaps that small part of him that hadn't yet succumbed to alcohol thought better of pushing his luck. "Whatever," he said, a small effort to save face, and made his way, a trifle unsteadily, back to his table.

"Thanks," the blonde said. "You're a hunk."

"No problem," I said, ignoring her come-on. "I can't stand a guy who pushes himself on a girl who doesn't have the time of day for him."

"Lucky for me," she said. When I said nothing, she added, "Would you really have fought for me?"

I chuckled over her choice of words, recalling a discussion with Darlene over David's unwillingness to fight for her in the aftermath of his affair, and shook my head. The girl seemed to mistake my reticence to respond for humility. Finally I said, "It wouldn't have come to that."

"You're cute," she said in reply to my discomfiture. "Buy a girl a beer?"

I heard my teammates chuckling over some private joke.

"I'm a married man," I said a little too forcefully, realizing I'd been twelve years out of this game.

"We just made the playoffs," Trexler said, an effort to get the girl to notice him. "You should be buying us a round."

The blonde ignored Trexler's comment. "I'm not asking you to sleep with me," she said with far more maturity than her age betrayed. "It's just a beer with a Tiger." When I nodded, she told the bartender to bring her a light beer.

"Aren't you here with friends?" I asked, hoping to prompt her departure even as I enjoyed her flattery. It was my experience that women always went to public restrooms in pairs, and the same could be said about going clubbing.

"My girl is over there," she said, indicating a table for two at which a young woman sat, alone. She, too, seemed out of this woman's league, overweight and devoid of much sense of fashion or cosmetics. Perhaps the blonde feared competition and so chose to go clubbing with someone who offered little, although her confidence seemed to indicate she was used to success in procuring whomever she wished—as well as those she didn't wish.

I was uncomfortable with the moment, but a part of me also enjoyed the attention she was lavishing upon me, which confused me. In a poor attempt at making small talk, I said, "She doesn't seem your type."

The blonde laughed. "She's not. I'm not gay."

"That's not what I meant," I said.

"Then say what you mean," she said, eager to further the conversation. While she waited for me to reply, she took a swallow from her glass. As she drank, I watched several droplets of water fall from the bottom of the glass, seemingly eager to land between her ample breasts. I looked up at

Trexler just as she finished; he seemed fascinated with the water's progress as I imagined it working its way deep into her cleavage. I looked from Trexler to the blonde to see her run her tongue, moist and pink, across her lips, shiny with too much lip gloss. At another time and under different circumstances, I might've found humor in the image of someone kissing those slippery lips only to slide off and find their nose embedded in her ear.

Embarrassed, I stammered, "Never mind." I regretted stepping in to liberate her from the clutches of a drunken college kid. I should've kept my mouth shut and left this damsel to extricate herself from the clutches of caveboy. Today's liberated women boasted that they could take care of themselves. I shook my head, hoping she would take her beer back to her table while at the same time wishing she wouldn't. She made my wish come true.

"So what's it like, playing baseball?"

"We're paid well to play a kid's game," I said in an effort to downplay my celebrity and remind her we weren't alone.

"You have a girl in every city?"

"No," I said. "I have a wife in Chicago."

"Lucky her."

"I'm a lucky man," I said, wanting to end the conversation. I wasn't used to women, other than Darlene, flirting with me.

Darlene. I suddenly recalled a casual comment she'd made a few months ago while we were entertaining friends: "No young woman would be interested in a thirty-six-year-old ballplayer in the twilight of his career." Perhaps that was why I found it gratifying to have my ego stroked by this younger woman—she had eschewed the come-on of someone closer to her own age for an aging ballplayer. *Harmless,* I thought. *In a public setting and with my teammates around me, it won't go any further.* Yet it felt wrong. Darlene hadn't intended insult with her comment, but my ego had been somewhat bruised nevertheless. Feeling foolish over my reaction to her remark, I'd said nothing then, but now I wished I had. No one wants to feel as if their spouse takes them for granted. Unfortunately, it wasn't until this moment that I realized that that was how Darlene's remark, coupled with the fact my career was nearing its end, had left me feeling: undervalued. Maybe when I got home I'd relate to Darlene this whole affair and we'd both have a good laugh over it.

"We should get back to the Apollo," Reynolds said, and I silently thanked him for making that suggestion.

"Wait," the woman said, opening her purse. A moment later she handed me a pen and pushed her bar napkin in front of me. "I'm Regina," she said.

As I scrawled *To Regina, Backstop* across the paper, she asked, "The Apollo up in Harlem?" Reynolds concurred. "I'm from Harlem," she finished as I pushed the paper napkin back across the ring-dotted surface of the bar.

"Thanks," she said, folding the napkin and depositing it into her purse with her pen, and I wondered that she hadn't bothered to ask the other guys for their autographs. After a long pause during which I deliberately avoided making eye contact, she added, "Well, I'll be getting back to my girl. Thanks again for the autograph."

I only nodded to her and watched her departure through the mirror behind the bar, the gentle sway of her hips snug in the miniskirt a little more affected, perhaps for my benefit, than when I first saw her come out of the restroom. I glanced at the other table, where the kid also watched the blonde, with overt lust. I realized then that it hadn't been the flirting that had left me tense. It was because of the arousal with which she'd left me, and that was something I hadn't felt for another woman since I'd met Darlene. I'd noticed pretty women before, but never had I felt that I was, as Darlene once said, "in harm's way." I concluded it probably would not be a good idea to relate this encounter to Darlene. To do so would serve only to keep alive its memory.

The blonde and her friend left McSorley's ahead of us, perhaps wishing to avoid the unwanted overtures of that other patron after we left.

"I'm Regina," Radford, said in caricaturistic imitation. "We know what *that* rhymes with."

"Backstop," Reynolds added in good-natured ribbing. He knew I wasn't the type to cheat on Darlene, even while, in my mind, I already had. "What's wrong with you? What were you thinking? You could've gotten yourself some strange."

"Yeah," I said, not bothering to mask my annoyance. "Maybe you didn't hear me tell her I'm a married man. Besides, she's just a kid."

"Nothing wrong with young stuff," Trexler said, who, as a first-year ballplayer, was young himself.

"You should know," Radford said, giving our diminutive shortstop a shove.

"Well, you know what they say," Reynolds said.

"No," Radford said. "What's that they say?"

"What happens in New York stays in New York."

"Very funny," I said, waving at the bartender to cash us out.

I AWOKE THE NEXT MORNING THINKING OF DARLENE, in anticipation of her warm embrace, her soft, sensuous kisses, her way of welcoming me home, which was never typical.

I showered, dressed and headed down for breakfast. When I returned to our room to finish packing, John, already packed, was getting ready to head for breakfast. A few minutes after he left, as my bad luck would have it, a knock sounded at my door. Thinking it was room service, I opened the door to find the blonde from McSorley's standing there. I'd forgotten her name and had even managed to push last night's images out of my mind as I looked forward to being with Darlene in a few days. Without waiting to be invited in, she pushed her way past me while I managed to stammer, "What are you doing here?" It was obvious what she was doing here, wearing another miniskirt and a tight top that, with its horizontal pinstripes, accentuated her full breasts.

"I just *had* to see you again," she said with a husky voice as I watched her overly glossed lips form the words. When I said nothing, she added, much more playfully, "Are you going to just stand there all morning or are you going to close the door and kiss me?"

"I told you, I'm a married man."

"She doesn't have to know."

"But I'll know. You need to leave." *I* need *you to leave,* I thought, cursing myself for being an early-riser and John, too, for being a late sleeper. *Why couldn't I have been the one to leave for breakfast a few minutes ago?*

"Dude, you look hot," she whispered.

"Look, miss—I don't even remember your name."

"Regina," she said without seeming the least bit put off. "I could tell last night you liked what you saw," she added with a sly smile, placing her hand on my chest and pushing me backward, in effect closing the door I still held partially open.

I heard it click behind me and knew I was in trouble.

"You like my legs, don't you?"

Had I been so obvious last night? I'd noticed pretty women before, without lusting for them and without incurring such a result.

She held herself against me, pinning me between herself and the door, and I felt the unyielding firmness of her breasts against me.

"I know I liked what I saw—then and especially now, now that we're alone. Tall, handsome baseball player with big, strong arms. Shy, too, playing hard to get—that's *such* a turn-on. You don't have to play anymore. I'm *so* hot for you," she purred, rubbing the front of my jeans. "Mmm ... I can't wait to have you inside me."

I pushed her hand away and said again, "Look," but this time I was unsure what to say. "You're a beautiful young woman, but that doesn't mean—"

She cut me off by kissing me, her lips oh so soft and oh so wet—and I didn't slide off of them—and I felt my resolve weaken more. I pushed her away and told her my teammate was due back shortly. But she must've sensed in my words a plea rather than outright refusal.

"Then we'd best have at it," she said, pulling her top over her head to reveal her dancing breasts.

I stood there a moment, aghast at my misplaced desire, oblivious to Darlene—who a short time ago had been the origin of that desire—her trust, and my vow to remain faithful.

IT WAS OVER IN TEN MINUTES. She never even took off her skirt. Without a word, she pulled on her top, confidently adjusted her breasts, and departed, secure in the power her body wielded and in her ability to seduce me, leaving me to regret for the rest of my life my disloyalty to the woman with whom I'd spent years building trust. A wiser man than I once said, *It is better to suffer wrong than to do it.* Never were those words truer than at that moment: I would much rather come home to Darlene's confession that she had been untrue to me than to inflict on her my cold, hard truth.

By the time Hart returned, I'd thrown up my breakfast and showered again, experiencing only humiliation at being unable to cleanse away my shame at having put up so little resistance.

Hart took one look at me, sitting on the edge of my bed, and knew something was awry.

"Backstop," he said. "What's wrong? You look as if you've just gotten terrible news. Is Darlene okay?"

"Darlene is fine," I said, thinking she soon wouldn't be. If Hart could see through me so easily, Darlene would require no effort to see my guilt. "Come on," I said, grabbing my bags, "let's get out of this ugly town."

THAT NIGHT, in our room in Detroit, Hart again asked me if everything was all right. I'd been uncharacteristically quiet during the flight, and out of concern he'd asked me twice what was troubling me; each time I waved him away.

"No," I said, "nothing is right." And then I confessed to him what had happened last night and that morning, while he'd been at breakfast, sparing none of the vulgar details. I expected him to rebuke me, mildly, perhaps quoting some proverb from the Bible, but he surprised me.

"Backstop," he said. And then, "We should've gone to breakfast together."

"John," I said. "You're a late sleeper. We've never gone to breakfast together." Under different circumstance, I'd have thought my reply humorous.

"This game," he said ruefully, "being away from our families, is trying."

"That's no excuse," I said, suddenly wondering if John had managed to remain faithful to Trisha all these years. But I couldn't ask him that. This was my burden to bear, alone. "I love Darlene."

"I know you do."

When Hart said nothing more, I asked him what I should do.

"It's never happened before?"

"Never." And then I said again: "I love Darlene. You would know if I'd done this before."

"Of course," he said, and then apologized for asking.

"John, I have to tell Darlene."

"Of course you do. God's Word teaches honesty in all things."

I hadn't heard John's agreement. I could only think that I could never bear this alone; furthermore, that Darlene had a right to know. "I'll never be able to keep this from her. She'll see straight through me. If she doesn't know the minute I walk into the house, surely she will when I take her to bed."

"You need to tell her," he said. "But not by phone. You need to face her."

"I'll never be able to come to terms with this, John."

"This is still fresh on your mind. We have a three-game home stand before the playoffs start. You will have at least that long to accept that it happened."

"Never," I said, fighting back tears.

"You're human," Hart said. "God understands your weakness."

"But Darlene won't."

"She's an understanding woman."

"She won't understand this. *I* can't understand this." For the first time in my life, I hated this kid's game I'd always loved to play, certain it was about to repay my love for it by taking Darlene from me.

"I'll pray for you," Hart told me, which was little comfort to me. "And you should pray, too, for forgiveness and guidance, and for Darlene's understanding."

I took Hart's advice and prayed that night as I lay staring at the ceiling, unable to escape into sleep. If God forgave me, I couldn't forgive myself. Guidance certainly wasn't forthcoming, nor was I assured that Darlene would understand.

I punctuated my final plea with a silent *damn*.

DARLENE SAW THE UGLY TRUTH OF WHAT I'D DONE AS soon as I walked in the door; I offered as little resistance to her questions as I had the woman in New York.

I lost track of the number of times I apologized; Darlene wept but betrayed no anger, which surprised me—perhaps that would come later—and muttered, "I should've known this day was coming. You've always had a wandering eye, always enjoyed signing autographs for pretty women."

Again I was forced to consider if this were true, as the woman in New York had also noted. I'd always accepted with grace the flirtations of autograph seekers even as I never reciprocated. Yet even if it were true, that I'd taken notice of a beautiful woman as I would a nude painting or some other work or art, I'd never before lusted for another woman. Darlene had always been enough for me.

"What were you thinking?" she asked.

"I wasn't."

"Oh, yes you were, Backstop. You just weren't thinking of me."

"No," I replied, hanging my head. "But that doesn't mean I love you any less."

"Doesn't it?"

Men often confuse sex for love, whereas women, I read

somewhere, are less likely to fail to make this distinction. Even so, no doubt because of our confusion, men are capable of indulging in sex without love, as I'd learned in New York. In that moment I'd managed to put aside my love for Darlene, and so she was right to question my love.

"No, it doesn't," I said, not wanting to concede her claim. "I made a huge mistake. I wish I could undo it, but I can't."

"No, you can't."

"But we can put this behind us."

Darlene smiled wryly, her eyes red with tears, and said, "Typical Backstop, always looking ahead to tomorrow. Lose today, look ahead to a win tomorrow; win today and look ahead to doing it again tomorrow. Poor night at the plate, always tomorrow to do better. We can't just put this behind us and move on because I haven't yet been able to grasp the enormity of this."

"I want to fight this, for you and us."

"You should've fought harder in New York."

"I know," I said. "You can't know how I feel."

"Nor you I." She waited a moment before asking if I'd at least used a condom, and I understood the vulgar image that must've played itself across her mind's eye.

"Of course," I said.

"Of course," she echoed in ugly imitation, and I realized the idiocy of my answer, as if that somehow had made it okay. "I know they're not part of your travel kit, so I guess I have her to thank for coming prepared."

"Darlene," I said, not knowing what to say; and not knowing, I could only let the sound of her name hang in the air between us.

"I think you should leave."

"Do you think that's best?" I asked, knowing that it wasn't best for me, knowing also that what I wanted mattered little right now in the grand scheme of all this.

"I need time to think."

I packed a few things, wondering if this is how it had played out those many years ago with David—that Darlene had asked him to leave, voicing her need for time to think. At the front door I turned and said, "We need to talk some more. I'll call and let you know where I'm staying."

More tears spilled over, ran down her cheeks; I reached to wipe them away— "*No!*" she said, flashing anger. "You *don't* get to console me."

If I thought I couldn't feel an ounce more pain than I had these past several days, I was wrong.

I left wondering if I'd ever again feel the soft texture of Darlene's cheek against my hand.

I'D COME TO LOVE DARLENE FOR MANY REASONS, not the least of which was her ability to avoid avoiding confrontation. I called her from a hotel that night, but she let the answering machine take my call. I left my number, reminded her I was leaving for Detroit for the start of our playoff series with Minnesota, and told her again we needed to talk.

Then I called my mother to tell her what I'd done, and Nestor, to apologize.

The room was cavernous, yet the walls seemed to close in on me. Not knowing what else to do, I called Hart.

"Hello, John," I said into the phone.

"Backstop," John said from the other end of the line. "How did Darlene take it?"

"Not well, and neither am I. She asked me to move out of the house." I heard John sigh.

"I understand your pain."

"Do you? Do you really, John?" I wondered again if he, too, had been a casualty of a similar seduction at some point during his career, but I refrained from asking. There are some questions a man doesn't put to a buddy let alone a teammate.

"No, I guess I don't understand it, not from a personal perspective," he said, surprising me with the warmth in his voice. "But that doesn't mean I can't empathize."

"I'm sorry. I didn't mean to take this out on you."

"Of course you didn't."

When I said nothing, Hart went on: "What's to come?"

"She told me she needed time to think."

"Give her time, Backstop."

"Yeah, that's exactly what she asked me for—time. We can't work through this apart, John."

"No, but you need to give her time to consider whether she wishes to work through it."

"That's supposed to make me feel better?"

"Of course not. Yet the choice *is* hers, Backstop. You have no right to decide for her."

"I suppose you're right." I'd given up everything the result of one stupid act. I sighed, told Hart that I'd called Darlene's father.

"I know you were very close to him."

"He was like I wish my father could've been. I needed to apologize to him."

"How did he take it?"

"He was as disappointed in me as my mother was when I told her the news. Maybe more." I felt the tears threaten to spill over, gave up the fight, let out a great sob.

"It's okay, Backstop," Hart said, probably because he could think of nothing else to say.

"No, it's not," I argued. "I can only imagine how my own father would've reacted. Nestor was much more civil than my father would've been, but he was angry, too. I'm not his flesh and blood. I hurt his little girl."

I waited for Hart to say something. When he didn't, I cursed myself, said, "All those months during our courtship I told her she could trust me, and all the years I spent building that trust. All a lie."

"No, Backstop. Not a lie."

"Then what?"

"The human condition. We're not perfect, far from it."

"Not every man has cheated on his wife. I imagine I'm in the minority. Nothing to be proud of, certainly nothing in which I should take solace, that I'm not the first. Nor that I'll be the last."

"Only God knows what's in a man's heart."

I thought about that for a moment, what John was intimating. "I don't imagine Rosalynn Carter took Jimmy's admission that he'd lusted after women in his heart as hard as Darlene took my news."

"Perhaps not. But we're all capable of failing."

"Not something I'm used to, John, failure. I've always tried to live to a higher code."

"You know what God says about pride, Backstop."

"One of the deadly sins."

"Lucifer was exiled from Heaven over pride. Perhaps God intended this as a lesson to you, about pride."

"I have *Him* to thank for this? I was perfectly happy in my marriage, content with my career, with walking away from the game in a few years, maybe finally starting a family. He couldn't be happy for me? He had to test me, knowing, omnipotent as He is, that I would fail?"

John was silent in my ear. Was he unable to refute my argument or just letting me vent? Certainly he couldn't be questioning his own faith, or what he believed to be God's plan.

I felt as if I were about to be exiled from the Eden that had been my marriage. "It's better I put out my own eyes than to lust," I said, paraphrasing one of Christ's teachings. "It's sinful behavior to envy, to give in to gluttony. Yet it's just as sinful to take pride in our accomplishments, a life well-lived. Life truly is a lose/lose situation."

"The man who wishes to follow Christ must give up everything."

I shook my head, fully aware Hart couldn't see me. "I won't pretend I understand what that means."

"Jesus told Matthew, 'Follow me and let the dead bury their dead.' He meant, in the first instance, the spiritually dead. To win eternity, Backstop, we must give up everything of this earth."

I didn't hear Hart's explanation. "You have no idea how sorry I am."

"I know you are. And God knows, too."

I snorted. "Yes, you, John, and God. But the one person

who matters most will never believe another word that comes out of my mouth."

"You don't know that."

"I love Darlene. More than I love baseball, more than life."

"She loves you, too, Backstop. Even now. Give her time to miss you, your life together."

"I know I've broken her trust, but I fear that if too much time goes by, she may decide she no longer loves me."

"Sadly, that's for her to decide, alone. You can only tell her how sorry you are, and try to reassure her of your love from a distance."

"I know, John," I said. "But what if it's not enough?"

"Time will tell."

"Yeah, time." I thanked John for use of his ear, and for his advice, and hung up.

I turned on the TV to catch a rerun of *All in the Family* on some cable channel. It was the episode in which a waitress flirts with Archie and she entices him to meet her at her apartment. Once there, his guilt forces him to flee after they kiss. When he confesses to Edith, she is devastated. That Archie couldn't go through with the encounter meant nothing to Edith; in her mind he committed adultery the moment he returned the waitress's flirtation.

Sighing, I turned off the tube grieving for poor Edith. Archie was the one thing she always counted on, and he had let her down. In that moment, I realized that infidelity comes in many forms. A flirtation, as Archie and I both discovered, is never innocent. That night at McSorley's, I'd enjoyed the flirtations of a stranger. By participating, I'd even encouraged it. Add to the mix that I considered withholding from Darlene the events at McSorley's, and I was guilty even before the morning after.

I could do nothing more but wait for sleep, painfully aware that Darlene hadn't called back. It seemed she knew something of the art of avoidance after all.

AFTER WINNING THE FIRST GAME OF THE LEAGUE DIVISION

Series, the result of strong pitching, we lost three straight to lose the Division and end our season. I had a miserable series, hitting .210 and providing no offensive support whatsoever. I felt I'd let down our team, but I cared little. The only team I cared about was broken, in disarray, and its future looked bleak.

JONES APPROACHES HIS THIRD AT-BAT TENTATIVELY. As I surmised earlier, Fernando is so far inside his head he probably doesn't trust that this is game seven of the World Series. After fouling off two fastballs to fall behind 0 and 2, he rolls over on a slow curve and hits a soft grounder to short to start off our half of the eighth with an out.

As I dig into the batter's box, I can hear the chants of the home crowd— "Let's go Tigers!" I'm charged, but I clear the sounds of the game from my head and look out to Fernando to try to gauge how he's going to attack me this time. He got me on strikes back in the second, but he needed his entire arsenal to do it; and I tagged him for a single in the fifth when he relied on his heater.

When he doesn't shake off the sign, I guess he's starting me off with something off speed. Sure enough, I get an outside curve, which misses for ball one. The next pitch is a fastball inside—a purpose pitch to back me off the plate and set up what I guess will be another outside curveball. When Fernando doesn't shake off Evans, I commit to jumping on the curve, which Fernando delivers, and I hit it hard, taking the ball the opposite way.

I hear the crowd erupt in anticipation, but I'm not sure I've gotten enough of the ball to send it out. As I run down to first I watch the ball, its trajectory high, certain I've put too much air under it. Gallegos is back to the warning track, seemingly camped under the ball and I slow my pace, sure I've hit just a long out, but the upper deck porch that hangs out over the first row of the lower deck has robbed many a right fielder from making an easy putout, and tonight I'm fortunate that it gratefully accepts my gift. I watch the fan in the front row who catches the ball leap with joy, fists pumping.

I round first base and the din of the home crowd grows deafening. Still, I show no emotion. I've certainly hit longer homeruns in my career, but none were as important as this one. I've always been careful not to show up opposing pitchers; and this homerun, as important as it may be should we go on to win—we still have three more batters to face in the ninth—I treat no differently than the three-hundred-twenty-four I've already hit in my career.

I round second base, conscious of the hitch in my gait, the result of my swollen and aching ankle, aware of my knees, which both seem to ask me, "How much longer are you going to ask this of us?" I pick up Preston, our third base coach, applauding with a big smile on his face, and it occurs to me then that this might be the last time I round these storied base paths, so I resolve to enjoy the moment as best I can. Preston holds out his right hand and, rounding third base, I slap it and feel the sting of his left hand on my backside.

All too soon I reach home plate, where McCandles is waiting for me, hand outstretched for me to slap, although he, too, is aware the game is far from over.

I head for the dugout and glance out to center field where Cobb once played—a silent acknowledgement of the greatest Tiger of all—and I recall the debate Darlene and I once had about whether a man's evil nature can, or should, be forgiven for the good he contributes. Right or wrong, Cobb's evil nature was set aside when the Hall of Fame recognized his many contributions to the game of baseball. It hits me then, as I doff my cap to acknowledge the cheering fans, that if a bad seed is capable of doing something good, then the obverse must certainly be true. I've tried to live my life according to a high set of standards but fell short, failing often where baseball was concerned—maybe also where my mother was concerned—and miserably with Darlene. That failure resulted in my hurting the one woman who means the most to me, as well as disappointing myself and my mother.

But my failures do not, by themselves, make me a bad person, nor should they take away from the good I've contributed, to both baseball and my marriage. In that moment, I resolve not to give up my fight to win back Darlene.

The crowd is jumping, electric with anticipation as I head down the steps of the dugout, greeted by a series of high-fives and a host of encouraging comments. I touch all the hands but ignore the comments as I approach my spot on the bench next to Stewart, who is standing and all smiles.

"Way to go, Backstop!" he shouts at me, clapping me on my back. "Don't get cocky," I tell him as I sit on the bench. "We've still got business to tend to."

Stewart falls silent and I immediately regret what I've said. He's just a kid—earlier I'd told him to enjoy the moment because he might not ever get another just like it, and now I've placed the weight of this World Series game seven squarely on his shoulders.

A moment later, he turns to me and asks, "We've got the top of their lineup to face in the ninth. How do you think we should attack them, Backstop?"

I look at Stewart, see the seriousness etched on his face, and suddenly I know without a doubt, for reasons I can't explain, that Darlene is watching tonight—that she's watched every game since this series started nine days ago. I don't know which is funnier, the look on Stewart's face or the question he's just asked, and suddenly I burst out laughing and find I can't stop. Stewart looks at me as if I've just slipped into madness, which only fuels my laughter to greater heights.

In that moment I know, beyond a shadow of doubt, that with a one run lead and with Darlene watching, we will win this game and the World Series—the Tigers' first championship since 1968 when, as a kid, I watched Denny McLain bloop a pitch for Mickey Mantle, the dreaded Yankee, to hit over the fence. *Damn it, Dad,* I think, glancing to my left and nearly expecting to find him sitting alongside me as he did those many years ago, *it was just a game!*

Not wanting to be left out of the joke, although he can't

possibly have a clue as to what the joke is, Stewart looks at me a moment longer before joining my laughter.

Finally my laughter subsides and I tell Stewart, elbowing him in the ribs, "You idiot! Just go out and do what you've been doing!"

Ninth Inning

FERNANDO RETIRED MCCANDLES AND RADFORD, both on fly balls to center, to end the eighth, and we take a 1 to nothing lead into the top of the ninth. As Stewart completes his warm-up tosses, looking confident, the crowd begins to chant "Let's go, Tigers," and when Gallegos steps into the box, the chant stops, only to be replaced with a thunderous and sustained cheer of anticipation.

Gallegos has always been a nervous batter, stepping out after every pitch to go through a series of nervous tics—adjusting the Velcro straps on both his batting gloves, twisting at the waist twice each way, bending over to stretch—before stepping back in to wave his bat over his right shoulder in what seems to betray tension rather than menace, his fingers continuously fidgeting on its handle as he awaits the delivery. Gallegos understands what's at stake here. He represents the tying run and he needs to get on base for Richards to move him into scoring position for Reese to drive in. I glance up at Gallegos to make sure he isn't cheating, and flash one finger to Stewart.

The din of the crowd lessens as Stewart goes into his windup only to return at an even higher decibel when Gallegos swings and misses at a low inside fastball.

He immediately steps out of the batter's box to go through his routine. *Whatever gets you through the at-bat*, I think.

Gallegos checks his swing on our next offering—a slider in the dirt—but we manage to get him with a changeup on which he rolls over to hit weakly to second base. The crowd roars its support. I look around me, intent on enjoying this moment as much as I can, aware there are still two tough outs to come, and note that not a single seat in the house is occupied.

We fall behind switch-hitting Richards, who is batting from the left side, on a fastball high; we double up with another heater that Richards turns on and sends deep into right field. The crowd, which has been deafening, falls silent as it watches the trajectory of the ball. I stand to watch it, and I picture myself, a la Carlton Fisk in the 1975 World Series, waving with both hands to push the ball foul as Fisk did to push his long ball fair—and sure enough, the ball, with enough distance to tie the game, hooks just outside the foul pole.

Welke hands me another baseball and I call timeout and trot out to talk to Stewart.

"How are you feeling," I ask him.

"Like it's the top of the first." He's running on adrenalin.

"Then what are you doing leaving your fastball up?"

"It won't happen again," he tells me, and I believe him.

&

"IT WON'T HAPPEN AGAIN," I told Darlene through the phone. The holidays had come and gone and I was still living out of a hotel.

"How can I be sure? You assured me it would never happen at all."

I started to say, "Trust me," but cut myself short, knowing those words would carry little assurance. My actions had shown my words meant nothing.

"Backstop?" she asked, indicating her question was not rhetorical.

"I know I hurt you," I said. "You have no idea how much it pains me, too, what I did. I don't ever want to feel this way again. I'm sorry."

"How can I be sure you won't ever do this again?"

"By letting me prove it." When Darlene said nothing, I added, recalling my advice during our first year, that there could never be a reward without a risk. "You can't ever be sure unless you give me the chance."

"Ah, Backstop," she sighed through the phone as if she hadn't heard me. "How could you do this?"

I had no satisfactory answer, so I remained mute.

"Is this some late career effort, a sort of midlife crisis, to hold on to your youth?"

"No," I said, wondering if she might be right.

"Then what is it?"

"Foolishness," I said, trying to convince the both of us. "I was stupid. Weak."

"You've always had an eye for a pretty girl."

"That's the second time you've said that, and maybe it's true, but that doesn't mean I've always desired to cheat on you, or that I've cheated in my heart."

"After twelve years of marriage, maybe I'm not enough for you."

"Off course you are. This isn't about you. It's about me being stupid."

"You had to prove to me you could still turn the head of a younger, prettier girl?"

Darlene's question indicated to me that she, too, had considered whether her comment last year had impacted my actions.

"You're still the most beautiful woman in the world to me."

"Then why?"

I had no answer, which prompted her to fill in the blank: "You couldn't resist temptation?"

"As silly as that sounds, maybe that's the reason. It certainly has nothing to do with you. I made a stupid mistake—the biggest of my life. But you ... you've given me the happiest twelve years of my life."

"It's not like you haven't been tempted before—it goes with the game."

Not like that *I haven't been tempted,* I thought. *At McSorley's, in public, it's easy to resist. But a woman comes to my hotel room and takes off her clothes ... Not an excuse, but before that happened, I only* thought *I understood temptation.* I said none of this to Darlene; it would only have sounded as if I were trying to justify my actions. John Hart: *Perhaps God intended this as a lesson to you, about pride.*

"Ah, Backstop," she said for the second time, "I hate you for what you did."

"So do I," I said. "But do you hate me?"

"Of course not. If I did this would be ever so much easier. I don't hate you, but you've caused me to doubt love, as well as my trust in you. Without trust, we have nothing."

"I understand that, but if you cut me loose to try love with someone else, you'll still have to build trust. Why not let me rebuild our previous trust?"

"I'm not cutting you loose."

Although she hadn't spoken it, I tacked on to the end of her statement a silent "yet." Still, I wasn't beaten. "But apart like this, how can we hope to close the door on that part of our past?"

"It took me a long time to close the door on my past with David. I imagine this will take longer, if I'm ever able to."

"I'll quit the game."

"I can't ask you to do that."

"You're not asking."

"The Tigers made the playoffs last season for the first time during your tenure. With a healthy bullpen staff next year you could go all the way. If the Tigers win it all and you're not a part of it, you'd only resent me."

I chuckled, but my heart wasn't in it. "You've learned a lot about the game over the years."

"You once told me that to love you would result in my coming to love the game."

I sighed into the phone, said, "We've so much history together, Darlin'. We've bonded in so many ways. I don't want to lose all of that."

"I don't either," she said.

"Then tell me what to do, what you want."

I heard Darlene sigh. "I need more time."

Frustrated, I said, "You asked David for time, too. I don't mean that as an ultimatum. I'll give you all the time you want, Darlene, but you need to understand that that doesn't mean I won't fight for you and us. But I can't do it alone, not from this hotel."

THE OFFSEASON PROVED LONG. I spent many hours in silent consternation. When next I talked to Hart, I told him, "I have no idea if this has any bearing on the why, but last summer she told friends that no young woman would find an aging ballplayer attractive."

"Backstop, you need to stop looking for reasons."

"How can I when Darlene keeps asking me why I did what I did?"

Hart took a moment to compose a response. "Backstop, attractiveness has nothing to do with what that woman in New York did. If it hadn't been you, it would've been another."

"But it wasn't another—she had four of us from which to pick. Why did it have to be me?"

"It was you who stood up for her. Your admission to being married only sealed the deal."

"If that's supposed to make me feel better, it doesn't."

"No, and it shouldn't. What you did was wrong and there is no justification. But money is power. You not only have money, you have fame—a dangerous aphrodisiac to some women. That you denied her advances only drove her to seduce you or bust."

"I was weak," I said, despising myself for my admission.

Hart sighed. "A woman's ego has been likened to expensive china. We must take care to tell her she is as beautiful as the day we met her. We must forgive her for the lines in her face, her aging body. But if a woman's ego is like china, a man's sense of self is as fragile as the finest crystal. Tell him he is no longer attractive to another woman and one risks shattering the crystal."

When I said nothing, he suggested I not give up.

"I UNDERSTAND YOU'RE TALKING TO DAVID," I said into the phone.

"How would you know that?" Darlene asked, belligerent.

"Your father thought I should know."

"My father? Why are you talking to him?"

"Because he's the closest thing I have to a father. I've been trying to make this right, while you've taken to rekindling flames with a former lover. If it's revenge you want—"

"I don't need revenge to cheat—you taught me that."

Ouch. "I'm sorry," I said. "I didn't mean to accuse you. But David?"

"I didn't contact him, he called me."

"How did he—"

"My mother." When I didn't say anything, Darlene added, "We're just talking."

"About what, how he once told you what you needed, that I couldn't provide it, that he's available if you want to go back to him?"

"It's none of your business."

"The hell it's not! Despite what I did, you're still my wife until you tell me you're not." I took a breath, counted to five. "I can understand you leaning on a girlfriend, but what advice, what possible comfort can he provide you?" Darlene remained mute. "This isn't right, Darlene. I hurt you, I know, and I hurt myself. I hurt us, damaged what we shared. I made a mistake, a one-time—"

"How can I be sure it won't happen again?"

"She was a stranger."

"That's supposed to make it okay?"

"Of course not, but you and David have a history. Find some other way to punish me."

"This isn't intended to punish you."

"It certainly feels that way."

"And it isn't about rekindling an old flame."

"Then what do you hope to accomplish? If you have any desire to allow me to make this right, this isn't the way to go about it."

"You can't make it right, Backstop. What's done is done. You can't mend the broken trust."

"No, I can't," I said. "Not if you won't let me try."

JOHN HART HAD TOLD ME LONG MONTHS AGO NOT TO GIVE up. I didn't; but neither did Darlene give up on her stance that I not be allowed to move back home. I spent the winter living in the hotel and hanging around the shop, which

Darlene allowed. I alternated between trying to get her to talk and pretending all was well between us. I didn't ask about David—I didn't want to know. I took her to dinner often, but she remained aloof, giving me little indication that she was working through anything. Or that we were any closer to resolving anything, and our date nights brought little of the pleasure of our courtship days.

My mother passed away in February, just two weeks before I was to head down to Lakeland. Weighing in at a whopping ninety pounds, Mom had been experiencing abdominal discomfort. On a Friday, my sister Karin took her to the emergency room at St. Mary Mercy Hospital in Livonia, where she was diagnosed with a urinary tract infection. Karin called me in Chicago and told me they had her on an antibiotic, and that she expected to bring her home on Monday. She called me again on Sunday afternoon to inform me that they'd discovered a blockage in her lower intestine, the result of her Parkinson's slowing her digestive process. They advised Karin against surgery, which they explained would largely be exploratory and would serve only to traumatize her, likely extending her life by a matter of days.

Because of my baseball career, Mom had assigned Karin as her patient advocate and had advised her of her wishes to not be kept alive beyond her body's capacity to sustain her. Given the circumstances, Karin and I agreed to transfer Mom, against her doctor's wishes, to Angela Hospice, which was around the corner from St. Mary. Her doctor expected that she wouldn't survive the trip, but Karin and I agreed she would receive much better care at hospice, where they would monitor her discomfort very carefully and administer morphine whenever she needed it as she waited for death, whereas at St. Mary they would administer morphine on a strict regimen every two hours.

I flew to Detroit on Monday to await the inevitable. On Thursday, I spooned some tapioca, one of her favorite desserts, into her mouth. "It's delicious," she said after I asked her if it was good. A few minutes later, she slipped into a coma, from which she never regained consciousness. On

Sunday, she passed away—she simply exhaled and never drew another breath. After what she had endured in her battle with Parkinson's, she certainly deserved an easy death.

Mom hated the idea of an open casket—"I don't want people looking at me," she said, and made it clear she wanted to be cremated. Knowing this, Dad opted for cremation, and after he passed we purchased two niches in a wall at St. Hedwig's Cemetery in Dearborn Heights.

While we planned Mom's memorial service, to be held that Friday, as estate executor my sister informed me that she wished to sell the niche our mother was to occupy next to our father and inter her with her parents at White Chapel in Troy. I argued that that was not with Dad's last wishes and asked whether Mom had specified that she be laid to rest apart from him. Karin told me she hadn't. As executor, she didn't need my blessing, but I thought she wanted it for appearances sake. Should anyone in our family question her, she could in good conscience say, "My brother and I decided this together."

I thought long and hard about my sister's intent. She blamed Dad for our mother's medical condition and obviously felt Mom would rest easier apart from Dad. Surely it no longer mattered to our parents, so I wasn't sure I wanted to ensure my father's last wishes were carried out, or merely wanted to prevent Karin from resting easier in parting them. In the end, I gave in to Karin's wishes, a decision I regret to this day.

Darlene flew out for the service, and while she was cordial to Karin and the rest of my family, many of whom she'd never met, she kept distance between us. We talked little and made no mention of my infidelity or our future. This wasn't the time or place to discuss our marital discord, so I derived little comfort from her presence. After the service, she immediately flew back to Chicago, leaving me stung. As I once told Darlene, I'd been grieving my mother's loss for many years, so her passing was a relief to me that her suffering was at an end. What grief I felt was over Darlene's treatment of me.

I went down to spring training a week late, feeling out of sorts and still smarting from Darlene's nonchalance in Detroit. I couldn't imagine what might be going through Darlene's mind while the distance separated us, and I rued the start of the season. That she might decide she no longer loved me weighed heavily as an omen, as did the knowledge that David had the next eight months to wreak havoc.

My mind was anywhere but on baseball as the grapefruit season opened, and for the first week I had a terrible time at the plate. Finally, the skipper took me aside to ask if everything was okay.

"The loss of a mother is tough," he said.

"No, it's not that," I said, wondering how much I should say. Finally, for sake of the team, I said, "Darlene and I are separated."

"I'm sorry to hear that," he said; then, after a moment, he added, "You know we're going to need your head in the game once the season starts if we're to make a run."

I nodded. "I know, Skipper. I'll be there."

"Good," he said. "I know we can count on you." Then he ambled off to leave me to my own thoughts.

I realized I could do nothing about Darlene once the season started except to call her every night as I'd always done. I had to let the cards fall as they may where we were concerned, doing my part in the fight, letting her know I still loved her and wanted nothing more than to close the door on last September and step through another door, this one to the future, with her by my side. I'd let her down, but unless I got my head back into baseball I'd let the Tigers down, too. And whether or not we made it to the World Series, I didn't want to end my career like this, playing like Mantle, and like many other ballplayers have in their final seasons—going through the motions, a shell of their former selves, remembered for not getting out of the game soon enough.

The next day, as I was running sprints down the left field line, McGillicuddy, who'd retired several years ago to become our bullpen coach, called me aside.

"I'm sorry," he said. "I overheard the skipper telling

Preston about Darlene and you."

I bristled, but realized I hadn't told him to keep what was going on in my personal life to himself. I said nothing to McGillicuddy, only hung my head. I hadn't told the skipper the reason for our separation—only Hart knew that and I trusted him to keep it to himself. Yet I could count on McGillicuddy to speculate the worst. My dislike for him notwithstanding, I kept my shame to myself.

"Of all the ballplayers I've known," McGillicuddy added, "I'd have bet on you two to make it."

"Thanks," I said, not knowing what else to say, surprised by his sincerity and angered by his assumption we were split for good. I went back to my sprints, keeping to myself my hope that Darlene and I could still work it out.

After my talk with the skipper my plate production started to come around, and by the time opening day rolled around I had my confidence back to where it had been prior to last season's playoff series with Minnesota.

TO MY SURPRISE, I had a career year, batting .306 and hitting thirty-one homeruns with a hundred-six runs batted in. I won't say my separation from Darlene was good for my game, but I was committed to not letting it disrupt my game.

My visits to Chicago were less frequent than they had been during previous seasons, since Darlene still resisted the notion I be allowed to move back home. At least she consented to picking me up at the airport and to continuing our customary date nights. I had no idea what she might be thinking about how my life on the road might have changed since she threw me out, nor did I ask about hers; but I suspected, wanted to believe, that she was, in her own way at least, fighting to hold on to some familiar, comfortable part of our past life.

We never spoke of what had happened in New York, nor did I bring up moving back. I didn't want such discussions to distract me from the game, and I felt all that could be said about the episode had been said. If Darlene felt the same way, she never let on. I was grateful that she didn't wish to distract me from the season I was having—for all I knew she was planning on serving me divorce papers as soon as the season was over. Yet I would've gratefully discussed anything she wished to bring up, hopeful that we could bring our separation to a resolution. I kept to our routine of previous seasons, calling her every night, a silent affirmation of my whereabouts, telling her I loved her, and attributing to her the season I was having. In time she seemed to return to her old self, laughing, congratulating me for having a good game and season, and also assuring me she hadn't stopping loving me.

My hope that all might yet turn out happily ever after began to escalate.

BEFORE GAME ONE OF THE WORLD SERIES, I called Darlene. "I wish you'd come out to watch," I said.

"I'm sorry," she replied, "I just can't."

"Other plans?" I asked, trying to be funny. When she said nothing, not offering even a laugh, I feared the worst. Before I could stop myself, I asked if she were still seeing David.

"I haven't been *seeing* David," she told me. "We spoke a few times, the last time in May, and we had lunch once. You were right about him—he wanted to use our separation as a way to get me back into his bed."

"Thanks," I said, "for telling me that. But why did you wait so long to tell me?"

"I didn't want to distract you from the season you were having."

"So you just left me to assume—?"

"I couldn't be sure you cared."

"Ah, Darlin'. What have we been doing these past seven months, since the season started? My calls, my efforts to show you I still love you, care about you, about our life?"

"I know what a creature of habit you are, how superstitious you are. How could I know your good season was the result of your denial of what happened and a fantasy that nothing was wrong? Or even that you'd found someone else.

You've always needed harmony in your life off the field to play well."

"Wow," I said. "You wanted time, you said, so I gave it to you. But I also told you I was ready and willing to fight, to discuss anything anytime you wanted. I know my being on the road made that difficult, but you're more important to me than anything."

"Even baseball?"

"Even baseball."

"There's something else you need to know," she said.

"Go on."

"You were right about my wanting to punish you, with David, which is also why I didn't tell you I wasn't seeing him anymore. That's something I'm not proud of."

"I understand."

"I don't think you do. You don't know how close I came to exacting revenge, Backstop."

"What stopped you?"

"I couldn't do that to you, or to myself. I know how it pains you, what you did, and I didn't want to put myself through that. It's bad enough being the recipient."

"You have no idea how much I wish I could undo that." I sighed, and a moment later I added, "Damn, I wish you'd come out for the series."

"I'm sorry. I just can't."

☙

WE FALL BEHIND RICHARDS 2 AND 1 ON A CHANGEUP IN THE dirt on which he doesn't offer, and we come after him with a slider that he laces hard to right field. After the long foul, McCandles is playing deep, but he charges hard and because the ball is hit so hard, he manages to make a sliding catch for the second out. The crowd can taste the Championship, the Tigers' first in twenty-eight years.

Reese steps up to the plate and the tension is palpable; yet Stewart stalks the mound with confidence as the crowd voices its support around us. I squat, oblivious to my aching ankle and barking knees. Convinced that Reese will be looking for something hard that he can drive out of the park, I call for a curveball. Stewart leaves it up and Reese watches it go by for ball one. I don't want to risk falling behind 2 and 0 on something off-speed, so I call for a fastball down and away. Stewart delivers and Welke surprises me by calling strike one—I was convinced the ball missed the corner, but Welke was lined up on the inside corner. Reese steps out and glares at Welke, telling him, "They don't need your help."

I flash three fingers to Stewart, and Reese swings over Stewart's slider as the ball drops out of the strike zone.

I call for another curve and Reese, showing remarkable patience, watches it go by for ball two.

I fire the ball back to Stewart, who immediately looks in for the sign. I flash four fingers for a changeup and Stewart rocks back, preparing to go into his windup. Reese calls time and steps out to make Stewart wait. After taking a couple of practice swings, Reese steps back in to await Stewart's offering.

Stewart brings his changeup and Reese sees a fastball, swinging hard and, as the ball drops, he beats it hard into the dirt in front of home plate. I'm up as the ball bounces straight up and I take six steps toward the mound to field it. As I plant my right foot to make the throw to first, my foot slips on the autumn dew and I drop to my knee. With Reese's speed, I have no time to stand and replant my foot, so I fire the ball from one knee to Radford who short-hops the ball for the last out, and all bedlam breaks loose.

Before I know it, Stewart leaps into my arms, his legs clasping my waist, and I'm aware, as if for the first time, of the roar of the delirious fans. A moment later our bench clears, joining our fielders, to mob Stewart and me, still between home and the mound. I shout to Stewart above the din, "You did it, Stew!" and he shouts back at me, "No, *we* did it!"

We suddenly find ourselves at the bottom of a pile of our jubilant teammates to the delight of the home crowd.

Moments later we begin heading to the clubhouse to break out the champagne, and I glance toward the visitor's dugout, where the visiting team sits in silence watching our celebration. *We were the better team when it mattered*, I think. Yet they pushed us to the wall, taking us to a seventh game when we were favored to win in five. I nod and hold up my left hand in silent salute. I spot Evans, my counterpart behind the plate, who gives me a thumbs up.

Stewart has his arm around me as we make our way toward our dugout and I remember a promise I made back in the fourth inning.

I head over to where Bobby and his dad are waiting. I ask Bobby for the ball and a pen and, as I scribble *To Bobby, Backstop, World Series 1996* on the ball, Bobby tells me, "Great game, Backstop." I hand the ball back to him, putting my hand on his shoulder. Both Bobby and his dad thank me while the fans around them stretch out their hands for me to shake. I'm not sure the smiles on Bobby's and his dad's faces aren't bigger than the smile I'm wearing. "Thanks, Bobby," I say and head for the dugout.

IN THE CLUBHOUSE I'M GREETED BY RADFORD, who pours champagne over my head. "Where've you been, Backstop? We were beginning to think you were going to stand us up."

"Sorry I'm late," I tell him. "These old knees aren't what they used to be. I wouldn't miss this for the world."

I take the bottle from him and pour champagne into my mouth, letting it overflow and run in torrents down the front of my chest protector.

I set the bottle down and start to take off my gear, but Stewart grabs me in a bear hug and says, in imitation of the Bud Lite commercial, "I love you, man! You called a helluva game!"

"Couldn't have done it without you, Stew."

Stewart grabs the bottle I set down and pours more champagne over my head. "Man, you're the best. *This* is the best! It *can't* get any better than *this!"*

Yes, it can, I think to myself, an image of Darlene in my mind; but I don't rain on Stewart's parade. "Enjoy it," I tell him. "You've earned it."

"Enjoy it!" he yells at me, shaking the bottle and letting it spray over anyone within reach. "Oooooh, yeah, baby, enjoy it! I'll never shake off another sign from you! You da man, Backstop!"

By now I've gotten my chest protector off, and the skipper comes by to embrace me. "Thanks," he whispers in my ear, "for being here for us—for getting us here." He, too, recalls the miserable spring I'd had.

"Thanks back at you," I tell him, "for showing confidence in me last spring, and for putting me behind the dish for this series." The skipper knows my disdain for playing first base.

"It's where you belong," he says, adding, "I wouldn't have wanted you anyplace else. Hey," he says as Miller douses him with champagne, "save some for the MVP," and he takes the bottle from Miller and proceeds to pour more champagne over my head while the rest of the team chants "MVP, MVP."

Fox play-by-play commentator Joe Buck, already doused with champagne, comes over to have a word with me.

"Backstop," he says, "You've been the anchor of this Tigers team for more than a decade. It seems you're the unanimous choice, among your teammates, for the series MVP. You've had a solid career, a great season, and a great series both at the plate and behind it, so I can't imagine the media or Major League Baseball will dispute that."

"Thanks, Joe, but I couldn't have done it without my team." A clichéd response, but true.

At that moment Stewart pushes his way into the shot to hand me a bottle of champagne. In his best imitation of Buck, which is remarkably good, he says, "For your contribution to the 1996 World Series Champion Detroit Tigers, please accept this award for World Series MVP."

I laugh and, holding up the bottle as if it were a trophy, say into the camera, "Thanks. I'm humbled and honored—but I'd like to dedicate this award to my wife Darlene, out in Chicago, who has always been my most valuable player."

"This is for you, Darlene," Stewart says before planting a kiss on my cheek. I laugh and push him out of the shot as Buck, laughing, takes back control of the interview.

"Backstop, you've spent fourteen years playing baseball. I suspect Tigers fans want to know if you'll be back for a fifteenth year."

Normally, I'm put off by formulaic questions, especially those concerning my retirement; but for the sake of the interview, and uncertain just what might lay in wait for my future, I say, "I just want to enjoy this moment and give my knees a couple of months off before I think about next season."

"Thanks," Buck says, "and congratulations to you and the World Champion Detroit Tigers."

Eventually the media departs and our celebration becomes a little more subdued, with some players breaking into smaller groups, others departing to celebrate elsewhere.

Stewart comes by with Trexler and McCandles in tow. "We're heading to Greektown to celebrate," he says. "Wanna come along?"

"Thanks," I say, "but I'll pass and head back to the hotel."

Stewart is unable to mask his disappointment. "Okay," he says, and then he embraces me again, clapping me on my back. "Thanks, man, for making my dream come true."

"Stewie," I say, "this is every ballplayer's dream. *You* made it come true."

"Thanks," he tells me again as I think about my dad—how he tried to deflect me from making my own dream come true, and how I'd let him, for so long, distract me from really enjoying this game for what it is.

"You're a bona fide star, Stew," I say. "Don't forget that, but more important, don't let it go to your head."

"I won't," he says, and for the second time this night I believe him.

I trade congratulations and embraces with Trexler and McCandles. I tell McCandles, "That was a highlight reel catch you made," and the trio departs for Greektown.

Thinking I'm alone in the clubhouse, I sit to remove my shin guards when McGillicuddy sits down next to me.

"Congratulations," he tells me. "You played a helluva series."

"Thanks."

After a moment he adds, "I mean that."

"I know," I reply softly, looking at him. It's true: We wear our lives on our faces. Because he has no portrait in his attic, McGillicuddy bears the sins of his career on his face—weariness in his eyes, a certain sadness in his expression and in his overall demeanor. Gone is the supreme arrogance of only a few years ago, and I regret not meeting this McGillicuddy when I first broke into the game.

"We've had our differences over the years," he tells me, "and I know you don't like me, but I want you to know you were right. I screwed up my marriage. I don't know what happened between you and Darlene, but I sincerely hope you work it out."

"Thanks, Mac," I say. A moment later, as McGillicuddy stands, I add, "We're working on it."

"Good, I'm glad to hear that," he says, and leaves me to my thoughts.

I OPEN THE DOOR TO MY ROOM AND MY EYES IMMEDIATELY go to the phone to see if the light is blinking to alert me of a missed call. My heart leaps to see it flashing; but when I replay the message my heart sinks to hear John Hart's voice congratulating me. Hart retired before we broke camp in the spring, the result of a bad shoulder. I listen to his voice say, "God bless you," before he hung up.

I sigh and head for the shower.

I'M SITTING ON THE EDGE OF THE BED. My ankle is still sore, but my knees are grateful for my taking the weight of their world off them. When I started this game, I'd wake up the next morning with sore knees, but I was able to walk off the tightness in a matter of a few hours; tonight I know my knees will hound me for a few days for the torment I'd put them through these last ten days.

I'm conscious of the silence of the room, a stark contrast to the sounds of the game and the ensuing celebration of a few hours ago. My eyes tear up as I think of Darlene, so far away, leaving my celebration incomplete. *I'm sorry*, she'd told me. *I just can't.*

I'm no longer certain that she had watched the game. I think about calling her, but it's late. These World Series games start later than regular season games to accommodate prime time ratings, and the post-game clubhouse celebration got me back to my room late, despite the time difference.

Never in my life have I felt so alone. I curse myself yet again for my moment of weakness, for bringing ruin to our life together. *No better than McGillicuddy once was*, I think, wanting to punish myself.

I hadn't wanted to go out with Stewart and company to celebrate. I was tired and sore, but more importantly, I had been anxious to get back to my room to see if Darlene had called. And she hadn't. *Just desserts.*

I slip under the sheet and lie on my back staring at the ceiling wondering what is to come.

Joe Buck: "Will you be back for a fifteenth season?"

It would've been easy to have answered, "I'm done. I won't be back. I'm getting out of the game a winner, on top." *To work on being a better husband.*

But now I'm uncertain. I imagine going back to Chicago to find divorce papers waiting for me. That would be like Darlene, to wait for the season to end before serving me.

I can't imagine losing Darlene and this game in one fell swoop in one year. Prior to tonight's game, win or lose, the thought of retirement seemed right, and I welcomed it; now the thought of returning to Lakeland in the spring, to my life with my old friend baseball, seemed preferable to life without Darlene. Baseball had never let me down, as I had let down Darlene and as it now seemed she was letting go of me. Still, I knew baseball would one day abandon me, as my skills diminished and I found I could no longer compete with the kids who are coming into the game—bigger, stronger, faster, more skilled.

As I wipe away my tears the phone rings, sounding loud and ominous in the room's stillness. I beat back my hope as I pick up the handset.

"Hello."

"You're in," I hear Darlene's voice say.

"Where else would I be?" I say, my heart beating quicker, as it always did whenever I heard Darlene's voice on the other end of a phone.

"I thought you'd be out celebrating."

"Celebrating," I say with a wry chuckle. "Isn't that what got us to this place?" When Darlene says nothing, I add, "I'm glad you called. It wouldn't have seemed a win without hearing your voice."

"I called a few minutes ago but didn't want to leave a recorded message."

"I was in the shower." And then, "Thanks. This is much nicer than a recording."

"Are you alone?" Her voice sounds thin with distance.

"Darlene," I say, incredulous. "I've been alone since you asked me to move out."

"You have?" Her voice, in its disbelief, sounds warmer.

"You asked for time, which I had no choice but to grant you. I didn't use that time to—"

"I wasn't sure."

"My god, Darlene. All the years we've been together—I know I let you down, but I thought you knew it wasn't because I stopped loving you or had a tendency toward unfaithfulness."

"I kept telling myself that, but I wasn't sure, even as you assured me. Broken trust can offer a convincing argument."

"You can be sure."

After a few moments, Darlene says, "Congratulations."

"What, you watched the game?" An attempt at humor.

"Of course I watched."

"I kept telling myself you were, but I wasn't sure."

Darlene laughs, and I realize how much I've missed that sound over the last year. "We still think alike, don't we?"

she says.

"Always have, always will."

"How's your ankle?"

"Sore and swollen, but I'm getting around on it."

"I could almost hear the expletives hiding behind your mask."

"A few."

"That was a wonderful thing you did for that boy, signing his baseball."

"I don't know that I didn't get a bigger kick out of it than he did."

"I know." And then, "You're a good man, Backstop."

"I try, even if I fall short."

"We all fall short," she says.

"I don't follow you."

"I'm sorry I didn't come out for the series. I should have, but I was thinking only of myself. And so I fell short."

"Understandable, but that doesn't make you any less a good woman."

"I also regret not being more comforting when you lost your mother."

"You gave what you could."

"No, in hindsight I think it was a choice."

"As punishment goes, I found it bearable."

A lull in the conversation, and I imagine Darlene, also lying in bed, cradling the phone.

"What *are* your plans for next year?" she asks finally, proof that she'd watched the post-game clubhouse celebration. "As your agent I need to know."

"Until you called, I was considering playing another season. Now I'm not so sure."

"So I could be out of a job?"

"Could be," I say, pleased not only with the conversation, but also with the familiar warmth of Darlene's voice. My hope for a happily ever after begins to return.

"Am I?" she asks, deliberately leaving her question unfinished, as if to test the validity of my statement a few moments ago that we think alike.

"Always have been, always will be my Most Valuable Player."

"And are you still?"

I chuckle. "Been rereading *You Know Me Al* have you?"

"Answer the question."

"I always will be your Backstop."

"You said many months ago, over the winter, that you couldn't hope to mend the broken trust unless I was willing to let you."

"I remember saying that. And I meant it."

"I think I'm ready to let you."

PACKED, I call down to the front desk to have them call me a cab to take me to the airport. After last night's game, I don't want to have to deal with shuttle passengers who might recognize me.

The elevator lets me out into the lobby, and as I head to the exit limping noticeably, Bastiaan, the young Jamaican doorman who's held the job the last few years, approaches me, his dreadlocks looking out of place beneath his cap.

"Let me take your bags, Mr. Backstop," he says in his thick, rich accent. I give him my bags and, as we near the exit, he adds, "A good game last night, Mr. Backstop. Congratulations for winning the World Series and for being Most Valuable Player."

I hadn't read the morning paper, so I was unaware that it had been made official. "Thank you, Bastiaan," I say. "It's gratifying to know I have at least one fan in this town."

"Oh, Mr. Backstop, you have many fans. From talk around the hotel this morning, I expect you might be the most popular man in Detroit."

"Soon to be forgotten," I say as I push my way through the revolving doors, with Bastiaan and his dreadlocks following.

Bastiaan situates my bags in the trunk of the cab and I pull a fifty-dollar bill from my wallet to hand him after he slams shut the trunk lid.

"Thank you, Mr. Backstop," he says. Then, offering me

a pen, he gives the fifty back to me and asks that I sign it.

"They must pay you well, Bastiaan, if you have no intention of spending this."

"No, sir," he says as I scrawl my customary signature across Grant's face. I'm not sure if he means the hotel doesn't pay him well or that he doesn't intend to spend the fifty, but I say nothing as I hand the bill back to him.

"Thank you, Mr. Backstop."

"You're welcome, Bastiaan," I say and turn to enter the cab. Before I get in, I turn back to ask, "Bastiaan, how long have we known each other?"

Bastiaan thinks a moment before venturing, "I'm not sure, Mr. Backstop. Two years is what I recollect."

"That's what I recollect, too," I say, then add, "Surely you know my last name isn't Backstop."

"To be honest, Mr. Backstop, I've always wondered what nationality that name might be."

"What do you think?" I ask, lobbing the ball back across the diamond.

Bastiaan considers his response carefully. "I'd guess Norwegian."

I smile and place my hand on his epaulet. "Norwegian it is, my friend."

I bend to enter the cab and Bastiaan bids me a good winter and tells me he looks forward to seeing me next year, with the hope of another run at the World Series.

I wave over my shoulder but don't look back. I'm going to miss Bastiaan.

Postgame Wrap-up

DARLENE MEETS ME AT THE FRONT DOOR AND, before I can say a word, puts her hand over my mouth and leads me to the bedroom where she helps me to undress. I watch her slip her snug jeans over her hips and ease them to the floor. I admire her shapely legs, and if my desire for her can grow any more, it does as she steps out of her jeans and over to the bed, where I unbutton her blouse. A moment later, it drops soundlessly to the floor as I softly kiss her navel; I hear her quick intake of air. I unhook the clasp on the front of her bra and it joins the blouse as she slips into bed next to me.

We make love with the passionate, frantic urgency of a year missing. We climax quickly, Darlene first, with my release in response to her breathless moans, the result of a years' worth of agonistic abstinence. Afterward, neither of us says a word; we just hold each other, kissing, caressing, exploring each other's body—not as if by rote, but with practiced loving familiarity—and we are making love again, this time each of us totally present in the moment, fully conscious of our partner, not lost in our own immediate need.

PROPPED UP BY AN ELBOW, I look down at Darlene, her hair tousled and her face and breasts glistening with a thin sheen of perspiration. I caress her face and she takes my hand to kiss its palm as she's done countless times before.

"I've missed this," she whispers, still somewhat breathless.

"What, my hand?"

"Ever the clown," she says with mock annoyance, pulling my head down to join my mouth with hers. When our lips part, she adds, "You, silly. I've missed you."

"As I have you. I love you, even if I failed to show it."

"I know that now," she says with a sigh. "Even my father assured me you did. But from the season you had, I had my doubts."

"Never doubt my love for you, Darlene." And then,

"You sound disappointed that I played well."

"No, of course not. You had a career year and capped it off with a championship—you made your dream come true." Her eyes well up with tears and she adds, "I'm so proud of you, Backstop."

Darlene looks pensive, so I prompt, "But." After a moment, she goes on.

"I couldn't help but feel, as the season wore on and it was clear you wouldn't endure a prolonged slump and that the Tigers were a team of destiny ... I couldn't help but feel that I'd lost you."

"You really *have* come to love the game," I say with a grin. "You even know all the clichés."

"What *Al* didn't teach me you did."

"Including what a fade away fastball is."

Darlene rolls her eyes, says, "A fastball hit so far it fades away over the fence."

We both laugh, and Darlene adds, "It came with the package. I never stopped loving you, Αγάπη."

"I've missed you calling me that." Then, in reply to her comment, "I had my doubts of that, when you persisted in not letting me come home, and when I learned you were talking with—"

"Don't say his name. He doesn't belong here in our bed."

"But you were never in danger of losing me. I only turned to baseball, lost myself in the game, because I feared coming home after the season to divorce papers. You asked for time—"

"And the last person from whom I asked time—"

"I'm not that other person."

"No, you're not," she tells me, holding my hand to her cheek and closing her eyes as I stroke its softness. "After fourteen years, I should know that."

"How often did I tell you, during the last year, of my desire to fight for you?"

"I heard, but I guess I just wasn't listening."

"A broken heart can be persuasive."

"Bruised and somewhat bloodied, but not broken. If it were, you wouldn't be here."

"I'm so, so sorry."

"I know you are." She sighs and I can tell the images of that night still pain her. They pain me, too, but I don't take my eyes from Darlene's. I place my hand atop hers. "Rest assured, Backstop, even as I forgive you, I'm not letting you off the hook, although I know I must if I'm to forgive you totally. But I'm disappointed that I abandoned you for an entire year. Why are you smiling?"

"Funny, but before the World Series I visited my dad at the cemetery, and I finally realized I no longer needed his approval for playing baseball." Darlene looks away, as if I've just struck her. I gently turn her face to look at me. "That's not a reflection on you, Darlin'. I wanted you to be a part of the season, especially the postseason. Wanting you to share it is far better than needing you to, isn't it?"

"I'm not sure I understand that, but it certainly sounds healthy."

"I need you to be a part of my life, but more important, I *want* you to be a part of it. I'm disappointed, too, that you chose to hold yourself apart from the season—even as I understood your why—but I realized that losing a baseball game was not a reflection upon me."

"And winning?"

"We won as a team even as, when we lost, we lost as a team. I contributed my share, as did the rest of the team."

Darlene laughs, says, "Thank Stewart for me, will you, for kissing you for me."

I join her laughter before saying, more seriously, "I took you with me to each game, as I always have." I think about adding that her absence during the last seven games pained me greatly in addition to disappointing me—my own bruised and somewhat bloodied heart—but think better of it; I don't wish to lay that burden on her in addition to the other—the one we needed to bear together. Instead I say:

"So in a sense, you could say I needed you with me."

"Thank you," Darlene says, stroking my cheek. In my

haste to come home I'd neglected a morning shave. Darlene has always liked my morning stubble. "Did you bring home the morning edition of the *Free Press?*"

"Home," I say. "Leaves me with a nice warm feeling." And then: "No, why? You know I gave up reading the sports section years ago."

Darlene says nothing, merely rises and goes to the closet. I watch her lovely figure, its feminine grace moving in total concert, and I feel my strength return. A moment later, she slides back into bed with what appears to be a photo album.

I leaf through it, recognizing headlines relating to moments throughout my career, and I realize she's been keeping a scrapbook.

"You've been keeping this all along, for twelve years? Why didn't you ever tell me?"

"I wanted it to be a surprise."

"Now I understand why my closet didn't come with the master bedroom."

"That's not why and you know it," she says, giving me a playful shove.

"A woman and her clothes," I muse. "Darlin', you have no idea how surprised I am—and how pleased."

You once said that a scrapbook tells a one-sided story."

"And that I don't need one to recall my career."

"Scrapbooks aren't just for one's own benefit, Αγάπη. They're also for those we leave behind—our children."

I close the scrapbook and set it on the nightstand. Then I place my hand on Darlene's hip, delighting in the soft down that covers it, and pull her to me to kiss her; I feel her hand between my legs.

"My god, you're insatiable," she breathes.

"We've a lot of lost time to make up."

Darlene moans her assent ... whispers in my ear, "Αγάπη μου αγάπη μου λίγο καιρό" (love me little, love me long).

"Forever," I promise.

2001

I RETIRED A FEW WEEKS AFTER THE TIGERS WON THE World Series and never regretted going out on top. I didn't need my knees to tell me it was time.

Less than a year later, Darlene gave her mother that grandbaby she'd been after her about. I've already showed him how to throw a baseball and swing a bat, and I look forward to teaching him about baseball—all the things my father left to me to learn on my own. Whatever differences we may have between us as he grows up, we'll always have baseball; and whether or not he decides to follow his old man into this grand old game is up to him. I intend to nurture him no matter what he decides to do with his life.

I've taken up playing the piano again, and I'm writing a sports column during the baseball season, only now for the *Chicago Sun*. Darlene recently brought up a discussion we'd had long ago about me writing my life story in baseball, and I'm starting to give that serious consideration. A lot of former sports figures seem to be writing autobiographies, and there seems to be a large market for them. Darlene assures me my baseball career is a heck of a lot more interesting than many of theirs, although I'm not sure she's just telling me that to entice me to start writing so that I'll spend less time at the shop, where I still serve as unofficial buyer, stealing kisses from her when the help isn't looking, and generally distracting her from her professional duties.

I'm delighted to learn that my name appears on the Hall of Fame ballot, my .297 lifetime batting average a duplicate of Kaline's. Whether I'm elected in my first year of eligibility or any year thereafter is unimportant. I consider it an honor just to have been nominated, just as I consider it an honor to have played this kid's game I still love so much—the ups and downs, the winning and losing, the streaks and the slumps, the good and the bad. It brought out my best, as well as my worst. Darlene saw me at my ugliest. She could've looked away, walked away. But she didn't. That's love.

Winning was gratifying, the icing on the cake; but it wasn't everything. Winning back Darlene's heart was everything and more: She is my most treasured victory.

— JCG; January 2008/October 2009

Be sure to catch ***One Hot January,*** the second book in the January Trilogy
By J. Conrad Guest

"Written in the tradition of Raymond Chandler, mystery and intrigue along with wants, desires and regrets prevail for private investigator Joe January. When he takes on a case involving a missing person, he gets a lot more than he bargained for—a conspiracy and a strange artifact that holds the key to a possible alternative reality. Set in New York City, 1947, *One Hot January* takes us back to the age of a Bogart cool, clever, sharp-tongued, fedora-wearing hero, complete with a smarts to handle the unforeseen, and an underlying vulnerability."
—Deb Ledford, Author of *Snare* and *Staccato*

Coming soon … ***January's Thaw***, Book 3 in the January Trilogy

You may also enjoy these other Beckoning titles from Second Wind Publishing, LLC.

A Love Out of Time
Mairead Walpole
Soul-mates, twin flames, "split-aparts" ... philosophers, poets, and priests have pondered their existence and their nature. Such a love can transcend death, stand the test of time, and make all things possible. Some know the truth, while others hope and dream.

Indian Summer
Dellani Oakes
A unique regency novel of a girl's coming-of-age. The Spanish call it "quinceanera" a girl's 15th birthday. Gabriella Deza, innocent daughter of a nobleman in 1739 St. Augustine, Florida, finds herself caught up in international intrigue and romance.

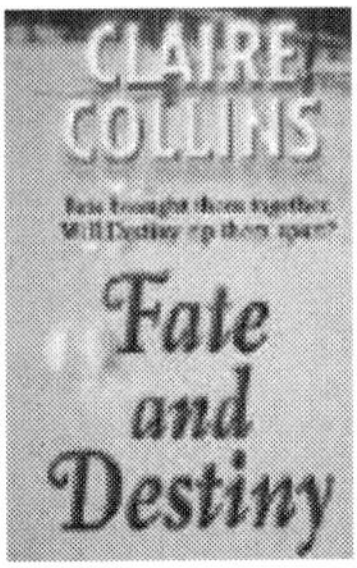

Fate and Destiny
Claire Collins
A romantic thriller set on a snowy mountaintop. During a blizzard, Andrew's dog, Shadow, finds Destiny—a beautiful woman left for dead, but very much alive. With her she brings mystery, danger, and passion to the little cabin.

Hand-Me-Down Bride
Juliet Waldron
Based upon the story of the author's great grandmother, who was a real life mail-order bride. Sophie agrees to marry a wealthy man she's never met—but life has other plans.

Lacey Took a Holiday
Lazarus M. Barnhill
A desperate act of love creates a cascade of changes. Lacey, the most unlikely heroine, has been betrayed and abused by the men in her life. Andy has lost everyone he ever loved tragically. This 1920s mountaintop romance breaks every rule.

Night and Day
Sherrie Hansen
It's midnight in Minnesota and Jensen Marie Christiansen is dreaming of a rosy future. It's daybreak in Denmark and Anders Westerlund is waking up to a world full of stark realities. When parchment paper and faded ink meet computer screens and fax machines, the old-fashioned magic of a great-grandmother's letters sets the stage for a steamy Internet romance ...

Author's bio:

Having lived his entire life in the Detroit area, J. Conrad's dad took him to his first Tigers game when he was seven—a Tigers win over the Angels during a time when the Angels played for the whole state of California and not just Anaheim.

J. Conrad dreamed of a pro ball career, but when he turned forty, he realized that dream was no longer in the future but instead the past. It was inevitable that at some point he would write a baseball novel. In *Backstop*, he combines his love and knowledge of the game with the heartbreak of betrayal and its subsequent redemption.

His first novel, *January's Paradigm*, was published by *Minerva Press*, London, England. *Current Entertainment Monthly* in Ann Arbor, Michigan, wrote of *January's Paradigm*, "Personal identity—the slipperiness and the malleability of it—makes up the major theme of the story ... (readers) will not be able to put it down."

10918025R0

Made in the USA
Lexington, KY
28 August 2011